"DON'T LOOK INTO ITS EYES!"
BEN WARNED.

"You'll see things; promises . . . promises that won't be kept! That's their power. They show us everything we want. They use our own desires against us, then offer us the sickness in our souls as something to be craved. But they're liars!"

Warren screamed and grabbed Dixon, prying at his strong fingers in the need to be with Susan.

"Warren!" Dixon shrieked. "Susan is dead!"

"*Warren.*" Susan's silvery voice sang in his ear, and he could not keep himself from reaching out, wanting her despite the terror.

"*Be with me, Warren.*" Her face was wicked with delight as her fingers drifted nearer and nearer.

"In the name of Christ!" Dixon raised his cross defensively, and the horror yanked back with each stab of the threatening symbol.

"*You bastard!*" she was shrieking. "*You can't kill what's already dead!*"

"A vampire novel you can get your teeth into, and then it returns the favor."

—J. N. Williamson,
author of *Shadows of Death*

BLOOD LUST

RON DEE

A DELL BOOK

Published by
Dell Publishing
a division of Bantam Doubleday Dell
Publishing Group, Inc.
666 Fifth Avenue
New York, New York 10103

ISBN: 0-440-20567-0

Printed in the United States of America

Published simultaneously in Canada

April 1990

10   9   8   7   6   5   4   3   2   1
OPM

Many people, directly and indirectly, deserve credit for the input and inspiration I received to write this novel. Rather than attempt to list them all, I will name some of the main contributors in acknowledgment and dedication: Bram Stoker, the Reverend Montague Summers, Charles Williams, C. S. Lewis, Christopher Lee, Peter Cushing, Hammer Films, Dennis Wheatley, Stephen King, E. W. Kenyon, Jim Fields, Scott Schad, the cast of the 1973 Hale High School production of *Dracula,* Dr. Franz Hartmann, Leonard Wolf, Mark Irwin, my parents, stepparents, grandparents, in-laws, and most especially my editor, Jeanne Cavelos, my wife, Davi, and children, Cindy and Chris.

"The blood is the life. . . ."
  Bela Lugosi in the 1931 film *Dracula*

"For the life (soul) of the flesh is in the blood. . . ."
  Leviticus 17:11 (Amplified Version)

I

1

He awoke to hunger—greedy hunger. Last night's feast had been interrupted and his needs were unsatisfied.

But tonight would be different. His study of this city had been thorough, and he knew where it would be best to go next.

Rising, he saw the darkness through cracked, oversize windows, smeared and dusty from disuse, and smiled, inhaling the fetid air obscenely. Soon it would all be like this dank and deserted warehouse. Soon it would all be under his dominion and he would be free to move on—and in a few years, the many, many seeds he had planted here would develop and grow on their own, and begin to spread. But slowly, and over such an extended period, that no one could ever find them all . . . and they would be difficult to trace back to him.

And when it was all done, he would command thousands . . . millions.

Still, he would have to be careful. In the last place his desires had overcome his plans, necessitating his departure and a lengthy journey.

He walked the pitted floor, kicking aside the wasted condom of some past teenager's sexual initiation, then picked it up and grinned. There was no such protection from the gifts he brought, and though the threat of discovery was far behind him now, he wished he had been able to deal with his pursuer as he had the others: to make him submit to what he feared most, and take his essence from him forevermore.

But that man would not trouble him again now, and could never divulge what had happened. He was dead.

Yes. But for him especially, the short torment had not been enough.

Taking another deep breath, he stood and brushed damp dirt and metal shavings from his sleeve. If any others back there knew of him, they would never find him. He had left quickly, and in the day, when they wouldn't expect to see him.

He kicked one of the soggy cardboard boxes and laughed as discolored bottles of cleanser fell onto the floor and shattered, hearing his own echoing cackle mix with the sound in mild disappointment. He would have to make up for the failure of that departed opportunity here. But eventually his ends would be fulfilled even in that last town, as his power became complete with the passing of time.

Time was his, and if he used it correctly, he would not fail.

2

The crystal domed clock resting on the television said that it was only just before eight, but loneliness made it seem past midnight already. As usual, Warren was gone, and she was alone.

Susan glared at her dull features skeptically, then made herself smile, brushing back her thick brown hair until it framed a still soft and modestly attractive face. She pursed her lips, posing, hoping to be impressed by the seductive power she urged through the skimpy nightgown under her robe, the seductive power of a mature twenty-eight-year-old.

But what the use? She was *alone*.

"I sure as hell never knew it was going to be like this."

The words faded almost as soon as they were out of Susan's

mouth, and she shuddered, turning away from the full-length mirror and walking back to the portrait albums and yearbooks she had spread out on the couch yet again tonight. She interlaced her fingers so tightly that they hurt and sat down hard on the brushed material.

"Damn you, Warren!" she tried bitterly, wanting the words just to hang there and wait for his return. She wanted to fill the blue living room with her depression and betrayal so as to stifle him, but those words broke the silence for only an instant, then were gone.

Warren. Damn Warren, screw Warren . . . *fuck* Warren! She whined the words in his absence and then they were gone, too, and when he came back, he would never know she had said them; never know how she really felt—

And what would he do if he did?

Yes, what would he do? Would he even fucking care?

What would his precious congregation do?

Susan sighed. They would stare in disappointed silence and shake their heads. Warren would merely suggest counseling. He was a great one for talk. "Let's talk it out," he'd say.

Talk it out. She was so damned tired of that. Warren was gone all the time to his meetings and visitations, always caring for and helping others, and with her he only wanted to talk.

Talk.

"I'm tired of it, Warren," she murmured to the oak-framed painting of a seascape with gulls floating timelessly in the air above green water.

"Fucking sick and tired."

She *was* tired—tired of him always gone or coming home exhausted. Maybe those people who clamored for his time needed help, but so did she. She needed her husband—she needed companionship! He was so obsessed with assisting others, but he didn't even guess her own dissatisfaction. Susan twisted her lip sourly. Why couldn't he just see her needs? Just once?

"Because I'm his fucking wife," she whispered aloud. Warren was so wrapped up in it all, he was nearsighted. He could see problems from a distance, but up close it was as though he were blind.

Her eyes moved around the room, bypassing its spacious, Early American majesty and finding anger now at the wealth Warren had been born into—so much that it meant nothing to him. He spent money on everyone, even sending it off to people and countries he didn't know, as if in atonement for his lucky fortune.

And especially on her. He bought her everything she wanted, bought her "toys" to keep her occupied in his absence.

But it meant nothing. She needed *him*—she needed her husband. Getting up in the silent house, Susan walked restlessly to the baby grand piano he had given her just this past Christmas and hit three keys simultaneously. The uneven chord jarred back her destroyed hopes of being an acclaimed pianist. Destroyed when she lost two fingers in the car wreck last year. It underlined the loss of her once great expectations of being Mrs. Warren MacDonald, and in retaliation she played "Chopsticks" with furious intensity, then pushed herself away from the hated gift. Warren had given it to her after the loss of her fingers and ability. Instead of the encouragement he'd pretended, it was a dark reminder of what she could never be.

Susan fought tears and wandered aimlessly across the snowy shag carpet on bare feet, betrayed and alone, to find herself back at the mirror on the other side of the retangular room. She stared at herself once more—imagining herself as one of the posing models in a men's magazine.

So why didn't her sexuality intrigue Warren?

The dark frown pulled her face back to anger. As usual, it was back to him again, and because of him and who he was, she was beyond the interest of other men. Even when she would actually flirt earnestly she drew no reactions. Everyone knew who she was, and of the complications that could come from an affair with a preacher's wife.

It trapped her, so she had only herself.

Staring at her slender body wistfully, Susan dreamed of a muscled lover moving against her and enfolding her in his arms, his rough hands stroking her shoulders, gliding at a snail's pace to her breasts to knead her dark brown nipples, his smooth lips kissing her savagely and tasting her while he tore the opaque negligee from her with a hot, passionate sweep. His tongue would run warmly across her shivering, naked skin.

"Oh . . ." Her fingers began to slide down her stomach.

The doorbell chimed as she moaned again, tearing her rudely from the vivid reverie. "Fuck." She blushed angrily and pulled the cotton robe tight around her. Who could it be at this time of night? But then, she knew it was someone looking for Warren. It was always someone to see Warren.

The chimes rang louder.

"Fuck." Frustrated even by herself, she broke away from her desires and walked as slowly as she could to the door, peeking out the peephole to see a man in a gray-black overcoat. She held her breath and didn't answer, wanting to slip back into the memory of her imaginary lover. She waited for him to walk away, but he smiled, as though he could see her. Susan's heart thudded as she stared back into his blue eyes, and at last her hand turned the dead bolt and opened the heavy barrier. "Y-yes?" she asked, her knees weak.

The tall man smiled, and Susan crossed her arms to pull the robe closer around her, suddenly embarrassed to be standing there with so little underneath. He was handsome—very handsome. His thin face was sturdy and firm with a vague underlying passion. His hair was a peppery gray and he had a black moustache that was stark against the winter pale of his skin. The outline of powerful muscles bulged even through the badly tailored black polyester suit and coat, and when he stepped nearer she was awed by them, feeling very small behind the glass door she could not keep herself from cracking open.

"I'm selling a new line of cleansers for the home," the man drawled smoothly and quickly, holding up a big scarred sample case. He took another step forward and tried to peer behind her. "If I could come in for a few minutes I'd like to demonstrate them for you."

An unexpected giddiness gripped her and she blushed, entranced by the powerful eyes. "Uh . . . my, uh, husband's not home right now and it—it's rather late."

A bushy eyebrow slid up and he nodded, not concealing his disappointment. "I see. Well, I wouldn't keep you long . . . and

I imagine you're the one to make decisions on this sort of thing, aren't you?"

"I—I'm hardly dressed," she stammered, trying not to stare into those eyes.

He smiled again and held out his hand. "Believe me, the hours I work at this, I'm used to demonstrating to beautiful women in their nightwear. If it would make you feel more comfortable, I can wait while you change."

Beautiful. His word flew through her. "N-no," she stammered. "I guess it's okay." Her eyes stayed in his and she opened the glass door wider and touched his fingers, shivering at their chill. "Good Lord, you're freezing. Come in and warm yourself up."

He let her pull away and stepped inside, making her flinch as the air entered with him. Her lips twitched uncertainly as he took her arm, and the ice of his flesh pulsed hypnotically, dragging her into his easy smile. She blushed as she found herself retreating back to her fantasies.

"Where would like the demonstration?"

The gruff, sensuous voice brought her back and she led him into the living room. Freed from his eyes, she swallowed apprehensively. *This isn't a fantasy! It isn't!* A fear took root in her gut. Except for the fiction of those erotic daydreams, she'd had no experience with strange men.

Because she was a preacher man's wife.

"Why don't you just sit down on the couch and I'll show you what my rug cleanser can do." His voice droned on.

Susan watched him, seeing the strong muscles she'd already guessed at as he took off his coat. She was tingling in the images of her fantasies as they once more rose to life in the deep-set gaze that gripped her tight. She craved his potent masculinity, shivering at his rippling muscles while he poured green liquid on the rug and began to scrub the carpet.

They were the muscles of her imaginary lover. And then he faced her with a sly smile that made her weak with arousal. Time stood still as her need built . . . and built. . . .

". . . so you see how much work this can save you?"

His words gave her the certain safety she craved. She'd never seen this man around here before and he would move on to other blocks tomorrow. No one would ever know he was here with her, and even if they did, what was wrong with listening to a salesman's pitch?

And—and he'd called her beautiful.

"This little item here," he was saying with practiced ease, "is just great to shine up wood. Look what it does to your coffee table." The salesman motioned her closer and she stood up, feeling the drops of sweat on her cheeks. The robe was too heavy on her shoulders now and she shook it off cautiously, exposing the slight baby-doll covering of her nightie. She stepped to his side, acutely aware of his body.

"Getting a little warm?" He grinned.

She smiled back with unthinking lust, forgetting who she was. Nothing seemed important any longer—nothing but satisfying the urgency within her. Clumsily, forgetting the practice with her imaginary lover, she pushed against him, guiding his hand up under the thin fabric to her bare stomach. She shivered at his hardness, holding him close and rubbing up and down against him. Her fingers stroked him fearfully, then squeezed into his hard buttocks.

"Tear the gown from my body," she commanded huskily.

A knowing familiarity stirred his eyes as he dropped the polish and slipped an arm around her. She shuddered in unhidden ecstasy at the strength and cool touch of his flesh, then at the rapture of fulfillment as he did as she asked, listening to the musical rending as she was freed from the confines of her brief clothing. She felt his rough fingertips move between her legs, and he eased her onto the couch and knelt before her . . . then tugged the panties down her creamy hips, down to her feet, forcing her to gasp as his cold hand spread her legs apart and his tongue licked between those lips.

Susan cried out in unexpected ecstasy when his furious talent slid over her with gradual speed. "Y-yes . . ." she breathed. "Oh, yes . . . more. . . ."

3

"I really appreciate you coming over like this, Warren," called Carmen Richison's soft contralto voice from the kitchen doorway. Warren turned and looked through the Victorian-style house that was his last stop tonight. Its architecture shamed his own more modern home down the block, but with all the homeless people around nowadays, it was hard enough to justify the expense of what he already had.

"I'm glad to help." He smiled gently as he sat on the plaid divan and rubbed his hands to dismiss their lingering chill.

"You really do. I get so lonely when Chuck's out of town—especially now, after the holidays." Carmen carried two wineglasses into the living room and past the large console TV, shaking the shiny tresses of her long blond hair. They bobbed over her naked shoulders and the thin straps of her low-cut lavender dress. "It's nice to have a concerned neighbor like you come over to look after me."

Frowning to hide his blushing pleasure, Warren combed his brown hair out of his eyes and shifted uncomfortably on the divan. He thought about Chuck Richison, so often on the road as he wheeled and dealed. He was far more wealthy than Warren, building his fortune daily, and despite their differences, Warren had a certain admiration for his good sense. Besides, Chuck was one of the few people who listened to his sermons attentively when he found time for church. That alone had been enough to create their light friendship, and Chuck's greed had seemed to drop off lately, too, especially since he married Carmen. Warren hoped dearly that she would prove his salvation . . . that is, if he could manage to keep them together.

"I really do appreciate your company," Carmen repeated, forcing him to meet her blue eyes.

"As, uh, your minister and Chuck's friend, it's the least I can do," he replied quickly.

Carmen walked toward him, displaying her youthful buoyancy

with every step—she was only twenty-two—gave him a glass, and sat beside him to sip from her own, giggling when he scooted farther away. She smoothed her hem back over her knees, then peered at him seriously, making her face knot up in a way he rarely saw, even these past four or five nights that he'd come over. "I just get so lonely sometimes," Carmen went on with a lower voice. "It's nice to have someone to talk to."

She continued, but Warren was barely listening, thinking of Susan instead. Wasn't that what she always complained about? That *she* was lonely?

Yes. But he was only doing his job when he wasn't with her; comforting and supporting the members of his congregation. After all, he was always nearby and not gone from her at night as Chuck so often was from Carmen. It wasn't as if she hadn't known it would be like this sometimes too. They had been over it time and again before the wedding: His being ordained committed him to helping others and to being on hand when they needed him. He was a minister, whose calling was to minister. And yet it still stood between them and brought out their almost nightly exchanges. Her early promises of understanding and support had disappeared over the years, and now she openly challenged his devotion.

But he was just doing his job.

"You know"—Carmen's voice broke in on his thoughts—"sometimes I dream of being married to *you,* Warren." She giggled again as he stared and opened his mouth. "I mean, Susan's got it made, you know? You *never* go out of town."

Warren hid the smile that tried to creep over his lips. "Susan thinks I'm gone too much," he whispered aloud, feeling the frequent accusations she threw at him rise against Carmen's approval. His face reddened with guilt as soon as the words were spoken and he took a swallow of the mellow red wine.

"She's crazy," Carmen said, then fluttered her eyelids with a new chuckle. "How about if you and Chuck swap us as partners for a while and then we'll see what she says, huh?" She looked down at her unmarred hands, stretching her fingers. "Or maybe I shouldn't even joke like that to a preacher. . . ."

Burning in another blush, he tried to meet her grin: "We both know it's only a joke, Carmen." Warren pushed back his jacket sleeve and checked his watch reluctantly, knowing he should go. He'd come by as he promised he would, and knew it would do no good to continue discussing the problems in her relationship with Chuck again.

"How about some cheese?" Carmen asked, getting up and going back to the kitchen.

He shook his head, but she was already gone. He just felt so tired . . . especially because today's exhaustion was still heavy on him. It made his willpower sag. Warren forced his attention back to earlier this evening when he'd found most of the troubled people he had looked in on last week back to normal at last, their illnesses gone. . . .

Unfortunately, each was now presenting him a second task of reviving their newly troubled marriages. Those other problems were quite different from that presented here, though, and disturbed him even more: They were very sudden marital disintegrations, perhaps best summed up in the case of Leslie Gordon. Once a selfless woman, she was now more and more interested in what *she* was getting out of life, often at the expense of others. It had been a virtual overnight transformation, and distressed him with the coincidence that Leslie had been one of the first to fall victim, less than a month ago, to a peculiar illness.

Yes. The strange flulike ailment was capturing so many now, and always with these same aftereffects. Warren remembered the morning when he was called to Leslie Gordon's home to find her pale and nauseous, full of an inexplicable shame and guilt. The previous evening was a blank to her. As they talked, he tried to use his knowledge of psychology to help, but in the course of this past week the trouble had come back, except that now she had nightmares she could never quite recall. He could feel her earnest distress at his very presence. Her husband told him secretly, in depth, of her recent antagonism, but even he didn't know the reason why; his wife Leslie no longer spoke to him. She didn't speak to *anyone,* but sat staring silently and blankly out the window every night.

The way Susan sometimes did.

When Carmen came back with a plate of crackers and cheeses, he looked up at her sly smile, then put down his unfinished glass and stood up, stopping her. He looked at the soft rise of her breasts, then quickly away. "I"—he shook his head, walking across the room and feeling a new pressure of guilt for being here so late—"I think I need to talk to you and Chuck together, Carmen," he managed, ignoring her sullen pout. "If you want to work this out with him, then he should hear what you're saying too. You two haven't been married that long, and there are always a lot of problems in new unions, especially since you're so much younger than Chuck is." He faced her, not looking away this time. "If you want to work this out . . ."

Carmen put down the plate beside his wine and followed him past the coffee table, taking his hand. "But what if I *don't* want to work it out, Warren?" Her deep eyes slid over him, then over the still-life paintings adorning the living room. "I don't like the things I have to put up with, and you can't tell me it's going to get all better, because I know people who have been married for years that have trouble too." Her fingers stroked his skin delicately, bringing goose bumps. "Just look at you and *Susan.*"

Swallowing hard, he wanted to explain how the turmoil in his own life had begun only because of that wreck Susan had been in, but he had told Carmen that before and knew it would serve no purpose. "God gave us all the ability to talk to each other, Carmen, and he expects us to use that gift and work these things out with what we have. You've got to overcome your difficulties and so have I, and if you need help in talking to Chuck, that's what I'm here for." He walked to the front hallway closet to take out his overcoat, then dragged its sleeves over the arms of his suit, listening to her approaching steps.

"Well, maybe you're right," she murmured at his ear. "I guess you *are* really helping me, Warren. You're helping me to get it all clear in my mind. I really appreciate—"

Buttoning up his overgarment, he stepped to her front door quickly.

"Can we talk some more about this tomorrow?"

Hiding a shudder, he felt the longing to stay here with her now, and to come back as she suggested—as he had promised Chuck.

"Warren?"

He closed his eyes, imagining her in the ways she said she imagined him, as though she were his wife, but fought those impulses as hard as he could with the knowledge that Susan needed him; that with the thoughts alive in him now he could not excuse his remaining away. "I don't think I can come tomorrow night," he said finally, with a sigh.

Carmen stood stiffly for a moment, then shrugged. "Will you call to make sure I'm okay?"

His fingers brushed over the cool doorknob and he made himself turn back, seeing her posed with one hand on a very shapely hip, the other under her sulking mouth. Her eyes were wide and sad.

"I—I'll call," he promised, and struggled to get out as she turned up her lips in a promising smile.

"Maybe I can change your mind about coming over when you do, huh?"

Without answering, Warren pulled open the door and stepped out into the frigid night, breathing in its iciness to dispel Carmen's temptations. He looked at his darkened home down the block, past the swaying, leafless tree branches, then walked with guilty relief to his Mercedes in the driveway. He sighed and got in, driving the short distance slowly.

Maybe tonight Susan wasn't waiting. Their ongoing battle was taking a toll on him, and with the outside troubles developing now he was in no mood to get into it tonight. He just hoped she'd gone on to bed this once.

Warren turned into his own driveway a minute later and got out of the car bleakly, continuing to watch the single-level house for telling signs of her ambush, breathing in the night air warily now. He shook his head and looked up at the bright moon in the cloudless sky, then to his gray shadow on the white-brown lawn, letting his thoughts return to that woman Leslie Gordon again. In a very short time she'd become another person, and he hadn't the slightest idea why. Why? It didn't make sense.

Walking through the dead grass, he went over the puzzle with frustration. Menopause, perhaps? She was near the age, but that reason wouldn't explain the others, and there were so many such cases now that it was hard to believe in coincidence— Melanie Winthrop, half Leslie's age, was going through the same thing, after the same sort of overnight illness.

It was strange. He had discussed it with the doctors who'd

examined some of the people he could now only think of as patients, and was frustrated when they passed off the incidents as a touch of a virus or the flu, followed by mild depression. Everyone seemed to pull out of it—at least physically—so it was easy for the doctors to dismiss. But not for him.

Quietly, Warren unlocked the front door of the house, then stepped inside and flipped on the hall light. As he glanced at his watch once more, the growing certainty that Susan hadn't waited up for him this time surprised him anew, but he just thanked God and yawned with relief, hung up his overcoat, and stepped into the living room. He flipped on another light cautiously and was quiet so as not to awaken her.

While he paused in the unusual silence, it struck him that maybe she wasn't here. Susan had threatened leaving before. The notion made him chew his lip. She had actually been the first to exhibit the intense selfishness that had been hovering recently. But hers had begun months ago, as he'd told Carmen, and he knew its cause was the loss of her fingers in the wreck.

Warren shook his head, remembering his attempts at counsel. She wouldn't go to a psychiatrist. She just quit trying, refusing to be a person on her own. She relied on him to make her something instead, and was greedy for his time now. She— His thoughts broke off as he saw her, sprawled on the frosted material of the couch, naked and fast asleep. Again he shook his head.

"Susan," he whispered softly, moving beside her. "Susan? Time to go to bed."

She didn't move. Standing back, he smiled sadly at her fading beauty. Her curves no longer excited him . . . but what could he do? He couldn't very well force her to snap out of it and once more be the person she had been. He could only encourage her as he already had. The decision was up to her. He wouldn't allow himself to interfere with her will—he could not make her be anything she didn't want to be.

"Susan"—he spoke a bit louder—"get up now."

When she still wouldn't stir he frowned, knowing she didn't usually sleep so soundly. "Susan?" He touched and tenderly massaged her arm.

There was no reaction.

Alarmed, Warren checked her pulse and sighed as he detected

her slowly beating heart. But the depth of her sleep made him look around for an open bottle of wine, and he moved his nose to her mouth suspiciously, then managed a faint smile. It was free of the frequent alcoholic taint, and sweet. Perhaps, he hoped, she'd finally begun her exercises and only exhausted herself after the months of inactivity.

Carefully lifting her to carry her to the bedroom, he held that hope dearly. Maybe he had finally gotten through to her. Maybe she was finally beginning to care about herself again, and how she appeared to others. He crossed through the doorway, laid her on their bed, and covered her gently with a blanket.

"Good night, Susan," he whispered softly, kissing her cheek, then went back to living room to check his agenda for the coming day. When he'd finally finished and put his notebook aside, he noticed Susan's robe and gown on the rug, and walked over to pick them up—

And stopped with wide eyes. The gown was torn to pieces— as though Susan had ripped its silken fabric viciously from her body.

II

1

When Susan awoke she was surprised to find Warren sitting in the straight-backed walnut chair beside the bed, reading. It increased rather than erased the foggy otherworldliness of sleep still engulfing her. Vague impressions flooded her consciousness and she tried to remember . . . something—something that had to do with the tingling pain where her legs met.

At the same time that pain shamed her, without her knowing why. She blushed and felt a loss . . . but of what? She couldn't recall. Only that it had something to do with the hurt and the hazy shadows of her dreams, dreams that were fading except for the knowledge she had had them.

"How're you feeling?"

Still blushing, Susan looked at her husband with round eyes. She wanted—needed—to hide the sensations within and yawned truthfully. Despite the sleep she knew she'd had, she was tired. "Fine. It—it looks late." She nodded at the sunshine coming through the window shades. "What's the occasion of your still being here?"

Warren shrugged, appearing so uncomfortable that she stared at him with more attention. He was so familiar, yet different—completely different. He was somehow distorted to her vision, as though changed during the night—as though he'd become more threatening to her and what she was, and what she wanted to be. It caused her to tense, and the dull longing in her heart blossomed . . . though she didn't know for what—didn't know what for.

"I was worried about you," he said in the bedside voice he cultivated. "How . . . are you feeling?"

"Worried about me?" she mocked. "Since when?"

He looked stricken, and she studied his increasingly foreign face—the high forehead above bright but not piercing eyes. They were set at either side of a thin nose that tapered to the faint beginnings of wrinkles around thin lips. Solid below was his deeply clefted chin, flowing into his neck, and a muscular body that was spoiled by the enlarging pot about his middle. She knew him by heart, yet somehow his very appearance held a growing aura of antagonism.

"I love you, Susan," he finally said. "I've always cared—"

"Shit," she muttered.

"Susan."

"Shit," she repeated, fighting back the pale smile of satisfaction the word gave her.

"It's not proper—"

"To hell with what's proper."

Warren frowned at her with apprehension. "Susan, do you feel all right?"

She frowned back, surprised by her words and the force behind them. Drawing back, she felt the strange pain throbbing through her become more acute, and she struggled against nausea. The brightness streaming in between the purple lace window curtains hurt her eyes and repulsed her. She felt repulsed by Warren . . . by this room . . . even by her own existence.

What the hell was wrong with her?

"Susan?"

"I feel like *shit.*"

His raised eyebrow looked as though he'd expected that. "What's wrong? Do you—what happened last night?"

"What—what do you mean by that?" she asked sharply, not understanding the strange guilt and vehemence consuming her. "Why would you care if anything happened to me last night? You weren't here. *You're never here.*"

"That's not true."

She pulled the thick blanket up to her neck, reticent to confide her feelings. "What makes you think anything happened last night?"

He locked his eyes to hers and adjusted his clear-framed glasses with a tremble. "When I came home you were lying on the couch, naked."

Her mouth quivered. "S-so what? M-maybe I was trying one last time to arouse your failing manly interest." But she wondered at his words and at what she *had* been doing. She could distinctly remember putting on her gown, and her robe. . . .

"If you weren't letting yourself go as you— Forget that." He put down his book without marking the place and nervously stroked one of her covered legs. "What happened? I found your gown and robe in the middle of the floor."

He reddened and her curiosity grew. What had gone on last night? She knew she was naked now. If he'd found her that way when he got home, why . . . But she couldn't remember. Only that she'd been standing in front of the mirror, dreaming of a muscular man holding her . . . a *real* man, his hand slowly moving between her legs as she carried out his desires with her own fingers, and— Why couldn't she remember?

"Your gown was torn to pieces."

She gasped, the recurrent fantasy of a stranger taking her, ripping off her clothes, and violating her, to her actual pleasure, vivid in her thoughts. Could she have gotten so carried away? But why—*why couldn't she remember?*

He hesitated. "Did you take anything last night? Medicine?"

Blushing, she shook her head, but felt a memory trying to emerge. Vague impressions of her dreams, made almost familiar by his words . . .

"No," she answered after a strained silence. "I didn't talk to anyone. I didn't even see—" Her voice cracked and fell as the unknown memory shimmered close. She swallowed hard. "You're the one who's popular. I can't even play for the church anymore, much less for people who really know music. I'm just a cripple—" She broke off, hearing a deep voice in her ear. It wasn't Warren, or anyone else she could name, but it was as if she had heard it before. The voice said simply: *Beautiful.*

"Susan,"—Warren moaned, and she looked up in surprise that he was still there—"don't start in on that stuff about being a cripple. You can learn to play as well as you used to, even with the limitations of your fingers. You need to come to grips with this. You need to . . ."

His words faded into the roar of her mind until she barely heard them: "You need to *look* at yourself, Susan. Actually, physically *look* at yourself like in a mirror, and tell yourself that you're—"

Beautiful, soothed that strange voice, overpowering Warren's monotone. *Beautiful . . . beautiful . . . your body, so tender and fresh . . . so sweet. . . .*

"Beautiful." Susan sighed, floating in the tones inside her head. "Beautiful."

"What?"

She opened her eyes and smiled, almost leering. "I'm beautiful," she repeated. "I can do what I want . . . anything I want."

Disbelief was on his face, then a stunned pleasure. "Yes—yes, you can—you can overcome by learning again. You can be better on the piano than you ever were."

The guilt still gnawed inside her, but she could ignore it. She *was* beautiful. Something had happened to her last night. She was a blur of physical weakness laced with a strange personal strength of will, and a guilt that was ebbing quickly now. Though she couldn't understand it, her fantasies had helped her—her fantasies. They filled her warmly and drove Warren farther away —her fantasy had taken his place, a fantasy she had made real, or at least more real than he was, more desirable. . . .

The vague images of her sleep were becoming clear, and a lust grew in her to make those images true again.

2

Elizabeth Potter looked up from the library's front desk with a searching grimace, frowning as the unmistakable odor of sour liquor puckered her nose. She swept her eyes across the rows of book-filled shelves and the dozen age-assorted patrons nearest her, finishing in the unblinking gaze of a middle-aged, red-faced man in a dirty plaid shirt and faded jeans. His icy eyes seemed closer than the six feet that separated them, and she looked away, knowing his kind—another wino or transient come in to get out of the cold. Still, his iciness seemed forced, overlying a seething passion he could not completely hide.

And now he was smiling at her.

Elizabeth clicked her tongue at the roof of her mouth and kept her eyes steady, ready to oust him at the slightest provocation.

To her surprise he came sauntering up to the wide desk with a mild and unhurried step.

"Where do you keep the card file here?" he asked.

She wrinkled her nose at his filthy scent, turning to look at a more pleasant man behind him. "We use the microfiche . . . sir. Over near the stairs up above." She pointed briskly at the machines beside the staircase, trying to load the reply with her disapproval.

He nodded heavily and brushed back a long lock of greasy hair. "Big place you've got here. Rather than have me spend a lot of time looking around, could you tell me where you keep your books on religion?" Long pause: "And where you keep the recent local newspapers?"

The questions and his precise manner surprised Elizabeth. "Uh, religion is on the second floor at the north side." She frowned. "The newspapers are in the room next to the microfilm machines, at the opposite end."

Keeping his eyes on her doubtfully, he rubbed his thick whiskers, then winked. "Thanks very much," he told her softly. "I won't trouble you long."

She hesitated, feeling that all this must be very wrong. A man looking like he did should have no business in her library. As he walked to the stairs and past a young couple holding hands, she gazed after him, nearly feeling his tired, dignified steps. But she didn't stop him and smiled secretly, wondering who he might be, and what he was hiding from.

But mostly, she remembered the air of profound suffering he carried, and the sinister gleam trying so hard to overshadow it.

3

A little before noon Warren came to the bedroom doorway and looked in on Susan. She stared back without recognition, caught up in the mazes of her mind. Warren's earlier questions and her uneasiness that something had happened to her—something important that she couldn't remember—had brought this on. Why was she so melancholy and physically exhausted . . . why? *Why?*

"How are you feeling now?"

"Huh? A little tired," she replied too quickly. But she wanted him to leave and didn't know how to tell him of the discomfort and guilt he was causing her. It might make him suspect that something was wrong—it might make him suspect . . . what? She shook her head and wondered if her sanity was slipping. Had her fantasy become so real?

But the still throbbing pain and her satisfaction told her it was real. She wanted him to leave her alone so she could think this out, so she could relive her obsession once more, and through that, try to remember it all. The tingle of her lust made her hate Warren for being there.

Warren glanced at his wristwatch, then back at the folding tray holding the scarcely touched breakfast he had brought in an hour ago. "Aren't you going to eat?"

"I'm not that hungry." She paused. "And—and it's cold now."

She fidgeted in the excitement to relieve her longing. "If you need to go somewhere, I'll be all right."

He frowned. "You usually want me to stay."

"Maybe," she said, carefully keeping her voice free of sarcasm, "maybe I'm finally beginning to realize that we both have lives, Warren. We can share with each other, but we can't hold one another back." A tiny smile tried to force its way to her lips as she used the very words he'd used on her countless times, but she wouldn't yield. "I've been thinking about that, and you're right."

The distance between them disappeared as he walked past her dressing table and the chest of drawers, came to the bed, bent over, and kissed her. She shut her eyes, his lips revolting her by their touch, but bringing back the memory of those shadowy lips of her dreams—lips so cool and sensual. . . .

"I love you, Susan," he said. "I know sometimes it's seemed I was trying to make things worse, but—"

"I know," she whispered, keeping her words slow and calm. "I understand. You were right. I can do anything."

Beautiful, she thought.

He hugged her and oppressed her with his tight hold. "I've got a lunch to go to and then I'll be at the church. I may have to go to dinner with Tom too—if you need me to come home, though, call, okay? If I'm not there, they'll know where to get in touch with me."

Susan nodded. "I'll be all right." She made herself hug him back, then choked back relief as he stood up and returned to the door.

"Do you want anything before I go?"

"I'm not an invalid." She laughed, and with an honest humor. It actually made her want to call him back to her . . . to share these strange sensations assailing her.

"I'll try to be back before eight." He pursed his lips in a kiss at the doorway. "Remember to call?"

"I will," she responded, and watched him turn and disappear into the hall. She hesitated, resisting the peculiar urge to call him back—and then her fingers were down under the bedcovers and caressing the sore pleasure spot between her legs. The pain of pleasure. She concentrated on last night, forgetting Warren and entering her fantasy once more. From miles away the front door creaked open and shut firmly, and on cue her lover shaped in her mind with all his pale ruggedness; his dark, peppery hair . . . and his *eyes,* the profound sexuality and deep power of his eyes. She wanted him again, reliving the pleasure that flooded back from the shaded memories she unveiled through her sheer will.

The release and power of the previous night's orgasm consumed her, and those hands—*his hands*—were on her flesh. His mouth pressed into her tender skin, bringing her frenzied gratification. And then the debauchery was complete—the surge of a new orgasm filling her. Susan wheezed and sagged in sensual delight, gasping.

Minutes ticked by and finally she came to herself enough to sit up and examine her still pulsating center of delight: the skin fiery red yet cool to the touch, and unbelievably, she could still see the ragged imprint of his toothmarks where they'd pulled out tufts of her curly hair and broken the skin. Almost fearfully, Susan moved a finger through the black fluffiness and touched the dried blood there, the wonder of last night's experience bubbling inside her. She knew she had to have it again. She had to have *him* again.

But how could she find him? She searched for a name but knew he hadn't told it to her. In frustration she tried to bring it all back, envisioning him as though he were before her now. If she could only see him, she was sure she'd recognize his distinctive features at once.

But where had he come from, and where had he gone? Could he and her experience just be a part of her imagination?

Her eyes fell to the imprints in her flesh and she knew he was not.

Susan got up and held tight to the carved bedposts. She was weaker than she'd thought. Walking slowly out the door into the living room, she made it to the couch and sat down, then awakened to a familiarity, and knew this was where it had happened. She sighed, his lean face in her eyes, then let her gaze trail to the coffee table, recalling her plans to clean and dust it.

It was shiny and sparkling as if new.

He had cleaned it . . . demonstrated a product on it. She remembered now—

Her lover was a traveling salesman.

4

At seven-fifteen Susan stepped out of the house into the night, closing and locking the door with nervous anticipation. Carmen, her neighbor down the tree-lined block, hadn't yet been visited by her traveling salesman and his wares. She hoped desperately that he would go there tonight.

The idea thrilled her as she hurried through the chill air down the sidewalk: Her subtly posed questions to Carmen had shown her a way to be with him again. Though she wasn't sure how it would turn out, knowing she could at least see him once more was exciting.

But once she saw him, it wouldn't be enough. If a memory alone could do so much to her, what would his actual presence do—what would *she* do, there, in front of Carmen? And if she did or said anything, could she trust Carmen to be discreet? Susan almost turned around, seeing her secure life in danger of being lost forever for one more short moment of rapture. But she went on, growing careless of the possible consequences as she remembered how he'd driven her to such heights of ecstasy. It was worth it all. She would gladly give up her life-style for him —for his touch once more.

Susan hurried across the dead grassy yards and up the stone walk and pushed anxiously at the doorbell under Carmen's mailbox, looking down the street to see if he was coming.

But except for the stray collie dog Warren sometimes fed, the block was empty.

"Hi, Susan," Carmen greeted her, making her jump. Susan took a deep breath and waited while the younger woman opened the door with a peculiar smile. "It's so nice to have you over.

I'm surprised we don't see each other more often—we live so close together. . . ." She stood back to let her by. "Sometimes it seems so lonely here in the middle of this big city."

Susan nodded in pretended sympathy, but she had never really cared much for either Carmen or her husband. Carmen was a flamboyantly attractive twenty-two-year-old who'd hit it lucky by meeting Chuck, twice her age and recovering from the untimely death of his first wife. Chuck owned a large business and had so much money, he bragged how long it would take to count it. But he worshiped Carmen and she had everything she wanted—including, rumor went, other men. Chuck was gone a lot and Carmen was well known for her mastery over the opposite sex. She made Susan envious.

But then, she, too, was beautiful. The salesman—the mysterious handsome prince who had saved her from the emptiness of her life—had said so. His eyes stared at her even now, half mad with lust, and he told her how beautiful and wonderful she was. She *was* beautiful—*as beautiful as Carmen.*

"Let me take your coat," her hostess said, reaching out for the heavy, down-lined jacket and hanging it in the closet. She shut the door and stroked her long, carefully braided blond hair, leading Susan into a front room that matched her own in elegance, even to the piano and the lush paintings. "How about a drink?"

"That would be nice," Susan said, feeling her heart beat faster. She rubbed her tight jeans self-consciously and sat on the mahogany sofa, her mind far away, but glanced up as the wet chill of a glass was pressed into her hand. "Thank you." She smiled quickly, looking at the drink. "What are we having?"

"Fire and ice." Carmen sat beside her and crossed her legs, exposing a lot of thigh as she moved and made the slit in her pink dress widen. "Brandy on the rocks. To warm your tummy on a cold night." She smiled with an honest shyness. "Really, I am glad you came over, Susan. Like I told Warren, I still don't know many people around here."

Susan glanced up at her husband's name with the memory of anger, but sighed and let it fall away. "Oh?"

Carmen cocked her head. "Yes. I saw him last night, but I guess he told you."

Not remembering, and surprised to find she didn't care, Susan shrugged. For once she was glad Warren had not been home the night before. She exhaled slowly, feeling how the salesman had moved inside her during that short time they were together.

"Warren's been nice to come check on me, but I . . . sometimes I miss another woman's company. There hasn't been much of that since I married Chuck and moved here." The dainty structure of her face became sullen, and Susan frowned at her unexpected admissions. Carmen's expression was frail with an honesty of truth, and she suddenly didn't seem the woman Susan had believed her to be. She was supposed to be so aloof —but Susan realized she didn't really know her at all except through hearsay. They'd spoken idly in church, and when they got together with their husbands, but . . . She frowned. Perhaps Carmen never had secret men over in Chuck's absence. Perhaps she wasn't a person to trust.

Maybe not, but did it make any difference now? This afternoon she'd gone over it time and again: She no longer loved Warren. He was repulsive to the touch.

"I miss my girlfriends from college," the younger woman went on. "I love Chuck, I guess, but it seems like he's always gone, and he never wants me to come along. He's afraid I'll be bored." She laughed dejectedly. "I'm bored when I'm left behind in this big empty house." She looked at Susan in a flash of sincerity. "I mean it, thanks for coming over."

Mild embarrassment made Susan look away. "I . . . wanted to come," she answered, flushing with the guilt that she'd ignored Carmen these past months as Warren ignored *her*. Since the horrid loss of her fingers she'd ignored everything.

Beautiful.

"So, where is Warren tonight?"

The question passed through Susan uncomprehended. Impossibly, it seemed she heard faint steps outside the house, coming toward the front door.

"Susan?"

Footsteps.

"Susan, are you all ri—"

The doorbell rang.

"I . . ." Carmen watched her, then put down her drink and stood up. "I've got to answer that. Just a minute, Susan."

She watched the younger woman—just a girl—go into the hallway, and Susan forced herself up to follow, then trembled as the front door opened, and listened.

"I'm selling a new line of cleansers for the home. . . ."

An estatic sigh bubbled inside her. It was *him*.

"I—I'm sorry," Carmen was saying, "I have company now. Maybe you could come back later."

"*No.*" Susan's feet crossed the space to the hallway in a frenzy, her need pumping in her veins. "Th-this is," she gasped, trying with the last vestiges of what she'd been to control herself, "the salesman I told you about, Carmen—the one who was at my house last night. *Watch his demonstration!*" She was once more drunk in the potent eyes outside the screened outer door, and her discipline vanished. "You'll be amazed. . . ." she got out.

Carmen stared at her, then at him. Susan felt cold as she thought she saw a fleeting look of annoyance streak his face and her heart skipped a beat. "Perhaps I ought to return another night," he said, frowning.

"*No!*" Susan burst out with fierce jealousy. He was staring at Carmen, and she at him, just as Susan had last night. The old sense of inferiority struggled in her once more. He was *hers*.

"Perhaps you could give us a short demonstration," the younger woman said weakly. She unlatched the screen and the lean salesman took her hand. "Oh, you're so cold—at least come in and warm yourself by the fire."

Susan heard her own words of the night before on Carmen's tongue with hot envy. She was oblivious to all but him, and as he stepped inside with his demonstration case she felt last night's passion bulge between her thighs, and tore at her blouse in that frantic lust, ripping off two buttons as she threw it off—she was clumsily unfastening her jeans and unzipping them, pulling them down. . . . She heard Carmen's disbelieving gasp as she kicked the pants away, and then her bra was on the floor . . . and finally, her panties.

She wanted him.

"Susan—" cried Carmen in a stunned tone. "*Susan!*"

Then the salesman's deep-set eyes turned, consuming Carmen with their power, and she could only stand there, her mouth open wide, choking as she struggled to speak. At last her face blanched and she sank to the floor in a limp faint. The salesman stepped over her, smiling to himself, and his fingers closed over Susan's wrists with intensity. He touched cold lips hungrily to hers.

"Yes," Susan sighed, "oh, yes. . . ." She shuddered in delirium as his power swept over her, and she let herself lie down on the rough, carpeted floor as he drew back . . . heard him close the front door quietly. Her body shuddered with anticipation.

But he bent over Carmen and began to remove her dress instead.

Susan weakly pushed up on her elbows to try to stop him. She was the one he wanted, not Carmen. He had said *she* was beautiful. But then he stared into her so deeply that she could no longer command her own body and fell back.

"I won't be long," he assured her with a voice that was almost cruel, "and then you will take your turn once more." He chuckled. "You are even more beautiful tonight."

Disappointed but strangely reassured, she relaxed with the heady anticipation, imagining herself to be Carmen as she watched him slip down her nylons and lay them aside, then force himself between her trembling legs and inside her. Carmen was awake now, and her wide eyes darted from him to Susan. She began to pant, then at last relaxed and moved with his long strokes. Susan smelled their musky union enviously but fought the emotion by pretending the woman's moans to be her own, slipping into fantasy and its warm security as the minutes passed. . . .

Carmen cried out feebly.

Silence. Susan trembled.

"Now you," whispered the deep voice.

Goose bumps tickled Susan's tingling flesh as she opened her eyes and watched the mesmerizing man move away from Carmen and come closer. She sighed, reaching her shaking fingers out to him, and at last saw the truth in his smile. It was at once more terrifying, yet more alluring, than any dream she could have. She knew she was going to die, but the gratification she would feel would make it worthwhile.

She craved that moment and opened her legs wide for its pleasure.

1

"She may die, Warren. We're doing all we can for her, but the way that psycho tore open her wrist, she's lost a lot of blood. She's still unconscious and seems to be slipping into a coma."

Warren MacDonald nodded at the steady voice and felt guilt. But how could he have known? How could anyone have known? Even if he had stayed home she might still have gone to see Carmen and he wouldn't have heard of this any sooner. He shook his head at the cruel injustice. Just this afternoon it seemed that she had regained the will to try . . . and now this.

"We'll do the best we can, Warren," the doctor told him without hope. He nodded at a balding, black-suited man of medium build seated several feet farther down the white hall. "We'll try. Uh, I think this gentleman's waiting to talk with you if you're up to it. He's with the police department. I can tell him to wait till tomorrow. . . ."

"I'm okay." Warren swallowed and pressed the doctor's hand emotionally. He walked over to sit with the policeman. He felt sick.

"Mr. MacDonald?" The detective was apologetic and touched his hand briefly as Warren sat beside him. "Do you feel able to answer a few questions?"

"Sure," he heard himself mumble, trying to grasp this situation but trembling all the same.

"Can I get you anything?"

"I just don't understand why someone would do this."

The policeman wiped his nose and loosened his red speckled K mart tie as he leaned back. "Yes, I understand, Mr. MacDonald. Believe me, I understand. But really, this incident isn't . . . uh . . . isn't as unusual as it seems."

Warren looked at him sharply.

"My apologies. I wasn't trying to be flippant. It is strange, but not singular. The officer who first arrived at the Richison house found Carmen Richison in a very weak state and unable to remember anything. She'd been sexually assaulted and is understandably in a very deep state of shock—can't remember what happened." He paused. "Your wife was lying in the front hall, and I'm afraid that she, too, was assaulted."

"Oh."

The detective picked at his nose with a long forefinger, looked at the dark result, and frowned hesitantly. "Are you in shape to handle this right now?"

He wasn't. The shock of it was far too great, and the guilt. If only he had stayed home or at least gone over to Carmen's tonight. . . .He didn't want to hear any more, but he had to know. Maybe he could somehow help the police find out who had done this. "Go ahead," he whispered.

The big man nodded. "If you want me to stop, just say the word."

"Yeah."

"Both women were orally assaulted. Uh . . ." The investigator drew a breath uncomfortably. "What I mean, sir, is that . . . this psychotic attacked them . . . and, ah, chewed them." He stared at his dirty finger again and wiped it on his slacks, then looked at Warren long and hard before continuing: "Your wife got it the worst. She—she's badly mauled. Then the assailant slit her wrists. When we got to her, she'd lost a lot of blood."

"The doctor told me that." His stomach rumbled and he felt blood drain out of his face. *Just one of those things,* he knew was the next remark. *It happens every day, right?*

"For all we know, this could be the job of a lone lunatic, or maybe some kind of a cult, but we have no way of telling just yet. There's an unfortunate history of this kind of thing. The

Manson murders, or what Richard Speck did to those nurses in Chicago . . . even Jack the Ripper."

"Yeah." Warren gulped.

The detective took out a paper card and gave it to him. Warren glanced down and saw the man's name was Robert Mishkin. Warren stared at him blankly, wide eyed and stricken, only wanting to see Susan.

"My home phone's on that card under the office number. Odds are that this guy's met you and your wife . . . or the Richisons. If anyone comes to mind, please let me know immediately."

"Did you get any fingerprints?" Warren clenched his teeth and held the scream inside. Susan . . .

Robert Mishkin held up his finger and prodded his left nostril again, wriggling it. "I can't say yet. I hope so. They're still running the lab tests, but even without the results my guess is that this may be the same man or group that broke into a house across town. The victim there couldn't remember what happened, either, and his roommate scared the intruder away before he could get a look at him. We're not completely sure, of course, since that instance was a *homosexual* attack. Whoever broke in had . . . chewed at the man's groin." Mishkin paused carefully. "There were distinct tooth imprints still in his skin. We're having the bite radius we figured from his wound compared to the damage done to your wife and the imprints on Mrs. Richison."

"But who would do things like this?" he whined shakily, near tears.

The detective shrugged. "There's a lot of sick people in a city this size, Mr. MacDonald. There's a lot of sick people everywhere, and if you want my opinion, they're getting sicker every day."

Warren shuddered, barely able to subdue his physical illness. "I've got to look in on Susan. I'll call, uh, if I think of anyone."

"Thanks. There's just not much we can do without a good lead." His lips stretched in a hard smile. "But don't worry. These guys have a way of tripping themselves up." Robert Mishkin raised his hand back under his nose, then suddenly moved it away and tightened his jaw. "Need someone to drive you home, maybe?"

"I'll call someone if I do. . . .Thanks."

"Good night, then. I'm sorry."

"Thanks," Warren repeated, watching him get up and walk down the tiled hallway to the elevator. He got up himself, gulped, then turned and walked the other way to the nurse's central desk. His mind was hollow, and he knew he was in danger of losing far more than just Susan; far more. He was in danger of losing her . . . *and his understanding of life.*

2

The stranger was back at the same time this morning. Elizabeth Potter hadn't even thought of the peculiar bum since he went up the stairs yesterday.

"Good morning," he said politely as he passed her.

"Good morning," she said, moving the brand-new books on the counter between them out of his reach.

He stopped and showed her his enthralling eyes, and she blushed and lowered her stare. "Uh, could I help you find anything?"

"No, thank you, ma'am," he said gruffly, and his winish reek made her winkle her nose as it had yesterday. He shook his head. "I'm just going back up to check the newspapers." He showed her a quick grin. "I won't be long."

Curiosity filled her as to what this walking contradiction was up to. "Are you checking the want ads?" Possibly, she mused, he had lost his job and was penniless, barely surviving as he tried to find another.

"Want ads?" He laughed bitterly and rubbed his whiskery chin. "No, ma'am, I'm going over the obituaries." He touched his forehead in salute and sauntered away to the stairs.

3

"Hi, Carmen. How're you feeling?"

"What—" Her eyes were half shut and she'd been rubbing one hand against the other when Warren's voice made her flinch. "Oh, hello, Warren."

Stepping into the small private room, Warren MacDonald put on his glasses and looked at the age-yellowed quilt covering her, then at the TV fixed to the opposite wall, soundlessly showing the thousandth rerun of an old *Twilight Zone* episode with William Shatner. A dark green robe was laid on the nightstand beside the miniature hospital Kleenex box, and the adjustable table waited near the window, shining in the red glare of the setting sun. That light emphasized the pallor of her face and made him remember how rich, how lustrous, her skin had been the night before last.

Swallowing, he remembered how he'd left her then, to go back home to Susan. He'd left in guilt, and now the same guilt burned in his soul for not having gone back—for not having looked in on her last night, anyway. And for not staying home with Susan again.

Carmen sighed.

He had to keep busy. He didn't dare think of Susan and what had happened in relation to himself. The guilt and frustration . . . the self-pity . . . was more than he could handle. He *had* to stay busy—he must help himself by helping *others. He must help others.* It was his job, after all. Surely Susan would understand. He walked closer to the generic bed and patted the ragged quilt with his fingertips. "How did you sleep?"

Her eyelids fluttered. "I had—I had nightmares all night." She licked her cracked lips. "I . . . oh, God, I want Chuck."

"Yes"—he nodded—"I called him last night. He's taking the first plane he can get on." *Nightmares.* "What did . . . you dream about?" he asked carefully.

Carmen turned away. "I can't remember. The last thing"—

she shook her head—"Susan and I were in the front room, Warren, drinking brandy and just talking . . . just talking and I—I . . ."

"Yes?" Ice surrounded his heart as he listened to her distraught voice. She was looking away as if embarrassed, like so many others he had talked to.

Like Leslie Gordon.

He cleared his throat, knowing the response in her face well, though he hoped it was just coincidence. After all, Carmen's reaction was normal for a victim of her sort.

"I don't know. Something . . . happened. Something . . . I think the doorbell rang, and then—then I can't remember. . . ."

Can't remember.

"I feel so funny. So . . . disgusting. Guilty." Tears were in her eyes and her face tore in unhappiness. "Like I've done something *awful.*" Carmen's bewilderment was horribly thorough and her eyes glazed over with it. *"But I don't know what it was."*

"Whatever happened to you didn't happen of your own will," Warren told her softly and without thinking, looking up at the TV as William Shatner tried to convince other airborne passengers that a gremlin was destroying the plane. "You shouldn't feel guilt," he went on, knowing the right things to say from his experience with other rape victims. He touched her nearest hand and took it gently. "You shouldn't feel guilt. If you were forced against your will, you don't even need to ask forgiveness —*you're already forgiven.*"

"But I feel so awful."

He lowered his voice cautiously, dragging a visitor's chair nearer the bed and sitting down. "Perhaps there's something else, Carmen. Something you've done that you feel has brought this on you? Maybe it—it's the problem between you and Chuck? Is there something else you need forgiveness for?"

"I—" Wide eyes stared at him. "I—God, I thought that's why you were coming over to check on me, Warren. God, you must know." Her face turned away. "I haven't been true . . . to Chuck." She sighed heavily. "There've been other . . . men. I . . . he's gone so much, and I don't have any *friends.*" She wiped her wet cheeks with the bedsheet. "Oh, God, Warren. I've lied and cheated him!"

Other men. Warren thought of the temptation he'd felt for her himself, even before this past week, then rubbed her hand with gentle reassurance, fighting those lusts that tingled below their friendship. She took his hand, and he pulled quickly away. "There is forgiveness in confession." He smiled uneasily.

A moment passed. "I do feel a little better." She nodded. "Do I—do I have to tell Chuck, though?"

Forgiveness is truth, and truth is love. "It would be better if you would." He moved his glasses back up his nose. "He can't forgive you if he doesn't know what you've done."

"It'll hurt him so," Carmen whispered pitifully. "I'm afraid."

Warren shook his head. "You don't need to tell him immediately, Carmen. I don't mean that. When the time is right, you'll be able to."

"When the time is right," she repeated. Her lips twitched uncertainly. "Are you sure?"

Warren made himself chuckle. "Of course I'm sure. I went to seminary to learn this stuff—trust me, I'm a minister." But he didn't have the feeling he put into the words. They hid a nagging doubt, and he felt that his belief in his effectiveness, his ability to help her, was being questioned by circumstances.

Carmen's eyes closed. "I trust you, Warren."

But he was frowning inside. She trusted *him.*

"I think I'll rest awhile now." She pulled the sheet and blanket up to her neck. "I want to be awake when Chuck gets here."

Accepting the abrupt dismissal, Warren stood and looked at the beautiful woman again, his thoughts swimming in her admissions, and his advice. *She'd been with other men.* He'd given her the benefit of the doubt all this time, assuming that her flirtations with him were the farthest she would go. But the rumors were true. He felt sorry for Chuck. Chuck believed Carmen to be utter perfection. The loss of his first wife made his love for her so furious that he would forgive her instantly, but the hurt of her confession would gnaw at him forever.

Warred shuffled down the whitewashed hall to the elevator, waited silently, then went up one floor. With a deep breath he started down the hall to his wife's room.

"Mr. MacDonald?"

"Huh?" He saw the emotionless nurse walking toward him and stopped, his mouth going dry.

She smiled without feeling. "We've been trying to locate you. Your wife's come out of it."

"Thank you." She turned away and he wanted to run to the room, but instead he walked unhurriedly, listening to his feet slap the slick floor. In a few moments he was there and stepped inside, making himself grin gratefully at the nurse and doctor on the other side of the bed. "Susan," he said, lowering his hand to the sheet that covered her body.

Her eyes were open, but her slack expression didn't change until he bent closer. Then her lips twitched bitterly. *"You?"* she wheezed.

"Susan," Warren murmured, sliding his fingers over hers. "I—"

A high giggle suddenly came up from her purple lips, and her red eyes blinked. "What are *you* doing here? I don't need you anymore. *Go back to Jesus!*" Her hoarse voice cackled brokenly. "Your God . . . loves assholes like *you,* Warren. *Jesus sucks.*" She gurgled, squeezing her eyelids closed.

Warren squeezed her hand. "Susan, you're delirious."

But her face lost its fuzziness as he spoke and her thin eyebrows came together harshly, filling her gaze with an instant, unmistakable hatred. "Oh, *fuck you.* Jesus . . . *sucks . . . because he doesn't suck.*" Her giggle rose with beginning hysteria and her fingers pressed into his coat sleeve. "And *you* never even kissed my cunt, *you Jesus-licking bastard! You were never even there where I could see you!*"

"Susan." He gasped, glancing at the doctor's steady eyes.

She pushed up on her elbows with a shiver and tried to reach out to him, slobbering. "Now—*I'll see you in hell, Warren,*" she hissed. "Only *in hell!*" she screamed, suddenly thrashing at him wildly, her voice breaking into a retching choke as she mouthed fierce, inaudible curses.

"Get the oxygen mask on her," the doctor said quickly, finally coming to life on the other side of the bed and grabbing her arm. The nurse pushed against him, trying to comply, but Susan fought them desperately, wrinkling her face with terrible lunacy, hissing and spitting—digging sharp fingernails into the doctor's forearm.

Dazed, Warren let the nurse push him back. Staggering from the cold bitterness of Susan's stare, he watched her yellow saliva mix with the doctor's red blood dripping on her face. She licked her torn lips savagely.

"Dear God," Warren whined, backing farther away as her words echoed haughtily in his ears and drowned out the noisy confusion of another nurse and an orderly crowding inside. Sickened, he watched Susan's chest heave and saw wrenching spasms jerk her body, and he didn't struggle at all when someone gripped his wrist, urging him farther back through the door.

He stared blankly as it closed with a loud click, his heart and legs turning to jelly. *Susan.* Ice overtook his soul. *Susan.* Her words taunted him against the muffled screams.

Susan.

4

"Excuse me."

Putting down one of the new books, Elizabeth Potter saw him again. The educated wino. She frowned. He was cleaner and neater this morning. The tangy scent of old rum no longer stuck to him so potently and he'd donned a rickety pair of glasses. Though he was still unshaven, his ragged hair was washed. She wondered if he'd read her thoughts. "Yes?" she answered evenly.

He laid a newspaper on the counter and waited for her to join him. "Can you tell me where to find this church?"

The newspaper was one of today's locals, *The St. Louis News.* She followed his finger to the continued story of the local minister's wife who had been attacked and had died from her injuries. "What church?"

"Warren MacDonald's church—the woman's husband. Valley View Methodist."

"You're not from around here, then," she said, more as a statement than a question.

The man gazed with sudden iciness, then nodded. "Hardly. I'm from a little burg west of Springfield. I just got here a few days ago."

"On business?" She smiled sarcastically, thinking of him as a wino chosen by winos the world over to find new forms of cheap rotgut and guaranteed a life's supply of liquid escape for his success.

"Of a sort," he said seriously, showing years Elizabeth hadn't guessed before. With his unwrinkled face and the smattering of gray in his deep brown hair, she had figured him as probably her own age or younger, but there was a certain wisdom mixed in the harsh gleam of his exact features and fixed eyes, though it was as incongruous with his physical appearance as his forced, polite manner.

"Valley View is over to the far southeast side of the city," she said finally, "just before you cross the Mississippi. It used to be the outskirts until they started all those additions five or six years ago."

He pulled a city map out of his coat pocket and laid it over the newspaper. "Could you pinpoint it for me, please?"

With the index finger of her left hand Elizabeth traced a route to the area from the library. He nodded and began refolding the map.

"Would you like me to mark it for you?"

"I'll remember." He smiled, showing her clean, white teeth that proved beyond a doubt he was not and never had been a street-living alcoholic. "Thank you for your help and forbearance."

A hundred questions were in her mind as he walked away, and she wanted to call him back, but stared after him instead, watching him to the exit. A moment later he was gone from her life forever.

5

Ashes to ashes . . .

Warren peered around the front grounds of the massive stone church self-consciously, hardly noticing the cold wind whipping through his wool overcoat, but no one was close enough to have spoken so quietly. *Ashes to ashes.* He finally pulled his collar up and shivered under the unwarming sun. The associate minister had used that ancient epitaph an hour ago. Ashes to ashes, dust to dust. Though he'd only said "ashes to ashes."

Why not? The meaning was the same, wasn't it? Wasn't the use of both phrases redundant, anyway? Yes. And it didn't change a thing. He sighed, still trying to believe it was Susan they had put into the ground, that she wasn't still alive. . . .

"Death can be a dark passing."

This time the voice *was* in his ear. "What?" Through tear-dulled eyes he saw the haggard man step out of the holly bushes beside him, and was angry at the unwanted invasion of his thoughts—especially by someone with unkempt, longish hair, frayed clothing, and a face too long unshaven, certainly after a handout.

"My name is Benjamin Dixon, Mr. MacDonald." He paused. "My deepest condolences, sir."

Warren nodded briefly and walked on.

"Mr. MacDonald—"

This time he stopped in unmasked annoyance and turned back to the stranger. "Well?"

Benjamin Dixon frowned, glanced cautiously at the street, then back at him with determination. His gruff tone became low. "How do you feel about the occult? About witchcraft?"

Containing an annoyance bordering on fury, Warren licked his lips slowly, staring the man down. "Should I know you, Mr. Dixon?"

"I'd be surprised if you did." He grinned raggedly.

Trying to stay the unkindness of his thoughts, Warren looked at the tangled bushes, comparing them to his emotions. He wanted solitude. *Solitude.* It was why he was coming here instead of going home to endure the sympathy of Susan's parents and his friends. They had gripped his hand while he stared at the lonely casket, saying words that reminded him of his own empty platitudes, and he'd only nodded, mumbling his thanks sometimes, but mostly just staring, struck dumb by the tragedy. He had wanted at least an hour or so alone, and walked from the cemetery by himself, longing for the reassurance of the treasured books in his office, to escape temporarily from what had happened.

"I'm a minister like yourself, Mr. MacDonald," Dixon said.

Looking at his shagginess again, Warren raised an eyebrow at the revelation, then finally extended his hand, relieved when Dixon took it only briefly and released it. "I won't keep you long," he promised.

"I would appreciate that," he muttered, allowing the stranger to take his arm and walk him to the church's rough front door. A door far older than Warren. It had stood there since well before his birth, set in by workers long dead. It would most likely be there long after *he* died. "My office is up those stairs," he told him, leading the way as they filed inside the enormous lobby. His voice softened as he gazed up at the oil painting of the white dove with the symbolic twig of peace in its beak, hung with care on the far wall. "Are you Methodist?"

"Nondenominational."

"Could I ask why you're dressed as you are?"

"We forgot to take the offering." He chuckled, then shook his head apologetically. "Sorry—long story. Right now I'm living off the land."

Letting it pass, Warren crossed to the stairs and started up, hearing the creak of the other man's steps behind, and led him past closed doors embossed with the names of the music minister and associate pastor, into a small paneled office. He looked at the framed verse of the Twenty-third Psalm beside the window and moved to sit behind his desk, nodding Dixon to a chair. "Now, then," he said, boosted by the familiar surroundings that enfolded him gently, "what did you ask me outside? I'm not sure I heard you correctly."

Benjamin Dixon sat back in the hard black plastic and straightened his glasses with a sly grin. "You might have better than you think. I asked you how you felt about witchcraft."

Warren looked at him long and hard, drumming his fingers lightly on the desktop. He didn't—wouldn't—look at Susan's picture behind the stand-up calendar. "I've just been to my wife's funeral, Mr. Dixon. Do you understand that?" He took a deep breath. "I don't know you, and I certainly don't want to get to know you or anyone else right now. No offense. I just don't feel up to a theological discussion." Making a sudden fist, Warren hit the desk forcefully, a gesture unexpected even by himself. His voice rose. "I just want to be left *alone.*"

Dixon folded his hands, rubbing the dull wedding band on his ring finger. His face was faintly sympathetic, but determined. "I'm sorry, Mr. MacDonald. I know how you're feeling now—believe me. I wish I *could* leave you alone. But I believe that what I know could lead us to your wife's murderer." He took off his wire-framed glasses, opened his coat to wipe them on his shirt, then replaced them on his nose. "Mr. MacDonald—"

"Who the hell are you—Father Brown?"

Dixon smirked and bent closer, letting his face darken. "Let me talk. Have the members of your church been falling ill in greater numbers lately? Something like a flu, except that when they recover, there are definite and unusual aftereffects?"

The words sank through Warren with their quiet knowledge. "Hold it—who are you really? How did you know that?"

"Educated guess." His eyes became sharp with a smoldering fire and he rubbed his whiskers thoughtfully.

Witchcraft. Warren remembered the detective and what he'd said about cults. A cult might've used Susan in some kind of ritual. And though Warren knew that witchcraft and the like was so much uneducated garbage, there *were* people—crazy people —who believed in it, and tried to work the so-called "spells." The policeman's words stayed with him, making Warren wonder once more if maybe a lunatic witch group *was* responsible, and if so, how this Dixon fellow knew about it. He leaned back in his chair, suddenly watchful. "What do you mean, 'definite aftereffects?'"

"Those who've been ill become 'cold,' " Dixon said. "That's

my word for it. They become less responsive to those around them—uncaring of the needs of other people. Does that describe what you've seen?"

"How do you know that?" Warren asked quietly.

"It's what happened in my own congregation, Mr. MacDonald, and possibly—*surely*—others before them. God alone knows how many."

"And you suspect witchcraft?"

"Not precisely."

Warren frowned. "Then why did you ask me how I felt about it?"

Pressing his fingers together, Dixon shook his head. He glanced at the portrait photograph of Susan. "One of the newspaper stories mentioned it, and I just wanted to see your reaction."

"If you know something," he said, reaching for the brown desk phone slowly, "maybe you'd better tell it to the police."

Dixon snorted. "And you think they would listen? You think *they* would admit to the existence of the supernatural?"

Warren thought of the *Twilight Zone* episode Carmen had been watching. His knuckles turned white as he grabbed the phone's receiver, and he looked carefully into the other's face. "If you know something . . ."

Reluctantly, Dixon stood up and backed away, running a finger along a line of thick books on the shelf beside the door. "What I have to say is for *you,* Mr. MacDonald. I wouldn't disturb you if it weren't so important. I—" Dixon came forward, dropping his palm to force the receiver in Warren's hand back onto the phone's cradle. "You *don't* believe in the supernatural?"

"Oh, good God." Warren shook his head in disbelief, trying to pull his hand from under the other man's strong force, only holding back his growing anger in deference of who he was and how he *should* act. *"What do you want?"*

Benjamin Dixon stared.

He sighed bitterly, tiredly. "I believe in it—to an extent."

"And witchcraft?"

"As a supernatural reality, no." Warren remembered the occasional doubts in his own beliefs and shuddered, seeing their sensibility once more against this man's implications. *How and why had he ever doubted?* "I believe in the existence of man-made evil, but not a supernatural evil."

Dixon rubbed his jaw testily. "Then what of damnation, Mac-Donald? Can't people be damned for what they do? *What if your wife is damned?*"

Warren's eyebrows rose high on his forehead and he felt the angry creases they made. "Mr. Dixon, I wish to be alone—*now!*"

The older man's eyes were heavy in a harsh sneer. "Then I'm sorry to have bothered you, *sir,*" he breathed, not hiding his own irritation. "Please accept my *apology.*" He released Warren's hand, taking off his glasses again as Warren lifted the receiver quickly and held it out of his reach. Shaking his head more mildly, Dixon put the glasses in his worn shirt pocket, softening his tone. "If you won't listen, Mr. MacDonald, don't think that the police will." He took a step back. "I'll only tell you to be careful tonight and to lock your door when you get home."

Ignoring him, Warren dialed 911.

"Good day, Mr. MacDonald," Dixon whispered, a pinched expression on his face. Then, as the operator answered, the man went to the door, stepped outside, and was gone.

"Emergency," responded a woman's voice in Warren's ear.

He hesitated, started to speak, then slammed the receiver down angrily.

IV

1

Late afternoon the next day Warren was back in his office. He sat down in the padded chair tiredly, relieved that it was finally all over. Taking Susan's parents to the airport and seeing them off, listening to their sad reminiscences of their daughter, had been almost more than he could bear. And Susan's mother was ill now, too, making matters worse—that strange flu sickness everyone seemed to be catching. She'd forgotten the previous evening entirely.

But her state could be as easily explained by Susan's death. He was just glad the older woman was gone and no longer under his keeping. It would be too hard to deal with another problem now.

Rocking his chair back and forth, Warren noticed the visitor's chair out of place and remembered his peculiar, unwanted guest yesterday. Thank God he hadn't seen the man today. The sadness and shock was passing at last, but left him with a hollowness that was even more grueling.

His fingers trembled as he took the appointment calendar book out of his suit coat. He didn't even feel fit for taking care of his mundane everyday business. He had skipped lunch already, and canceled two appointments.

Shuffling pointlessly through the stacks of paper on his desk and laying them back down, he remembered waking up alone in the big bed this morning, dreaming for a moment that Susan was up before him and cooking him breakfast as she used to. He even smelled the frying bacon.

It had been too much. He couldn't stay in that empty house of sad memories and wasn't ready to go back to it even now. He'd built his life around his work and kept Susan to the sidelines, neglecting her, especially since the car wreck that had planted a new wedge between them. He'd opened that breach wider with his inability to face it.

If he could do it over . . .

No. How many times had he challenged that very thought in other survivors? It seemed he could instruct others on how to deal with death, yet couldn't even follow those simple guidelines himself. He wasn't following any of them—so how could he expect to help and lead others? He told them all that life goes on and love continues after death. There was no reason to be sad because love is joyful. Love understands that the departed have gone on to a better place.

Love understands, but the parting words from Susan's lips had come too close to destroying that understanding. She had spoken blasphemy and hate, like one of those freaks in the tabloid "reportings" of demonic possession.

Warren shut his eyes. He *didn't* believe in such things. He didn't even believe in *hell.* Long ago he had, as all Methodist boys do. He had believed in every biblical legend with all his heart, and knew of others who'd studied with him who still did. But his learning in liberal theology had destroyed those myths once and for all. How could a God of love, a God who *is* Love, spare any expense to save all humanity? How could there be such a thing as demonic possession? *How could the God he knew coexist with such a thing as a Satan or a hell and allow his beloved creation to go there, even of its own uneducated will?* Eventually His Love *must* win through, break apart all barriers, and bring even the darkest sinner back into His fold. There was no condemnation in Christ, after all, was there? *Wasn't that even written?* Warren held the thought tightly: There was *no* condemnation in Christ, even for those who weren't in Christ—who repeatedly refused God's grace. Even they must be saved. *In the truth of grace all must be saved and there could be no hell.* He had spent years in school learning that—men who had studied

God for more years than he'd even walked the earth had developed that doctrine, so who was he to question it?

But what of those who spent equally long years, and didn't agree?

Yes—he shuddered—like that bizarre, untidy man who had trapped him yesterday . . . and then dared to question Susan's salvation.

It made him twist his face bitterly. That very attitude destroyed those unsettling arguments. They condemned, and Warren *knew* there was no condemnation in Christ. The Bible was a book, containing God's will, but still had been written by men, who *were* fallible. Christian existentialism held that the mythical imagery of the New Testament was merely a natural vehicle for expressing transcendent power and action in terms of this world and human life, and that the real thing of importance was not the imagery but the understanding of existence the myths enshrined.

Warren frowned. For the first time those teachings disturbed him. Could they be heresy, as so many fundamentalists accused them of being? Could he be wrong? Were his beliefs wrong?

And Susan—not only was he unable to cope with her death, he had failed her life. She had told him over and over again of her hopelessness after losing her fingers, and rightly accused him of being selfish when he left her to help others instead of her. She was right that he hadn't cared enough for her, even before that wretched accident.

The awareness hurt. He saw now that his attempt to set goals for her and force her back to what she'd been had merely been his attempt to sweep the entire incident under the carpet. He'd never considered what the misfortune had done to her mind and soul. And that, indeed, was the real problem. Love wasn't sad, and a real love could ignore the awful things she had screamed out to him. But had he really loved Susan?

"I did," he whispered. "I do."

A long agonizing moment dragged by, and he hoped it was true, but knew that his failure was that he hadn't loved her nearly as much as he loved himself—not as much as the sacrifices and plans he'd made for his own life. He hadn't allowed her loss of goals and desires to come between him and his for more than brief moments.

"God," Warren moaned aloud, "what kind of a man am I?"

What kind indeed? He was supposed to be the example for the body of people he ministered to. He preached love as salvation rather than salvation as love, and now found he didn't even practice those precepts. What kind of a man was he—*what kind of man could he be?* What business had he telling others what to believe, when he couldn't practice the truths he told himself—

What was truth?

God's Love was truth.

"God . . ." he moaned again, and laid his head on the desk. Dizziness unsettled his stomach, but he doubted that he could even find the energy to vomit. Too weak. *Empty.* Warren closed his eyes, struggling feebly against the self-betrayal and new tears, his thoughts crawling like an abondoned baby through the terrible shadows of long-ignored facts. His throat made tiny wet noises until he couldn't hold back the sobs any longer, and he succumbed to their rule hopelessly, finally drifting into sleep as the sun set.

When he awoke, Warren felt little better. He rubbed the tight skin of his eyes where the tears had dried, and shivered silently. The nightmares of Susan and her horrible last words had echoed through his dreams with a ghastly violence, making his sleep wearing and unrestful. If only—

He set his jaw, pushing himself out of the chair while feeling for the lamp switch on the desk, blinking at his watch as it came on with a dazzle. It was near eight—still relatively early. How many nights had he come home far later to his distressed wife? Where had he been when she needed him? Where had he been?

He gulped, tasting sour spit.

Out on his self-appointed mission to topple windmills, that's where. He'd gone out to conquer giants, attacking only windmills, and found himself back home as Quixote had; a well-meaning, destructive fool.

He wanted a drink. A strong drink.

Tugging on his overcoat, he found his keys. *He wanted and needed a good tall drink; he wanted and needed Susan.* And maybe if he drank enough, he would find her once more in his dreams, horrible though they were.

Warren walked to the door and went down the stairs in darkness.

2

The house was silent. Warren stood just inside the doorway and shivered, listening to the sounds of creaking tree limbs in the wind outside. Their moans made him feel bleak.

Breaking the stillness with a sigh, he turned on the hall light, gazing into the living room and seeing but not feeling the calm sea and landscape paintings Susan had placed on the walls. He avoided looking at the couch he'd found her asleep on the night before she died, and opened the closet to put away his coat, feeling her loss gnaw at him. He wished and prayed that it was just a horrifying nightmare that would change his life as Ebenezer Scrooge's nightmares had changed him.

But it wasn't.

Warren went to the thermostat to turn the heat on, then stood there a moment, rubbing his hands together. The furnace rumbled with reassurance. In the kitchen, he blinked as the fluorescent lights came on, then poured himself a half-glass of brandy. A small stack of unopened mail waited beside the breakfast he'd left uneaten; dirty dishes filled the sink.

Warren sipped his drink, then refilled the tumbler.

It felt good. He wanted to spend the evening remembering Susan. Drinking . . . and remembering Susan.

Glass in hand, Warren walked into the living room and knelt stiffly to build a fire. He stacked three of the seasoned logs, struck a match and twisted the gas knob, then shrank back and tossed it in. The dry heat bathed his cheeks, and as he waited for the wood to catch, his eyes traveled up to Susan's lush portrait on the mantel. She looked vibrant, full of life and determination.

He spun on one knee, feeling the intangible pressure of eyes on his back.

The room was empty. The house was empty.

But in the blowing of the tree branches outside the window, he caught a quick glimpse of movement. "No," he whispered. It had seemed for a moment that he saw a flash of two gleaming eyes, surrounded by a face—*Susan's face.* "No," he said again, and looked back into the bright fire. He remembered his counsel to bereaved husbands and wives: "You may see things," he told them. *You may see things.* But then he forced rationality; whatever he'd seen hadn't really looked like Susan, had it?

No. The momentary illusion hadn't looked like Susan except for those eyes, and they only looked as Susan's eyes had on that final night in the hospital. He took another gulp of brandy and forced a chuckle: other survivors said they saw visions of their departed loved ones, and whatever he'd seen looked more like a man.

He couldn't even have the right delusions.

"Silly ass," he snorted.

The house creaked.

"Warren, darling, did you have a hard day? I thought I heard someone in here."

Warren jerked to his feet, spilling his brandy. She was there: vibrant, seductive, and naked. An icy mist broke out above his eyebrows.

"You woke me," she said. "I fell asleep waiting for you. It's late, but I don't mind. You're here now."

"Susan."

She walked to him, touched his lips with her smooth, cool fingers. He trembled violently. Her fingers stroked his cheek. A chuckle escaped him. "A—a nightmare—" He gasped, laughing louder and shaking.

"What is it, Warren?" She chuckled with him. "What's so funny?"

"I—I dreamed that you were *dead.*" He tried to grin.

Her lips curved sympathetically as she leaned against him. Her solid fingers traced designs over his face. "A nightmare, my sweet? But it's over now." She took his hand and slid it across her breasts, and he moaned. Desires long ignored blossomed from his heartache.

She wrapped her strong arms around him. He let his hands caress her, moaning again as she began to remove his shirt.

"Just lie back," Susan purred. "You've been right all along, Warren, and I want to thank you. I won't even bother you about returning home late again." She dropped the shirt, unbuckled his belt, slipped off his pants with agonizing slowness. "We'll be partners now as we never were before."

He lay on the carpet, sighing with incredible relief—Susan was alive, and *changed*. His ideas were right, and now he could learn to be a better husband, a better man. He caressed her shoulder as she knelt beside him, then let his fingers slip down to her breasts, listening to her moan as he found an erect nipple. With growing excitement that made his shorts tight, he pulled her close, surrounding her cool skin with his lips.

Her hands moved up his chest and fumbled through curly hair, then lingered on his cheek. He turned his head and licked the taunting fingers, sighing with her excited breath at his pelvis. Nimbly, her ten fingers played him as though he were a piano—

Her fingers. His insides rocked and as he stared down at her hands, the warmth slipping from his face. Black horror clouded back into his mind, hammering through his quickening heart. "Your fingers."

Susan crawled up, touching her nose to his, her smile grown wicked. "Yes," she whispered in husky abandon, "I can play again, and I have you . . . again. I have you at last. Come, Warren. I want you . . . and you want *me.*" She slid on top of him and spread her legs over his, rubbing against him, reaching down to squeeze his shrunken balls temptingly. Her passion consumed his fears, and he panted with the need she impelled deep inside, even through the bizarre disorientation surrounding him. Then his stiffness knew the ice of her flesh.

"Susan!" he screamed.

Before his outburst died, it was drowned out by the shatter of smashing glass from the window. Pinpricks of the splinters struck him with the rush of freezing air. Susan shrieked in fury, and he blinked at the hatred contorting her face and the vicious shadow in her eyes.

"In the name of Christ, you will leave and not return! You are barred from this house!"

A man climbed in through the broken window onto the couch, then to the floor. His frenzied eyes stared beyond Warren at Susan. He took a shining ornament from his pocket and held it up.

Susan's eyes sank through Warren like hot metal into plastic. His heart skipped. "I *will* have you. You *will* be mine, shit husband, mine to control in death, *as you controlled me in life."* Her cold power drove against his thoughts, his words. She opened her mouth . . . and he saw her *teeth.*

"In the name of Christ!"

She was gone.

Chill and giddy, and desperate for Susan, Warren pushed himself to his feet and started for the door. A hand caught his shoulder, and he fell in the entry hall. He struggled desperately to free himself from the obstructing force, feeling cold sweat break out on his naked body as the black pit inside him grew dizzily . . . and grew.

V

1

Very slowly, the protective shroud of sleep lifted from Warren, and he shivered from the cold, trying to place himself. He remembered leaving the church and driving home. Had he been in a wreck?

The living room was dimly lit. He was home, lying on the front couch, the seldom-used anniversary blanket covering his naked body. A cold breeze sang through the room and big broken pieces of glass covered the couch around him. They glimmered in the reflection of firelight. Slowly, he turned to the fire's crackle and saw a man seated on the hearth, smoking a cigar.

Warren gasped and struggled to sit up, brushing some of the glass pieces onto the floor. "Who are you?" he burst out. "What are you doing in my house?"

The shadowy figure turned and Warren pulled the blanket back up to his waist. It was that badgering hobo minister he'd met yesterday, Benjamin Dixon.

"Helping you," Dixon said flatly.

"Helping me?" asked Warren, plagued with the impression that he should be able to remember why he was in the state he was in. How had Dixon gotten in?

"You're confused." Dixon eyed him with a narrow grin and started toward the couch. He tossed his cigar into the open screen of the fireplace.

"I am confused," agreed Warren. "I feel drained." Dixon guffawed and Warren stopped, suddenly angry. "Why is that funny?"

Picking Warren's glasses up from the floor, Ben Dixon shook his head. His appearance was much cleaner and neater than it had been the day before. He wore a heavy coat, clean turtleneck, and unfaded jeans.

"Here," he said gruffly, handing Warren the spectacles and following them with his discarded clothes. Warren blinked, his head pounding, and jerked back when Dixon dropped the bundle into his lap. "Put them on and we'll talk." The man rubbed a red nose slowly, and sniffled. "It's been a long time since I talked *with* anyone. It seems like a long, *long* time." He watched Warren carefully as he began to drag on his underwear. "Winos don't talk, you know. They just don't talk. They only mumble— and grunt—and they drink." A tiny smile crinkled his face. "But I've learned so much from them, you know? All they do is drink, or they think about drinking and how they're going to get their next one. They even dream about it. They wake up screaming in the night for a bottle of Ripple—"

"What are you doing here?"

"Put on your clothes, sir," Dixon repeated firmly, walking back to the window and waiting.

Fitting his feet into the slacks and awkwardly standing to pull them up, Warren wobbled on weak legs and tried to concentrate. The broken glass and the breeze at last connected in the frame of the broken window. *The man had broken in.* Warren's heart beat faster; *Dixon was dangerous.* Warren gritted his teeth, trying to shake off the fog enfolding him. He had to get out of the room and call the police as he should have done the other day. This man must have broken in and—

"Susan—" Warren struggled to keep his feet as a blinding memory of her broke into his thoughts and consumed him. *The memory of her in this room, tonight. The memory that she wasn't dead, and had come into this room, naked, and undressed him . . . and—* "Susan!" he shouted.

Strong arms held Warren up as his knees became weak—he remembered her perfect hips straddling his legs, a frantic lust in her dilated eyes, and then the explosive crash that tore her eyes from him. She'd turned a hateful glare at the breaking window, and at this man, climbing into the house. "Susan!" he screamed, making his throat raw. "She—she's alive!"

Dixon pushed him back to the divan and looked grimly into his eyes, keeping his hand on Warren's shoulder. "She *is* dead, Mr. MacDonald."

"She was *here.*"

"Yes," the older man said. "She *was* here."

Warren was dazed by the words and knew he must be enduring yet another nightmare. He had seen her, touched her, but could not dislodge the equal memory of her lifeless figure lying still in her coffin. "I—I want to wake up."

Dixon snorted, showing Warren a hot sparkle in his eye. "You'd be better off it you never did." He lifted the glass Warren had used earlier and sniffed it. "Do you keep liquor here?"

"What?" He trembled, remembering Dixon's commentary on winos. "I—yes . . . in—in the kitchen." He recalled pouring himself that drink, and the proof of that truth made the terror that he might be losing his sanity cling to him. He fought the images trying to surface from deep inside, but couldn't forget they were there. Images of Susan, standing over him and baring her teeth at this man as he held up a small cross, the canine fangs sharp and long; her face a contortion of animal fury. Warren shivered uncontrollably and the surrealistic vision faded.

"Lie back down. I'll pour us each a drink."

2

"You surely don't expect me to take any of this seriously." The words were a statement and not a question. Warren's faint was more distant now, and like a dream, the impossible memory of Susan tonight was slipping quickly into his subconscious. He felt better with his clothes on again and the new glass of brandy in his hand. He swallowed another sip, breathing through his mouth as it burned down his throat, and stood from his seat on the divan. He looked Ben Dixon in the eye.

Dixon didn't hide his annoyance. *"Seriously?* Maybe you'd rather I just let her suck your blood?"

Compensating for the alcohol, Warren carefully stepped to the broken window and examined the thick cardboard they had wedged in. His thumb still stung where a distorted triangle of the sharp glass had snagged him, and he rubbed the Band-Aid over it, then backed away from the draft. It would play hell with his electric bill. "It was a dream."

"Dreams *again?*" Dixon pulled another cigar out of his coat to unwrap, then snipped off its end with a small pair of scissors. "And I broke the window because I don't like to use the front door, right?"

"I don't know," Warren blurted out testily. He felt the horrible pressure of the scenes in his mind blast against rational fact, and his brain thudded explosively as he stared into Dixon's hardened eyes and mouth. "What's your explanation for being here? How do I know you didn't give me something to mess up my mind—some kind of drug?"

Dixon cracked his knuckles loudly and blew a long stream of smoke across the room. "Is your wife dead or isn't she, Mac-Donald?"

The memory of Susan's hate filled him with anxious dread as it had the night she died. She'd stood—*he'd imagined she stood* — right before him tonight, her body toned and perfect, the way it had been on their honeymoon, on her face a vicious, bitter grimace he'd never seen there even when he'd watched her die.

The very thought made him blush. She *was* dead. Dead and buried . . . he had mourned for her with her parents—

And almost made love with her an hour ago.

"Well?"

"I . . ." Sanity compelled Warren to say Susan was dead, or that he himself was insane. But if he had dreamed those horrors, how could Ben Dixon know any of it? If he were alone now he knew he could easily discount it all as one more nightmare brought on by his loss—but not with this man here. The only possibilities left were unacceptable.

."There's *not* a rational explanation," Dixon told him sharply, pulling the words straight from Warren's thoughts.

Warren glared, backing away. "There must be," he muttered. "It's insane. You—you said Susan was a vampire." He spat out the word with distaste.

"Yes."

The clock chimed ten times, breaking into Warren's feeling of unreality. He knew this calmly lunatic man believed what he said. "How," he asked desperately, lowering his voice, "how did *you* know? What happened to *you*?"

Dixon shook his head and puffed his cigar, sending the stale odor drifting toward Warren: "The only alternative is to accept insanity."

"Have you?" spat Warren harshly.

"Not me," the big man said with sudden intensity. "Not me. Rather, the world we live in. The world that's made such things possible."

Warren finished his brandy, unable to dispel the vision of Susan standing there naked, sexy, and drooling for him . . . and baring those impossibly pointed teeth. It seemed her mouth had grown larger and larger, her ten beckoning fingers growing longer and longer.

It was impossible.

"My wife," Warren whispered indecisively, "lost two fingers in a car wreck several months ago. When I—*if,* I mean. *If* I saw her tonight, I saw her with a whole hand—her fingers were all there. How could that be if any of it really happened?"

"An illusion." Dixon stood and walked confidently to the fireplace, took the poker, and adjusted the logs, making the wood spark with a snap. "Vampires are human bodies inhabited by demons. But I guess that's harder to accept than some kind of scientific theory of a mutant resurrection for a man who doesn't believe in the supernatural power of darkness." Ben Dixon dropped the poker and closed the fire screen, glaring at him. "Good God—don't you know what the hell you've just seen and escaped? She is dead! She's been embalmed. Her soul is gone. What you saw wasn't her! She is dead and it's too late to help her. A demon has assumed her body to bring others into its power, and you're vulnerable. You are vulnerable whether you believe in it or not." He stomped to the divan, chewing his lips. "No man is without sin, so we're *all* vulnerable." He paused, lowering his voice, his gaze far away. "But she—it—knew your weakness, so it came here first."

It was all too much. Too unbelievable. The image of Susan and those teeth—her hate—was all that kept him listening. He could not forget that. He could never forget that, and knew it would be fastened into him permanently, next to his first glimpse of death when he'd witnessed his grandfather's heart attack in 1965. It was one of the bad things that stayed with you, returning at unexpected times; a thing that couldn't be ignored or forgotten. "What happened to you, then?" He breathed the question. "What brings you here?"

Dixon's dark eyes sparkled with measured hostility, but he gazed at the clock on the TV, then sat on the limestone hearth and crossed his legs, his voice the dull throb of a quiet engine. "My own church was nearly destroyed by the . . . vampire." He wrinkled his expression in distaste. "It was only by chance I discovered him. I didn't believe it—didn't want to believe it even when I was forced to. It's just not something you expect ever to have to believe. I had no idea of what it was capable of, or how smart it can be—the fiend responsible for this only takes a little blood from each of his victims. It doesn't kill them, but they're tainted." He stopped as his voice grew thin, and swallowed hard. "The infection is in them, and when they die, they become what he is."

"But Susan—"

"I don't pretend to know what happened there." Dixon tapped the growing ash from his cigar into his cupped palm, then dropped it past the screen. "The long and short of it is that your wife is damned. She was damned by her own will whether she consciously realized she was making a permanent choice or not." Dixon wiped his lip and sighed.

A tree limb slapped the house outside, and Warren looked at the cardboard over the window nervously, an icy chill growing in his stomach. "I can't believe it. You can't know that."

"No?" He swallowed with difficulty. "Well, I hope I'm wrong there." Then he frowned and pointed at Warren. "But you've got to believe it—you don't have any choice with your beliefs now, MacDonald. The sun rises and sets whether we want it to or not." Dixon started to say something more but stood up instead, crossing to him, his face as cold as the breeze trickling into the room. "If you *won't* believe me and what you've already witnessed, we'll try out the evidence of your eyes again. I'll do whatever it takes to convince you." He walked to the entry hall with determination. "Get up and get your coat."

"Where—where are you going?"

"*We're* going," Dixon said gruffly, "to kill two birds with one stone. And one of the birds is a vampire."

"You need help. I'll refer you to someone. Come to my office tomorrow." Warren's voice was a monotone.

Ben reached out and closed solid fingers around Warren's wrist, jerking him to his feet.

"I don't want to go," Warren said.

Ben Dixon smiled with that awful gleam in his eyes and his features twisted without humor. "I told you it doesn't matter a damn what *we* want, anymore."

Warren didn't struggle. Ben was bigger and bulkier than he was, and the pressure driving the man made him stronger yet. As Ben pulled him toward the door, Warren's head turned, Susan's picture above the mantel holding him, her eyes holding him. His sanity, his faith, were captured in her determined, demanding gaze, and at any moment her long fingers might close and crush them.

3

"It's freezing," moaned Warren. "Susan can't be anywhere out here." He pulled his coat tighter. The night's chill was bitter.

"But if you saw her, she was dead, so how could the cold affect her?"

Shifting his eyes away, Warren touched the icy fence they'd come to. "Stop it." Behind them his car sat very far away and very alone in the empty driveway. Ahead, the fence's wire squares framed gray tombstones. The crescent moon cast an eerie light over the sloping, shadowed grounds. His scalp twitched, prickling his hair.

"Let's go," Dixon said, poking his fingers through the fence. He climbed noisily and awkwardly, then dropped down to the dry, rustling grass on the other side.

"Even if you are right about all this," Warren said, "how do you know she—Susan—hasn't already come back"—he flushed, his face warm even in the subzero temperature—"to—to her grave?"

Dixon glared tiredly through the fence. "Haven't you listened to a thing I've said? *It* lusts, MacDonald. My God, didn't you see? She had you and lost you. She was practically frothing at the mouth." He put a hand in his pocket and fished out his tarnished cross. "They're *fiends*. Only the one who started it all has learned to control its hunger for the sake of self-protection. Its victims are just newborn babes, hungry for their first drops of blood. She had to have it. Just like those stinking winos I slept with. She had to satisfy her lust."

Breathing hard, Warren tried not to think of Susan, not to see her.

Dixon was smirking with a surly confidence.

"You," Warren whispered. "God, have you stopped to think how ridiculous you sound?"

"Truth often seems ridiculous," he murmured roughly, shoving the cross back into his pocket. "The men who believed the world was round seemed ludicrous just a few hundred years ago, but time has proved them right." He dug his fingers into the fence, as though to climb back over and drag Warren after him, and his eyes shone. "Time proves truth, not men."

Warren hesitated, wanting to go back to his car and just drive away, but he needed to prove that this man was wrong.

"Come on, MacDonald."

Silently, Warren counted to ten, then pushed his hand up to grab the high fence pole, wedging the tips of his shoes into the square holes. His hot misty breath surrounded him like a cloud as he puffed and climbed to the sharp wire ends at the top as Dixon had, then carefully lifted himself over them to jump down.

Dixon chuckled, his sound loud against the distant express-way traffic. "To do God's work, you must have the faith of a little child. We have to regain our sense of naïveté." He waved his hand at the fence. "We must act like children and think like children: when I was a kid, I used to climb a dozen fences every day."

From the traditional elongated half-moons and crosses, to the rarer statuesque memorials, thousands of markers ranged the flat, tree-dotted cemetery. Warren had never quite realized how many of them there were.

Warren thought of the dozen people he knew who'd had the same symptoms as Susan. Susan's mother had been stricken last night much as Susan was the very day she died, with the harsh overnight illness that left its victims hollow and self-centered. Though he'd discussed the epidemic with no one, Ben had known the symptoms.

Warren followed Ben among the gravestones, wishing desperately that he had stayed at home.

"The victims become vampires," Dixon stated flatly, sparing a brief glance at him. "They become vampires *unless* they receive the salvation offered them, but the taint of their disease won't allow that. The victims move farther and farther from the light until they are the same in life as they'll be in death. They're damned. They're damned because they love and worship evil." He snorted, a self-righteous grimace twisting his features coldly. "They welcome their damnation with open arms, and with the sick state of this world and the people in it, who would even notice the difference?" His chuckle dripped animosity. "Who would even care?"

Goose bumps spread over Warren as Dixon's words saturated the strange, swaying shadows around them. "If they made a mistake, if they were attacked, they shouldn't be damned. That's not fair," he said, recalling the iciness of Susan's flesh and furious stare.

"Fair?" The driven man laughed again. "Listen: Anyone who receives the vampire's mark is damned unless someone who's free destroys that vampire before the victim dies! Someone like *us*, MacDonald. Only we can take away the cancer that incubates inside each victim. That's the only way to help them."

The wind whistled briskly as Dixon dragged him toward Susan's resting place. Dixon glanced at him and nodded, as if reading Warren's thoughts. "I know where I'm going. I watched her rise tonight, MacDonald. You watched her buried, but I watched her rise up from the ground."

The dirt was black and loose around Susan's grave. Warren recognized the flowers he'd selected that had seemed so irrelevant, so insufficient to mark Susan's passing. The white and yellow roses were already dead in the cold, their shriveled petals scattered on the dirt.

"At least it's in a clearing," the big man muttered, bringing out his cross once more. He released Warren to dig through his pockets and take out a small plastic bottle.

"Good God," Warren whispered.

"A funny thing, fear." Ben Dixon waved at the dead trees and grass dramatically. "It serves as a safety release in films and campfire stories, yet it comes back to serve against us. We find ourselves afraid of things that aren't even possible." He tugged another cigar from his pockets, unwrapped it, and dropped the cellophane to the brown grass. "It's just like when we were children, except that now we know we can't trust our fears. That's where we've lost our way, MacDonald. I've learned not to disregard my fears without proving they're unjustified." His eyes scanned the cemetery; then he bit off the end of his cigar and spat it out.

"Some people would call that paranoia."

"But my fears are justified," Dixon told him, lighting up. He exhaled, and searched for long minutes in the silence. At last he dropped his stogie. "They *are* justified."

Feeling the hammer of his heart return, Warren took out his glasses and moved away from the tree to follow Dixon's pointing finger. His own fingers were numb, trembling as he fit the plastic frames on his nose.

Between the stark, slumbering trees he thought he did see something moving, pale and severe against the night sky.

Susan.

Warren sucked in a lungful of air shrilly. No—he tried to calm his aching brain—it was only the caretaker . . . the caretaker or maybe even a vandal.

"You see it?"

Dixon's words made the slender figure more solid, and the realization became terrifying as the shape glided closer and closer. "I . . . see something," he admitted, *"something.
. . ."* An urgent tide of nervousness gripped him. There were no such things as ghouls and vampires—he knew that.

The pale figure was coming faster, appearing and disappearing between the trees, and he craned his head with sick fascination to keep it in view. Its dark, shoulder-length hair flowed behind it, catching the wind, and then it was near enough to leave no doubt that it was a woman . . . a naked woman.

Her legs and hips were sleek, firm. Her breasts tremored with each movement forward. Dark hair licked at milky shoulders.

"No." He gurgled, drooling saliva onto his chin. *"No."* He closed his eyes, trying to rid himself of the panic squeezing his heart in two, knowing too well that face from the portrait, the face that held his soul.

"Yes," whispered Ben Dixon. He grabbed Warren and made him look again. Susan's familiar, somehow staggeringly voluptuous features were distorted in a rare grimace of satisfaction. She looked right at him—into him. The enchanting eyes promised unending pleasure with the Susan he'd first loved.

"Oh. Oh, God."

Her love was awaiting. He only had to accept her and return her love with his—with himself.

"MacDonald!"

"Huh?" She stopped at the far end of the grave, mesmerizing him with the future only she could give him, sweeping him with desire. Her pupils dragged him inside. His left foot crunched the ground, drawn forward. His hand rose to her.

"Don't look into its eyes, MacDonald!" warned a voice.

Panting, he felt the fury of his heart and wanted to go to her, to reunite with her like a long-lost lover. But he couldn't pull away from the intensity of Dixon's grip. He struggled, the iron fingers biting through his wrist to the bone.

"Don't," scolded the hushed whisper. "You'll see things: promises . . . promises that won't be kept. That's their power, don't you see? They show us the things we want—*everything we want.* They use our own desires against us, then offer us the sickness in our souls as something to be craved. But they're liars!"

Warren screamed and he grabbed Dixon, prying at his strong fingers.

"MacDonald!" Dixon yelled, throwing them both to their knees.

Susan was dead.

"Warren . . ."

He fought against opposing pressure, finally staggering back to his feet. Susan was *here,* filling his mind with the recollection of how he'd abused her with neglect, how he'd let a marriage that had started so well slip into nothingness because he didn't want to take the time. She was offering him another chance. He had to be with her again, and make up for those months she'd endured alone. She floated over the clods of dirt, closing the distance between them with outstretched arms, pulsing hunger in her eyes.

Her red lips parted hysterically, drooling animosity, baring those icy, pointed fangs.

Susan was dead.

"Warren."

Her silvery voice sang in his ear, and he could not keep himself from reaching out, wanting her despite the terror. Her face was wicked with her delight as her fingers drifted nearer and nearer.

"Be with me, Warren."

"In the name of Christ!" As their fingertips touched, Dixon pushed in front of him, throwing him back. Warren crashed into the cold dirt, whining miserably. As he pushed himself up on a sore shoulder, he tried to make sense of the horror cringing from Dixon's cross.

Susan's features stretched, her teeth protruding viciously. Then her swiping fingers nearly grazed Dixon's cheek. He jumped to the side, raising the cross defensively, and she yanked back with each stab of his threatening symbol. *"You bastard shit of God!"* she was shrieking. *"You cannot kill what's already dead!"*

Dixon's other hand brought up the plastic container and began to pump, spraying the clear contents at the cursing creature before him. *"Blessed water, thing of hell, slake your damned thirst on the living water of Christ!"*

The thing that was Susan screamed and shrank in ghastly surprise, flailing her wild arms against the black sky. Open wounds streaked her face where the water struck and steamed in the cold night air. Pressing his advantage, Dixon jabbed his cross-laden fist into her cheek with a power that knocked her onto the ground, scant inches from Warren. He poured what was left in the bottle onto her quivering breasts.

"No—you fucking shit of a crucified master!" Susan's raw, ugly wail burst into the hissing air of her boiling and sizzling flesh. *"No!"* Blood squirted from the new wound spreading above her stomach, splashing noisily in chunky red globs to accompany her horrible, tormented howls.

Warren blinked, paling in uncomprehending horror as her own furious nails ripped into her flesh, ripping away ragged, wet strips—sending the stench of burnt pork coursing through his nostrils. Her gurgling decay bit deep into his paralyzed brain, and still more blood spilled up out of her mouth, splattering its frigid thickness all over his cheek.

Then, all at once, the wrenching sounds ended and Susan lay still. The whisper of Dixon's prayers grew louder. *"Back to hell in Jesus' name."* His strong words flowed through the stink darkening the icy air, and the paralysis binding Warren broke at last. He coughed violently, his mind swirling in rabid hysteria.

The empty container fell to the ground with a plop. Warren struggled to his knees, unable to tear his eyes from the bone-colored mutilated corpse.

It was Susan, and she was dead. Really dead. Her damaged fingers were once more only stubs, and her left breast was torn, its flesh burnt black. Warren gulped, holding back the nausea grappling up into his mouth, then forced himself to grab Dixon's reaching hand and get to his feet. The hole was still eating into Susan's body. "God. Good God," he gasped.

"God is great" came the sharp reply. He pointed at the etched expression of despair on Susan's unmoving, pale face. "Legend has it that when destroyed, the vampire returns to innocence—that the body becomes pure. That's a damned fallacy. No man is pure, or the vampire would have no victims. A pure heart would give the demon flight. Our only satisfaction is that the body can cause no more evil. It is an empty container of wickedness." Dixon paused grimly, then made his face soften with an effort, took Warren's hand, and pulled him away. "I'm sorry."

"Th-that stuff you poured on her," Warren stuttered. "Acid?"

Dixon shook his head. "Water. Water I'd prayed over and asked to be blessed. It is *God's* acid, burning the fallen in a holy, consuming fire." He stopped and looked at Warren sadly. "Come on, we've got a lot more to do."

Warren looked back at his wife's body, watching her flesh wrinkle and continue to steam. "Look . . . Susan . . ."

"It's dissolving. The decay parallels the damnation of the evil that inhabited it. The taint has destroyed her." Dixon hesitated, then put his arm around Warren and helped him to walk, quickly, back to the fence.

"Wait." Warren pulled away from him, trying unsuccessfully to see Susan as she'd been when they married, finding only her reeking decay. But he *had* loved her—and—*there was no hell, no damnation.* "We—we must go back and pray over her body."

"What for, MacDonald? It's gone. God destroyed Sodom and Gomorrah. He blighted the whole world with a flood. Would you challenge His decisions of damnation *now*?"

Warren went along with him.

"It's too late for her, MacDonald. We have been chosen, but we can only help those who are still alive."

VI

1

Miles away from St. Louis, Freeport was fast becoming a de-
ranged town, frenzied and fearful with the deaths that had
erupted after Ben Dixon's disappearance, but unaware of his
single-minded quest.

The citizens locked their doors carefully now, as Emily Knox
did tonight. She tried the doorknob and set her jaw with satisfaction, then walked through the hall to a chair in the den, turning
off lights as she went. The house was quiet in the aftermath of
helpful neighbors, and aromatic in the pleasant gifts of food. And
it was dark now, except for the overhead kitchen light that
burned over the two cardboard boxes of roast beef, chicken
sandwiches, and cookies in the kitchen.

The air was full of the emptiness of a house whose owners
were on vacation.

Emily turned on a reading lamp, sat on the firm divan, and
halfheartedly thumbed through the assignment in her freshman
psychology book. She glanced at the title, *Motivation and Emotion: Biological Motives,* shut her eyes briefly, then started to
read. Adam Knox watched her from the kitchen table, sighed,
and walked slowly to stand near her. "Are you okay, honey?" he
asked.

The words startled Emily and she looked up at the tall, gray-
ing man to force a smile. "I'm fine, Dad."

"Yeah." He stepped behind her and rested a careful hand on

her shoulder. "Thanks for moving back in. I—I'm still shaken over—"

"It's okay," Emily said quickly, already tired of his overplayed sadness. She wasn't deaf or blind. Although nothing was ever said, she knew Mom and Dad had been talking seriously of divorce. The hate in their voices this past year had proved that. Arguments over where to vacation became separate vacations, and she could pinpoint every major break between them in the conversations that had become shorter and shorter, but deadly with dislike.

"I can't believe," Adam went on, "that it happened to her. I can't believe—"

She frowned at him, and he stopped. "I have to study for a test," she said flatly.

"Yeah." He sighed, and smiled ever so slightly. "Yeah. Life goes on, doesn't it?" Her frown continued and he shrugged. "Anything I can help you with?"

"I can do it." *Yes,* she thought, *just as I've had to do almost everything for myself these past ten years.* Her parents had ignored each other when it got bad between them, and they'd ignored her, too, especially after she got her driver's license three years ago.

"Emily?"

She looked at him.

"We—we had our differences, but I loved your mother. I really did." He looked down at his feet, and she could almost hear his mind flailing for words. "I—I'll go feed the dogs, I guess. I . . ." He shook his head.

Emily looked back into her book, listening to his flat steps creep back to the kitchen.

They had buried Mom this afternoon, three days after the sudden, unexplained attack that had taken her life. The voice of the minister at the gravesite still rang in her ears, speaking with ignorant falsehood of Mom's Christian goodness. They had laid her to rest in that final hypocrisy, proving the limitations of the church Emily no longer attended. Emily swallowed, comparing the minister's hopes to the reality of the policeman's conjectures, surmising that Mom had been walking home from the bus stop when she became the third victim of the senseless killings no one could explain.

And it was even Mom's own fault in a way, wasn't it?

Mom took a job when Emily started high school, an indirect casualty of one of her own arguments. She'd badgered Dad again and again to find a better-paying position, and in what Emily knew had been one of his best moments, he turned the tables. Mom got a job, and Dad advanced in turn to a higher-pressured, higher-dollar chair in his company. Mom could have quit then, and things might or might not have gotten better if she had, but no one would ever know now. She stayed with it, even with the bad hours, and was coming home late, as usual. The streets were dark and deserted by seven P.M. in Freeport, and no one saw what happened. The patrolman didn't even find Mom until she'd been dead an hour. In the ambulance they tried to revive her and discovered her enormous loss of blood. That third death had been the charm, though, and now the town practically crawled with cops; but it was too late for Mom.

It hurt, though Emily hadn't been very close to either parent for years. It hurt bad, but Dad's mournful pretense hurt even more.

The back door opened and banged closed and she heard Yoda and L.D. yap cheerfully as Dad brought them dinner. She knew his pretense was for her, and she supposed she should be thankful he loved her enough for that, but it made her angry instead. It was as if he was trying to cover up the bitterness that had divided the family, as though she were too young and ignorant to be aware of it. As always, she was being treated like a child, as if he and Mom thought she would never grow up.

But Mom was gone. Emily could hardly even remember the last time she'd talked with her face-to-face. Since school began this year and she moved into the dormitory, she'd tried not to see Mom or Dad much at all. In ways it was almost as if a stranger had died, and she was here consoling another stranger for a tragedy she knew he didn't feel.

The dogs yelped suddenly, and Emily put down her book. They whined as though a siren were hurting their ears, or—she frowned—as though they were being beaten.

She went quickly to the back door, trembling with anger. If

Dad was mistreating them . . . She threw the door open to the brisk cold night.

"Dad?" Her bare foot had already touched the top step before she froze in terror, and for an instant she knew she must have dozed off. Emily threw her hand back and kept her feet by gripping the metal rails.

The paralyzing, malevolent visage of her mother glared up. She was crouched like a spider over Dad's convulsing body, hovering over his bleak moans as they joined the cowering dogs'. The bright porchlight glare illuminated the dark, soggy splotch spreading over his torn shirt and the torn skin of his shoulder, while Mom licked her wet lips and bent back down. A nauseating, horrible sucking sound began.

Goddamn. The hair on Emily's head prickled and the sound from her lungs was like the air rushing out of a flattened tire. With a deep gasp she clenched her eyes painfully and reached back to the doorjamb, pulling herself back into the house. Her heart was a jackhammer against her rib cage and when she opened her eyelids again, she didn't look into the yard, but reached for the heavy door and pushed it closed. Her damp, trembling fingers found the dead bolt and turned it and she leaned against the smooth wood until she could breathe.

A minute passed. Her stomach tried to settle. She went to the sink with legs that had become too long, filled a glass with water, sipped it, and fought to keep from vomiting. The pitch of the dogs' continuing low wails made her eyes fill with tears, and her hand shook. The glass slipped and dropped into the sink with a loud shatter. Goose bumps rose on her skin and she breathed deeply, forcing herself back to the door, pushing at the plaid curtains. . . .

Cold sweat broke out over Emily's body with the shriek of fervent new howls, their agony pinching her eyelids shut until she could no longer stand it. With a hard swallow she forced her fingers to touch the door's multipaned window.

The howls and yelps suddenly stopped.

Dead silence. Emily listened, straining to hear something . . . *anything,* but only the sigh of her lungs and violent beat of her heart reached her ears. Her shivering fingers slid over the cold glass. pressing the embroidered curtain far to the sides—

clanging the brass rings that held it to the tin rod. She opened her eyes.

The hideous scream that echoed in her ears then was her own. She gaped into her mother's distorted, grisly face, pale and hungry against the glass, smearing the red drops on her lips all over the window and revealing stained, pointed teeth. Emily stared helplessly, trying to dismember the awful urge to open the door and embrace her dead mother. But somehow, her hand found the knob and—

"Emily," said a soft, firm voice, "wake up."

Emily's eyes opened with the fog of heavy sleep. Her friend Karen looked down at her, and she felt desperate muscles slacken in the relief of safety. She was in Karen's apartment, sleeping. Sleeping . . . *and dreaming*.

"Are you okay?" Karen asked, sitting beside her on the big bed.

"Yeah," Emily replied, running her tongue over dry lips. "Just thirsty. I . . . I had a nightmare."

Karen's eyebrows rose in sympathy, and she sat down on the creaking mattress, closing the robe over her nightgown. "Shit. I'm not surprised after what you've been through. Stay there, okay? I'll get you a drink."

Fighting embarrassment, Emily watched her friend leave the room. She knew the cries of her restless sleep had awakened her again. But at least Karen cared. At least she felt safe here in Karen's apartment. Mom and Dad never even knew about Karen. It had only been a bad dream, anyhow.

A dream.

Emily covered her face with clammy hands and felt sick—a dream of the thing that had killed her dogs and father. A dream of the horror that she could tell no one. Not even Karen.

Because it was also reality.

2

The picture of Susan on the mantelpiece made Warren shudder.
In it there were no dark circles under the chuckling eyes. Her
closed smile was like an innocent Mona Lisa's. Innocent of life's
treasure and death's leisure. He shook his head. Or was that
saying the other way around—life's leisure and death's treasure? He gulped. But either way she had been innocent of life
and death, knowing only the magic sound her fingers created on
the keyboard.

Then her closed tango with music had been ripped away with
her fingers, and the tune in her eyes disappeared with it, snip-
ping away her innocence like the final shreds of her torn skin,
until she was the monster he had watched Ben Dixon kill an
hour ago.

"You see our mission now, don't you?" Dixon asked anxiously, sitting near the reborn fire in Warren's living room and
sipping from a mug of coffee.

Uncomfortable, Warren stood and crossed to him, then took
down the picture of Susan. He was lost in a jungle of emotion,
logic, and other intangibles. Only the rage at a life that had
betrayed his beliefs stood strong and clear. He pulled back the
mesh screen of the fireplace and shoved the portrait of Susan
that was no longer Susan into the crackling flames.

"She can't return again," said Dixon.

Warren turned to the frail cardboard covering the window.
"What about whoever did that to her?"

"You think it would attack so boldly after what happened tonight?" Dixon stood at Warren's side. "It will rely on lies to
destroy us now." His eyes were far away, the lids red-rimmed.
"It *won't* come tonight."

Warren nodded, though his mouth was dry.

"MacDonald?"

He turned back to the fire, squinting as it licked and charred
the picture. Susan's likeness, like Susan, was shriveling fast and

turning to dust. The crack of its hot glass joined the growl of his empty stomach, and he remembered too vividly the way he'd thrown up over and over again on the cemetery grounds outside his car. "I—I can't deny what happened."

"Considering what you saw tonight, I don't see how you could even try," Dixon snapped, stepping away to take a package from the coat he'd laid on the hearth. He opened the small cardboard box and, removing a cigar, lit it. "It's not a matter of understanding what is happening, or why. We have to act! God has placed His trust in us." Dixon began to pace before the hearth, dropping into a monotone. "The vampire I'm following doesn't kill. He spreads an infection, an infection that waits for death. But people die from other things, too, MacDonald. One of the victims in my parish died unexpectedly, then visited my home the night he was buried. Thank God it didn't take me as long as you to guess what he was." Dixon looked at him through heavy eyelids, then turned away to rest his hands on the chimney. "It was my son. Three days before, my wife, Carolynn, took him to choir practice against his will. He cursed us both. . . ." Dixon faltered. His face was red as he faced Warren again, his expression blank. "They—they had a car wreck on the way. Witnesses said they saw Carolynn fighting with Todd in the front seat as they came to a red light, and she didn't stop . . . *didn't even try.*"

"I'm sorry," Warren whispered with all the compassion he could muster.

Dixon's voice was slow and nearly unemotional. "They were keeping my wife's body alive on machinery and there . . . wasn't any chance she could continue without it. When the doctors told me that the day I buried Todd, I had to go home to sort things out. I just sat in her favorite chair, and when I watched the sun set, I'd nearly decided to let her pass on."

Dixon's hand shook and some of the brandy spilled to the floor. He gulped. "Then I heard the knock on the back door." Dixon stared glassily. "It—it was Todd."

Warren shook his head, and for a moment the images inside him became clearer under the pressure of the man's passions. "You don't need to tell me more."

Dixon paced before the hearth with heavier steps. "I went to the hospital to see my wife and be sure she was all right. I saw two small marks above her right breast." He lowered his tone still more. "I knew I had to destroy Todd if only to keep her soul safe, and I went to the graveyard to wait for him." He examined his hands and dirty nails. "And now, his soul is in hell."

Warren watched the flames roar against the screen, wishing they could remove the ice in his spine.

Dixon faced him, his crazed eyes opposing his stilted, frigid manner. "You have to forget all your preconceived notions."

Warren decided he disliked Dixon more with each word he said. He watched Dixon sit in the white armchair across from the divan, then dig dirt from his filthy nails with a weathered pocketknife.

"We have to find the damned thing behind all this."

Warren gulped. "How . . . the *hell* do you expect to do that?"

"I've been doing that," he growled, flashing his eyes and making a stain as he scooted to the edge of the chair. "That's why I'm here now—it's why you're still alive and standing there listening! Because I've been doing it. This is our duty, MacDonald! I thought of our next step tonight while we walked, and if we follow my plan, we *will* catch our prey through its own trangressions. It has left an obvious trail." Slowly, his irritation disappeared, replaced by a sly smugness. "We do have a point of contact."

"What?"

"The woman who was with your wife when she was attacked."

"Carmen?" he whispered. "But . . . she can't be damned."

"Is she without sin?" Dixon challenged.

Warren averted his eyes. "She's . . . so full of life."

"That only makes her a more likely candidate for death." Dixon took it up. "We must see her. It's possible she will remember something." He squinted at the stogie between his thumb and forefinger. "Maybe even more possible than with the other victims."

"Why?" Warren croaked. "Why her?"

"The creature was with her *and* your wife. Its attention was divided." Dixon scratched his cheek thoughtfully.

"Go on."

"It defiled them both to satisfy its lust, and while it fed on your wife, its power over this Carmen may have weakened." He got up and waved his smoke through the air, stepping toward Warren with a hot confidence. "Has the young lady been released from the hospital?"

"Her—her husband will bring her home tomorrow afternoon."

Ben Dixon tapped a finger on his arm. "A vampire's victim is connected to it in darkness. That's why they change as they do. To a degree she may even know its thoughts."

"So you want to go see Carmen and see if she can tell us something." Warren remembered Carmen's disorientation and fear, wanting the strength to oppose this man. But he had no strength. His own understanding of life and God was in shambles. "She isn't well," he managed feebly.

"I won't hurt her." Ben Dixon flexed his fingers and sighed impatiently, walking to the TV. "The disease is already part of her. Ignoring it won't help. It will only get worse. We must find the cause of all this, and this woman may be the only way. If we must bring her some pain now, isn't that better than an everlasting torment?"

The doctor's simple words to Warren days ago returned as if he were just hearing them. "But she isn't well. She was . . . badly mutilated."

"In her vaginal area?"

"Yes." He shuddered.

Dixon nodded.

"I thought," Warren said quietly, "vampires went for the neck."

"Storybook stuff," he murmured dourly. "Or perhaps pornography's influenced even the devil." Dixon winked, then turned solemn and touched the domed clock. It was nearly five A.M. "We need to see this woman as quick as we can, MacDonald. Each day this epidemic spreads farther."

"God." Warren felt heavy under the dread of what Carmen could become. "It won't be hard to see her," he said. "Chuck, her husband, is a friend." He looked away to the clock. "I'm tired," he muttered thickly.

"So am I," Dixon agreed, sucking on his cigar and picking up his coat, "and you're right. We need to get sleep while we can. We have a lot to do tomorrow. The horrible paradox is that we must fight them on their own terms, MacDonald, in their own time. There are too many places they can hide in the day. We must wait for their blood lust to reveal them."

Warren rubbed his hands, desperately wanting to be left alone. "Where will you go?"

"I've rented at the motel just down the expressway."

Warren yawned with relief, seeing his earlier glass still half full of brandy, remembering how he'd wanted to spend this evening.

"I'll call tomorrow after we've both rested, and we'll go to see your friend." Ben Dixon tossed his cigar onto the remains of the burning portrait, then walked past the TV to the front hall. He opened the door there and, looking into the darkness, noisily zipped his coat and turned up his collar. He stepped outside without another word, and Warren watched him cross the lawn to the street.

Warren shivered and closed the door, then bolted it.

Vampires. He imagined the way his associates would take this story, listening with sorrowful, patient incredulity.

But he had *seen* it.

Warren retraced his steps and his eyes strayed to the fireplace. The frame itself was crumbling to ash now. He wondered suddenly if Susan had somehow fooled them, had overcome apparent destruction to return secretly and await him now, in the bedroom, her sleek body naked under the sheets, her mangled hand whole.

In the bedroom. He swallowed. If only he'd been more understanding after that accident she might not have grown away from him as she had—as he had forced her to. She wouldn't have become a *thing.*

Warren felt the oppression of his guilt and tightly shut his eyes. A bead of sweat ran down his forehead. He cursed himself silently. Susan had come back to give him another chance . . . and he had helped Ben Dixon kill her again.

He looked down the central hall at the bedroom door. He'd destroyed his own marriage, and the horror of his failure waited for him in sleep. She was damned by him, and died in that damnation, seeking to bring him down with her.

He forced himself to the bedroom door, recalling clearly how he'd answered Susan's bitterness with platitudes, and how in his own emptiness he'd sought out Carmen. She was full of the vibrancy Susan had lost, listening to his every word, teasing him with her admiration and innuendoes that sometimes went too far.

And sometimes he wanted them to go farther.

Warren walked tiredly to the bed, pulled back the blankets, and sat down, kicking off his shoes. He'd used Carmen's own lonely frustration selfishly to ease his own.

Susan, Carmen, and Chuck. They were *all* victims of his betrayal, making him as much a dark night-thing as the creature Ben Dixon sought. The comprehension made him dizzy and he fell back on the bed, smelling Susan's lingering scent on the unchanged sheets.

He had failed; but could he rise above his past to satisfy those mistakes even now?

Or was he only working out an imaginary fantasy of redemption?

Love was redemption. But where was Love in this fiendish mystique of vampirism? Where the love in Ben Dixon's way of things?

He considered how he'd treated Susan these past months, knowing he was no better. With needling exhaustion he knew he must begin again, and somehow find the love and Love that he still believed in.

Without it he knew there was no redemption.

Without it there was *nothing*.

VII

1

With a start Warren opened his eyes to the afternoon daylight with the fear of being late. He was out of bed and at the closet before he realized he was already wearing clothes and that he wasn't late for anything. He had no appointment to meet.

In a peculiar state of unreality he stared down at his dirty shirt, the tear in his slacks. It made him slow down, and he touched the rip uncertainly.

He turned to Susan's side of the bed.

He brushed the gritty dirt powdering him as dry fear scratched his throat. Then a sudden, overpowering thirst urged him into the hall toward the kitchen. The cold of the living room stopped him, and he saw the cardboard over the broken window, the shards of glass on the carpet.

The phone rang, its electronic bell jolting him, then rang again. "Damn," he muttered, pushing his feet toward the divan and picking up the receiver as he sat. Ashes covered the fireplace grate.

"Good morning, MacDonald. MacDonald?" the voice asked.

"I'm . . . here."

There was a long pause before Dixon spoke again. When he did, his voice was low and guttural: "Yes. She came to you last night, MacDonald. It was real. I used to have to convince myself each day."

"Dixon?"

"It happened. It all happened," the man whispered. "She came to you naked to seduce you—to drag you down the path to hell."

Warren wiped moisture from his forehead. "Stop."

"Now it's our turn to drag them down to hell. Call your friend like we planned last night. I'm on my way over."

After listening to the dead line for several seconds, Warren replaced the receiver on its cradle.

He didn't like Ben Dixon, but the memories he could not deny forced him to pick the phone up a second later and punch the lighted buttons. When Chuck answered, he set a time that afternoon to see Carmen.

2

"How do you feel?"

Carmen looked at Warren with reticence. "Tired," she murmured, licking dry lips. "God, I feel tired." Her face was sallow, nearly matching the color of her hair, which tangled greasily around the ruffled neck of her flannel pajamas.

He tried to smile, fighting the vision in his mind's eye of her transforming into a slavering, seductive temptress as Susan had last night. He glanced at Ben Dixon and Carmen's broad-chested husband, Chuck Richison. They stood before wood cabinets and shelves filled with football trophies, photos, and memorabilia. Though they were woefully barren of even a solitary book, the warmth of the surroundings made him jealous with the life his own home had lost.

"I'm cold too. *It's cold in here,*" Carmen went on.

Warren hesitated. Her slippery tone contradicted her words. "What I mean is, how bad do you hurt, Carmen?"

Chuck's square, rigid face showed lines of worry, and he smacked a chaw of tobacco, spilling driblets of brown juice down a rounded chin. Chuck's hair had gone gray since his football years, and his face no longer held the carelessness of his youth. "They gave me some Tylenol Codeine 3 to give her," Chuck offered. "I got a prescription for more when it runs out."

"Good." Ben Dixon nudged Chuck's tall shoulder and tugged him out of Carmen's hearing. Warren watched her sullenly before he backed away to join them.

"How long do they think it will take her to heal?" Dixon was asking.

Chuck's squinted glance flickered to Warren, and back to the older man. "Physically, they think she'll be okay within the month."

"And psychologically?" he asked.

"They're not sure, Mr. Dixon—Reverend Dixon. They think —they think it might be a . . . long time."

"Maybe Warren and I can help with her recovery."

"Do you really think you could?"

Warren felt Chuck's hope rest on him with peculiar guilt, and wouldn't look up. "Uh, yes," he said. "We may be able to help." He searched Dixon for strength, but could not find it in his calm, cold glance. "Yes—I think we can help."

Chuck smiled with relief. "Thank God."

"But I"—Warren gulped—"I really don't know if it's the time *now.*"

Dixon frowned at Warren. "I disagree. If you'll allow us to begin tonight, the process may not take all that long," he said, echoing the sound of Chuck's hope. "I can't promise anything. Only that I—*we*—will do our best." He laid his hand on the back of a chair, "And with God's assistance we'll succeed."

The two men stared at each other, then Chuck finally nodded. "All right," he consented.

The older man led them back to Carmen's side. She moaned as they drew near, and Chuck watched helplessly, his face drawn and fists clenched tight. "What—what will you do?" he asked.

"We must bring her to a full realization of her memories." Ben Dixon touched her pale face, then folded the restless hands over her stomach. "Only then can we begin to try to rid her of them."

"You mean she has to face what happened?"

"In a manner of speaking," Dixon replied.

Chuck knelt beside Carmen and bowed his head. He was a better husband than Warren had ever imagined.

"We'll be as brief as we can," Dixon promised.

"If you think it will help." Chuck said it quietly, grief showing in his slack muscles.

"It would be better if you weren't in here." Dixon touched his arm to lead him away. "Your presence might inhibit her."

"I . . ." Chuck went with Ben. "Promise you'll tell me what she says."

Dixon set his jaw confidently. "We'll do our best for her." Then he shut the door to the hall and returned silently.

"Now what?" asked Warren, his mouth dry. Carmen's eyes were closed, but her face bore apprehension.

"Now we get to work." Kneeling where Chuck had, he took one of Carmen's hands, glancing at Warren when she stiffened. "Carmen?" he whispered.

She opened her eyes.

"Carmen?" he repeated.

"I hear you," she mumbled.

"I am Ben Dixon, a minister under God. With that authority I command you to tell me of the events directly leading to Susan MacDonald's death and your own incapacity."

"I . . . what?" Carmen stared blankly. "Susan's dead?"

"She is."

Carmen's emptiness became a disgruntled frown for a moment, but she regained herself quickly. "I told Warren all I could remember at the hospital." She lifted her head from the pillow and tried to rearrange it without energy. After a moment Dixon helped her, folding it in half to keep her head high, and she lay back again. "Susan came over to visit. We were having a drink. I think someone rang the doorbell." She stopped, as if reconsidering, then smiled briefly. "Yes—that's all I can remember."

"Who was at the door?"

"I don't know." She blushed and looked away. "I told you, I *don't* remember."

"It was a man, wasn't it?" Dixon pushed his face close to hers. "A salesman. He came in—*you* let him in, didn't you? And when he touched you, his hands were as icy and cold as the desire in your heart. You looked in his face . . . and you *wanted* him." He squeezed her hand hard. "Didn't you?"

"S-Susan said to let him in." She glanced at Warren, her face losing its slight color. "Yes—*yes,* he . . . was selling something."

"And you both wanted what he offered you," Dixon's flat voice stated. *"You* wanted him, and when he—"

"No! I didn't—Susan took off *her* cl-clothes." Carmen's eyes were big with fear as hot tears rolled down her cheeks. Her hands became tight fists, then opened and closed, again and again, matching the quickening rise and fall of her chest and the wretched gasps from deep inside.

"That's enough, Ben," muttered Warren hotly.

"Not yet."

Warren touched her warm forehead. "I said it's enough."

"Enough?" His voice was sharp.

"Enough!"

And Carmen screamed.

3

Carmen knew it was very late when she awoke from her perverse nightmare. The blackness that met her open eyes equaled the night enveloping her soul. Still pushing at her was the false memory of herself among a dozen handsome, muscled men— each with the body of Arnold Schwarzenegger and the face of Robert Redford—as she took them singly and made them her slaves. Yet she still wanted—needed—more! To satisfy her, she needed to torment . . . to *hurt.* She savored the cruelty and hatred as being everything she'd ever wanted and been forbidden by the false values she'd been brought up with. She no longer wanted to repress her real nature—rather, she longed for its fulfillment.

She wanted to fuck rather than be fucked. She wanted to control and dominate, to take without giving—

A rattling machine-gun snore broke in and made her look at her sleeping husband with distaste. The familiarity he presumed by being in bed with her repulsed her. She shook her head, her damp hair slipping against her moist skin. He no longer had the right. Her marriage to him was ended and she was linked to another—one who promised her endless gratification in simply yielding to her own desires.

Another. The lust built inside her—lust that had grown stronger since that wheedling preacher man interrogated her. He had driven his fingers into her skull, his words tearing back the folds shrouding the desires she'd veiled, the clarity he gave her disolving her fear at the dark spot in her memory, bringing to life the incredible, unbarred pleasure of her lust's consummation.

She craved the one who had brought her the ecstasy of such wanton pleasure. It was the meaning she'd dreamed of and searched for in Chuck's absence, and wanted now even as he lay beside her.

But not from him. Not from Chuck, who had intrigued her with the expensive gifts, showering her with luxury until she could not bear to say no. He'd slipped the heavy diamond-studded ring on her engagement finger that night not with the romance she had expected, but with air of a businesslike exchange.

She did not want anything from Chuck anymore.

"I want *you!*" she whispered to the shadows with an outpouring of soul-felt desire. "I want *you.*" She envisioned the tall salesman who'd enchanted her, imagined he was with her now, slipping beside her onto the mattress as Chuck slept soundly. She wanted his cold body close, his fetid breath stifling her.

The potent imagination made her throw off the bedcovers, and she pulled her nightgown up to her neck, forgetting Chuck's grating old-man snores. Her hands became the stranger's as she moved nimble fingers across the sticky salve that covered her lacerated vagina. Unfeeling of the pain she brought herself, she closed her eyes, her tongue lolling—masturbating herself into a sweating frenzy.

Beside her Chuck slept peacefully.

4

". . . another mutilation killing last night, drawing renewed efforts by local police as the pressure on them grows. The governor's office was inundated with calls today, and sources report that the governor is talking with the FBI and leaders of the National Guard. In many respects this assault was similar to the attack across the state that left St. Louis native Susan MacDonald, wife of Methodist minister Warren MacDonald, dead."

Ben Dixon nodded at the TV in agitation. "It's already begun," he whispered.

"You think—" Warren looked at the dead ashes in the fireplace that reflected the dust Susan had become. *Ashes to ashes.*

"Shh." Dixon shook his head.

". . . officers are uncertain as to the reasons behind this most recent killing. Federal agents are being assigned to the area and will not comment on their investigation at this point. We talked with a local housewife this morning at Dock's Thrifty Grocery Store to learn how the citizens of Freeport are reacting to this bizarre outbreak of murder."

From the smartly dressed newsman with the hot-pink tie the camera cut to a middle-aged woman holding a brown paper sack. She fidgeted nervously: "I don't go out at night anyhow," she spoke with a twangy accent. "I always lock my doors too. I think it's something like that Manson group doing all this—but I don't know why they can't catch them." She looked the reporter in the eye. "Maybe if the police would spend more time on this instead of writing tickets for people not wearing their seat belts—"

The newsman's picture flashed back on the screen. "That

was Doris Epstein of Freeport with her feelings on the terrible
panic beginning to grip that little town. We also talked with local
patrolman Tyler Harris."

A reporter in a long coat appeared against the backdrop of a
quiet residential street, holding her microphone out to a griz-
zled, balding policeman. "Is it true that your department is blam-
ing these assaults on members of a marauding motorcycle
gang?" she asked.

"We have no reported suspects at this time," drawled the
skinny cop, frowning coldly.

"Is it true that reinforcements are being called in from other
cities?"

The policeman's frown grew darker, and he hitched up his
gun belt. "No comment, lady."

"Do you think—"

"I said, no damn comment." He walked to the driver's door of
his car. "Read my lips," he went on. "No comment at all."

The picture faded without warning, bringing back the
anchorman in the newsroom: "We'll continue our updates with
more interviews concerning those involved in this massive investigation and the five terrible murders that have caused the
nation to stand up and take notice. Local citizens in the Freeport
area have been advised to lock up securely and to stay inside if
possible during the night hours. For an in-depth report on the
victims, let's go to—"

"God," responded Warren.

Ben Dixon's face was hard. *"Damn."*

Warren stared at him.

"That's my hometown," Dixon said tightly.

Warren looked back at the newscaster with a chill in the small
of his back. He picked up the remote and switched the news off.
"You—you think he—it—has gone back there?"

"I didn't expect it this fast," he muttered.

But his expression showed a different insanity than before,
and it frightened Warren as he recognized the other man's surprised fear. "We know where *it* is." Dixon nervously rubbed his
jaw. "This is only the spreading sin of its disease. One of its
victims has died and risen again. All of them carry the sickness
deep inside their spirits until their tormentor is destroyed. *If*

they die before it does, they become like it. They become vampires."

"But they'll be destroyed if we destroy the one that attacked them?"

"No," he whispered, grimly wiping the shine from his brow. His shoulders slumped. "God. There's just no end to it. Now there's another to destroy. *Another.* There's just no damn end!" He crushed his fingers together with frustration, regaining his bitterness with an effort. "How much must I do to prove myself?" Dixon stared at his rough hands, breathing heavily.

Warren waited, watching him, but said nothing.

"The damnation," Dixon finally continued tiredly, "has fulfilled itself in whoever died there, and now its victims will kill, and it will kill again. Holy Jesus," he whispered, his expression twisting to unmasked fear, "it's such a damned perfect plan. And we're the only ones who know."

"Good God!" Warren exclaimed in horrid wonder. "Where do you get this stuff?"

"Books," Dixon snapped.

"Great. Do they say how can we contain it?"

Dixon sipped moodily from his mug of hot chocolate, then slammed it down on the coffee table. "It's what I've been trying to tell you, MacDonald. If we don't destroy the protagonist now before others die, we *can't.*"

"But . . . what about this other one?" Warren insisted, not liking the way this development had taken Dixon unaware. "I thought you knew what you were doing."

"I do," he shot back, standing up. "I just—" He bit his lip hard, clenching his eyes. "There *is* another one. There'll be more than one—there've been other murders." Dixon fumbled for a cigar. "But we've got to get this bastard salesman first—we can find the others more easily later. They'll be stupid and not as experienced." The cigar flattened in his fist, and his face screwed up under the pressure of a new outlook. "This filthy bastard is trying to destroy us all!" he cried, turning panicked, malevolent eyes to Warren. "You should have let me continue with Mrs. Richison this evening. She's our only link."

Warren shrank back. "How can you justify tormenting her like you were? We can't—"

"We can! We must—don't you realize that we're up against the very beast himself?" Dixon's face was cold and hard, and in it Warren at last found one way in which his beliefs would guide him. A small amount of his original confidence and certainty flowed into him. "No. One soul is as important as a dozen, Mr. Dixon. I couldn't justify standing back to let you do what you were doing!"

Dixon's eyebrows came together angrily. "That woman relies on the destruction of the creature as much as any of the other victims—the very destiny of their souls relies on us finding it quickly. But you'd have us sit here and do nothing."

The room echoed in his alarm. He looked at his watch and spoke through clenched teeth: "I'm going to go now."

But Warren wasn't listening. His eyes were in the fireplace again and it seemed that he could see Susan striving to reform and rise in those ashes, that he could see her seductive body as he had upon her return, could hear her accusing him for her death. Then he saw others, rejected as she had been, forming into the army of hate the vampire was creating.

Dixon was pulling his coat on.

Warren jerked around at the zipper's sound. "Where are you going?" he asked quickly.

"A walk," he replied. "A walk, then back to my room at the motel."

"Are"—Warren's tongue was heavy—"are you coming back?"

Dixon hesitated, showing again that worried uncertainty the news reports had brought him. "Not tonight. I've got to be alone. I'll call you tomorrow."

"Tomorrow." The nightmares lurked in Warren's bedroom.

"Good night, MacDonald. I'll let myself out." Dixon stood, then walked to the unlit front hall.

Warren tried to speak but couldn't force out a sound. He sat immobile as the front door opened and solidly closed.

VIII

1

Emily Knox sat stiffly on the worn green carpet in Karen's apartment, her back against the blue sofa, staring at the TV screen. Her eyes blurred until the images became her mother, bending over her father, the fangs shining in the porch light. She gritted her teeth and picked up the videotape box lying at her side. It was heavy and she put it back down, picking up another of equal weight.

"I really don't think you should be watching this stuff, Emily," Karen said from the sofa.

Emily noticed her friend's untied running shoe on the box she was seeking and reached for it.

"Emily?" Karen's voice was nervous with forced humor. "We've already seen two of these movies. I don't really like them, okay? And . . ." She shifted with discomfort. "Why don't we take them back so we can get something funny—Monty Python or something . . . or a movie with Peter Sellers?" She bent down and waved a hand before Emily's eyes, but Emily didn't blink; she was far into the ideas these films gave her. She thought of the young Roman Polanski and bumbling professor attempting their pursuit of a Jewish vampire . . . and that British actor, Peter Cushing, in the role of Dr. Van Helsing, running hard across the long table to tear down the drapes covering a window. She felt the reassurance of his victory when sunlight flashed into the cobwebbed room of Dracula's castle, striking fellow actor Christopher Lee and turning him into dust.

Karen touched Emily's shoulder gently. "Hey."

Emily finally looked at her.

"Why don't we take these tapes back and get some Pink Panther movies?"

Emily suppressed her blossoming anger, knowing Karen was trying to help.

But Karen didn't understand.

No one understood. No one had ever understood.

"I don't think we should have picked these things," Karen went on. "I . . . shouldn't be letting you watch them."

You're not allowed to watch this sort of thing, Emily, Mother said in her mind, *they'll give you nightmares.*

"Damn it, Emily," moaned Karen, "you're having nightmares already!"

I don't want you filling up your brain with this kind of crap, Emily, Dad said last year, shutting off *Fright Night* as Karen was trying to do now. *I won't have you watching this junk.*

"I want to see it," she made herself say, driving Dad out of her thoughts to concentrate on Karen's downturned lips. Her friend wasn't like Dad and Mom or the others; she was only trying to help—trying to get her thoughts off death. Karen's concern was honest, and not structured by her desire to make Emily into a person she wasn't.

Karen cared.

"I'm okay," Emily said. "I can't explain it, but watching these helps. They help me deal with what happened."

Karen's eyebrows rose, but she closed her mouth and sat back. Though Emily wanted to, she couldn't tell Karen the truth.

Mom had sucked Dad's blood and life, filling herself with it until it drooled down her chin. And she would seek Emily out next.

Emily shivered.

If Mom could find her.

"This is *gross.*"

Emily watched Roddy McDowall, as the vampire hunter, push a heavy wooden stake into a vampire who had transformed himself into a snarling wolf. Blood spurted on the walls and floor in the movie, and Roddy McDowall watched in shock, tears welling in his eyes as the wolf stopped moving, and magically reverted into the naked, anguished form of a dying teenaged boy.

"I . . . I'm sorry," the vampire killer moaned.

And Emily began to think of finding Mom first. She would kill her just like that, but would never feel that remorse.

Mom had been a vampire long before she'd died.

2

Ben Dixon directed his scuffed shoes down the street and read off the stenciled curb addresses, fighting the gnawing questions of his quest. The stark, bare trees and darkened homes filled him with angry fear. Vampires seemed to be everywhere. Even when he looked at Warren, he sometimes wondered . . .

He rubbed his hands together. He knew he was toeing the line between sanity and lunacy; still he could not help himself. It made him shudder as he recalled the newscast. His own town of Freeport was already reeling as a result of the infection. Soon the damnation would spread through the state, and beyond into others.

The knowledge trapped him and he felt very alone. He didn't dare tell Warren anything after the irritation he'd shown during Carmen's questioning. He couldn't risk it.

There could be *no* risks now. He felt total hatred for this "traveling vampire." His wife and son were dead because of it— his son lost to him forever in the dark hell he understood too well. His ambitions were stolen from him. And even more, he hated the vampire because it had used against him his own hidden past.

Ben struggled with that hole in his soul and clenched his fists, bitter; maybe he hated the vampire more for that than for the destruction of his family. He hissed into the air. Even if his inspired mission to rid the world of this evil didn't keep him going, at least he had his lust for revenge.

When he reached the Richison house Dixon stopped, and moved to a stickery bush near the front door. Its pointed leaves were green and full and stuck his hand like a razor when he leaned against the wall to rest. Licking the pain thoughtlessly, he recalled his interrogation of Carmen and hoped he had said enough to jar the evil rooted in her sweet body. Although he'd told Warren they hadn't gone far enough, Dixon felt that his prodding might stir the slumbering darkness inside her, impel her to meet with the vampire by awakening the link between them.

Trying to ignore the cold, he scooted against the hard stone wall, farther behind the bush, and took out a cigar. He was accustomed to waiting now and reflected on these terrors that had changed his very perspective of life. Instead of viewing things as black, white, and gray, he saw them now as black or white. No gray. Gray invariably turned to black.

Ben lit the stogie and crouched with his back to the house, huddling and shifting his coat so it covered more of his legs.

It was cold.

And he waited. An hour passed, and his limbs stiffened. He dreaded his plot had failed. Or that he'd missed Carmen. If he had stimulated her wicked passions and she'd slipped out before him, her fate was upon his head to no avail.

The idea gnawed at him, increasing the pounding inside his skull that rarely left him alone anymore. *It had to be this way.* The zeal of his pursuit prescribed his methods, and even when he wondered if he shouldn't have given those methods more consideration, he knew there just wasn't time. The race was begun. Time stood tall against him and hesitation might mean the vampire's victory. After Todd's death he'd begun steeping himself in lore and driving the streets at night. He'd been Freeport's ghoulish watchdog, ending his rounds at the cemetery each dawn.

The vampire hadn't hidden there, though. Ben had followed his path of ill victims but had never seen the vampire itself until on his way home a few days after Todd's death. He could not remember how many weeks had passed since then, when he'd faced that reeking creature and come so close to tracking it to its lair and destruction. But it had tricked him, and now he must proceed so vigilantly that such a thing couldn't happen again.

He had come upon it quite by accident. Only days after his wife died peacefully, he forced himself to go out and eat. As he drove home, Ben cut through the unlit dirt lane the local high school kids called "the alley." The streetlights had been broken three times in the past month, and it was doubtful they would be replaced again. At least, the mayor had said, the kids weren't wasting money on motel rooms.

It was the same as any make-out point in America, except that any infraction at the high school resulted in the punishment of being brought to the alley for detention and picking up every fallen roach clip, cigarette butt, and bottle. Especially the beer bottles. The Freeport *News* published a running tally of the kinds and number of bottles every Friday morning, always adding a warning to teens not to be one of those horrid hippie freaks that hung out there.

But whoever came out for detention next would not have any great cleanup task. The alley was not in much use now that the weather had turned so cold. It looked deserted, and Ben was surprised to see no beer cans or discarded bottles in the ditches. Movement at the roadside made him bring his foot off the gas pedal. He slowed the car and stopped, then turned in the seat. Through the side window he saw the huge figure of a man bent over a pale white nakedness, his head buried between long, hairy legs. Uncertain if he should say something or not, Ben opened his car door with a peculiar excitement.

At the sound, the kneeling man jerked up and turned, his eyes endless tunnels ablaze in hate. It petrified Ben for a seemingly endless moment.

"Come," whispered the strong, quiet voice.

Ben flinched at the power enticing him. Forbidden pleasure beckoned in the eyes. His feet stepped unwillingly onto the icy ground and forward.

"I have searched for you, bitter man. But why are you bitter when you can have so much?" the unearthly voice whispered, and the figure took a step toward him. "More than you ever dreamed of awaits you, preacher." The vampire showed its dripping fangs, and he smelled its ripe stink as it shuffled forward. "More pleasure and delight than your God would even allow you is yours if you will just take it, the domination and use of men and women . . . yes, men. Like this one I drink now: Men to be yours to suck your trembling cock . . . and children . . . the taste of their sweet lives to nourish you . . . the entertainment of their bodies." The voice became a hellish imitation of Bob Barker, speaking as if describing perfectly reasonable desires, as if Ben deserved these things. "You need give me nothing in return."

Ben moved closer.

"You need give me nothing." The evil face gleamed and its red glistening teeth showed in the starlight. "I will only take away the chains that bind your soul. I will take your life but give you the lives of others in return—I will give your spirit the release into its truth . . . the truth you have sought to contain."

Ben reached the darkly clad man, hypnotized by his reddened eyes. "My—my wife . . . my son." He shivered with the shroud closing blacker around him. "I want them. . . ."

"You do not want them." The sly voice chuckled. "You took them in fear of your God. You say you love them, yes, but that love is weak and I can introduce you to greater things. You shall have them if you want . . . but you shall have them as more than you *hope.*" The shadowed man held out a hand. *"And I will even suck your dick for you, preacher man. I will suck you as you have never dared to guess. I will bring your chained fantasies to reality."*

Ben shuddered, thrown back into the memories that voice stirred. He felt the remembered mouth close around his trembling, growing penis . . . reliving it . . . becoming hard. He gasped with the intensity of that fought but never forgotten desire, touching his belt and not feeling the night's chill as he opened his slacks. The air caressed him like a tongue.

"Yes. . . ." The man touched him then, and took Ben's hand with cold fingers that made a thrill explode in his groin. He looked into the thin, handsome face, gliding his eyes over the body's hidden muscles; remembering Jack, that husky friend of years past, moving onto him atop the hotel bed where they straddled one another's naked bodies, where Jack shoved deep inside him and filled his body and mouth with forbidden fruit. . . .

"I will suck you deep into *my* soul, preacher," hissed the man as he pulled Ben into the ditch, then knelt and caressed him.

Ben swallowed, knowing he should not be here . . . should not be doing this. He had not seen Jack in twenty years . . . had never repeated those acts that had filled him with such guilt.

And such satisfaction. As if in answer the icy tongue licked him until he shivered, but in delight at the forbidden ecstasy he remembered from the past. . . .

"I have much to teach you that you have denied yourself, preacher. You have denied what you desire because of His pitiful sake too long. But tonight"—he laughed—"I will suck you dry, and you will suck me . . . and any other you desire." He reached over to touch the naked body on the yellow grass and Ben looked with him. "And you may have him as well, and the others like him that wait. Men, women . . . children. Even that boy, Jack, whose sperm you drank so long ago." He chuckled. "You will suck him until he screams . . . suck him better than ever before!"

Ben looked down at the supple, tuned body lying beside him, his own strength crumbling with the wet saliva bathing his scrotum. Then he saw the blood streaming from the savage marks below the body's stomach, splattered up on the hairy chest and hauntingly familiar face.

It was Daniel, his son's math tutor—a high school boy—*and his wound was the same Dixon had found on his son.*

A staggering surge from his balls boiled in him, wanting release . . . but— He flinched, feeling the razorlike teeth closing in.

He could suck, and feel the joy of another man's body entering him once more; taste the small boys as he swallowed them up . . . then drive himself into the contrast of young girls, satiating every lust he had locked inside his weary heart.

His eyes held on to the blood dribbling from the math tutor's groin.

Vampire. He would be a vampire.

"*No!*" he screamed, aching for the orgasm that built, and built. "God, *forgive me!*"

The vampire pulled back, laughing, sliding his tongue faster and faster under Ben Dixon's scrotum. "You are too late, *preacher.*"

Ben screamed, rocking back and reaching into his coat; blushing in horrid shame when he found the small cross at last and jabbed it into the air.

The laughter was louder as it danced to the side. "You're a fine cock-lusting soldier of your cross. The portrait of your Christian values!" howled the creature. *"You cannot stop me, charlatan! You are torn between the lies you live and your desires!* My mark is on too many now. My strength is in what I *know,* while yours is merely the faith of what you *believe.* It is a faith that will grow tired before the end, preacher, and you will long for this moment! Your faith will fail you and you will be mine yet."

"Damn you, bastard!" He pushed the cross an inch from its stained mouth and it stepped back, turned, and darted away on long legs. Ben felt his face turn fiery with humiliation, and weakly pulled up his pants, breathing hard.

Staggering to follow, he bumped against the young math tutor at his feet and hesitated. He lifted the young man and carried him to the car, laid him inside, and closed the door. Then he charged after the vampire into the wooded area at the other side of the lane. Tree branches stung his cheeks and hands as he stumbled in the murkiness, almost losing his balance twice as holes swallowed his feet. He didn't see the fiend again until he came to an open area. It entered a deserted shack, and he followed its noisy gallop, charging onto the water-rotted boards of the dilapidated building and inside. Only hints of shadow were revealed in the starlight from the door. The windows seemed covered or boarded over. His nose wrinkled at the filthy odor of waste and excrement, but he kept on, remembering his purpose against the stifled eagerness between his legs.

Swallowing his fear while he felt his way through the grit and cobwebs in close, dank rooms, he kept the small cross pressed tight in his squeezing palm. Then he heard the squeak of hinges, and the loud, rusty click of a lock. Then nothing. Ben backed away, lurching back to the short hall and the front room—the door he had entered still open wide.

"God," he gasped, running back to it blindly.

Halfway there, his right ankle caught against a broken board and he managed to catch himself, his left sole coming down on a protruding nail in the floor as the front door slammed shut. Ben gasped in pain, and the lock clicked. He was locked inside. Trapped.

Yes. Trapped and humiliated with his reborn sin. But at least the thing that had rekindled that lust was outside. He sighed and let his sweating body down on the bare floor to check his wound, his thoughts of pursuit far away. The nerves of his foot grumbled, unsure of how badly they were stabbed in the numbing cold. He ran a finger across the small hole at the bottom of the shoe, then put the damp finger to his tongue and tasted the blood.

All at once the piercing tingle of electricity charged the air and he opened his eyes wide, then flinched as the space beneath the front door burst into orange flame, spreading two feet past it over the dry floor—the smell and crackle of burning wood exploded as hot tongues shot up brightly across the floor planks. By instinct he could tell that the fire was not natural. Some force was powering it, driving it to consume. Heat cut through him as the flames ate into creaking wood. He struggled to one of the boarded windows to tug wildly at the lumber. Splinters slid into his fingers as the fire bit into him. Sweat was dripping off him by the time he managed to wrench the main board off. Ben felt his clothes start to burn. He screamed, grabbing the frame and feeling the now wonderful frigidity on his cheeks. He straddled the molding briefly, kicking away to hit the ground hard. Slobbering, he rolled back and forth to put out the flames. When he finally felt the fire was out, his sight had gone fuzzy, and it was all he could do to pull himself away from the sparks on the grass before he fainted.

When he recovered, the vampire was gone.

Sick-hearted and in pain, Ben staggered back through town, his car forgotten, to his home. He heard the sirens long before he reached the two-story dwelling, and stayed back in the shadows when he saw its inferno. He stared from the distance, afraid

to seek help from even the firemen. There was no way to know
who might be under the vampire's domination now.

Ben wanted it to believe him dead. He had to destroy it and
release himself from the damnation he'd strayed too near—and
the only way to remain the hunter was not to allow it to know it
was hunted.

Ben stopped at a convenience store two blocks away and
bought treatment for his minor burns, then withdrew all the
money he could at a Transfund with his bank card, and waited
for dawn. With that small amount he went to a secondhand store
in the oldest part of Freeport and purchased clothes. He
changed in the dusty store's bathroom, then walked out without
a word, hiding behind a Coke machine when he glimpsed the
vampire down the street, looking the part of a normal visitor
passing through. Following it discreetly, he kept well back,
though he suspected that during the day it had none of the
supernatural psychic traits it possessed in darkness.

The trail ended at a local rent-a-car, and Ben Dixon listened
closely as the vampire gave its destination as St. Louis, far
across the state. Due to his finances Ben followed by bus and, as
he'd hoped, picked up the trail once more.

Ben smiled. In a way, he, too, was undead. The newspapers
said he was believed killed in the fire that had consumed his
home: in a fit of depression after his tragedy he'd apparently set
the blaze himself, although remains hadn't yet been found.

Hopefully the vampire believed him dead too. He didn't want
to reveal himself until the last moment, when he hoped to take
the damned thing by surprise. He was trusting that Carmen's
evil-heightened senses were strong enough to lead her to the
vampire, but not to warn her of his presence.

The front door of the house suddenly creaked open, and Ben
Dixon looked up from his reverie. Through the holly bush he
saw her, a thick, padded coat over her long nightwear. She
slipped onto the porch and pushed the door quietly shut, then
hurried across the lawn to the street. Ben stretched painfully.
He limped on a leg that burned with sleep, but kept the pink fluff
of her gown in sight as he followed. The night's crisp tang was
steeped in his own heavy excitement.

The first few blocks were easy. Carmen never once looked

behind her. Then her stealth became obsessive and she glanced all around every five or six steps. Dixon wasn't sure if she was searching for the vampire, or if she'd become aware of him with her new power, and he dropped back to be safe.

The air became increasingly rank after they left the residential neighborhoods behind, and at last the young woman stopped outside of a dark, boarded-up warehouse. She hesitated, swaying in the light breeze, and Dixon knelt behind a car across the street. Carmen moved ahead mechanically, drawn by an invisible force. When she pushed open the door, Dixon started to follow, then hesitated, gasping in the snare of bleak memories. He wanted to go in—

But the memory of his temptation was too strong, and that lust imbued the dark building with allure and threat.

He suddenly did not trust himself to do it alone.

Ben felt the vampire's mesmerizing stare reaching through the covered windows for him.

He backed away, staring at the brick-and-metal trap of the building, suddenly wondering who was luring whom.

So what of Carmen?

He stepped into the street, hesitated again, then turned away from the warehouse, running through the cold back to Warren's home.

There seemed no way to stop the evil without sacrifice.

3

"Come on!"

Warren blinked his sore eyes, opening the storm door. "What?"

"Come on!" Dixon shouted, reaching in to grab Warren's bare arm.

"What? Where do you—"

Dixon's eyes blazed, but the uneasy fright Warren had seen

behind them earlier tonight was much more pronounced now. *"He's there!"* Dixon screamed, echoing his frenzy into the quiet night.

Stiffening, Warren took in Dixon's red face, his hard panting. He started to turn back for his coat, then frowned. "Where?"

"Come on!" Dixon shrieked, clawing Warren's forearm with jagged nails. "Don't you—" He took a deep, grating breath. "Your friend Carmen is with him—with it!"

Warren's mouth fell open as understanding sank in, but words wouldn't come. His jaw trembled and he jerked his coat out of the closet, then ran back into the hall to find his discarded shirt and shoes, pulling on the shirt as he hurried back. Dropping the shoes on the floor, he slipped them on and got his keys, then ran outside to join Dixon, slamming the door.

"What happened?" Warren gasped, getting into his Mercedes and starting it up. His eyes turned up the street to the Richison house, where Chuck was certainly still asleep inside, unaware of Carmen's danger. *He had trusted them to help her!*

Dixon got in the other side, slamming his door too. "This is our chance," he wheezed, still breathing hard.

"Where's Carmen?" Warren shouted, reversing the car into the street.

"In an old warehouse half a mile from here." Dixon waited while Warren turned the car that way and burned rubber. "It's there, MacDonald. I know that bloodsucking bastard's there!"

Warren wheeled down the road, slowing to avoid parked cars despite the urgency boiling into him. "What about Carmen?"

"The questions I asked her tonight brought her lust back into focus, I think. I waited for her, and followed her—"

"You *what?*" Warren yanked the wheel to make a squealing turn, almost losing control of the car with the sudden rage he felt. "And you left her *there?*"

Dixon shifted on the seat.

"How could you—" He wanted to scream the horrified emotions that were filling him, but could not find words.

"I—I couldn't go in," Dixon murmured, then laid his hand on Warren's shoulder with excitement. "But we have it, MacDonald. We have it and know where it is! Isn't that worth a sacrifice?"

"A sacrifice," he muttered sickly, Carmen's face in his thoughts. The plan he'd unwittingly assisted infuriated him. He knew that even if his own beliefs were flawed, his basic understanding of love was right. He couldn't imagine this man's methods in that understanding. "How could you!"

"That bastard has got to be stopped—*now.*"

"At any cost?" Warren shot back bitterly.

"It—it seems there must be a cost." He clenched his fists. "We have to get it! It's done too much already."

"You knew that what you said to her would push her into finding that thing."

"I knew it might. It's our best chance to stop it, MacDonald. And you would have been against it!"

"Damn you."

The frozen lawns of the residential neighborhood broke off without warning into trash bins, high fences, and silent tractors. Dixon pointed past them, and Warren squealed the Mercedes to a stop half a block from three old warehouses.

"That's it," Ben Dixon whispered excitedly, poking his finger at the nearest.

The building was an old janitorial shop that had been deserted for years. It was condemned and stood decaying, patiently awaiting the wrecking ball. Its faded brick and tin walls rose from the dirty sidewalk thirty feet high, casting eerie shadows. "Come on," Warren said, taking the lead and running across the street. They came to the dented metal exterior, and Warren stopped at the solid door.

"Are you ready?" Ben asked.

Warren's determination wavered, and he nodded jerkily, unable to speak.

Dixon forced open the door with one strong shove, making Warren admire his courage if not his motives. Warren followed Ben and turned on the flashlight he'd taken from the car, playing it through the musty structure. Splintered boards, soggy paper, and unidentifiable metal debris covered the cracked concrete floor. Piles of empty wooden crates were stacked haphazardly against the far wall, and curling old cardboard boxes were scattered everywhere, containing rusty sweeper parts. He kicked something and it rolled loudly across the floor, making him jump. It was only an empty beer bottle, its label faded into illegibility. Others littered the near corner with a variety of aluminum cans. Cigarette butts dotted the floor as far as he could see and the scrawled graffiti on the walls proved the caliber of the building's most recent occupants, and the length of time they had been here. "Jimmy Carter sucks Khomeini's Iranian cock" had been altered to accuse Ronald Reagan. Someone had added AIDS *Hotline* in fresh black letters to a faded phone number, showing the changing sexual climate.

And a putrid decay polluted the air. It was the smell of a dead rat found in the trap when you returned from a month's vacation.

"Reverend Dixon," hissed a loud voice.

Warren jumped in surprise, his heart a battering ram, and the named man grabbed the flashlight with an equal start, swinging its beam swiftly through the shadows. "I'm here," he answered with vicious defiance.

The huge open space chuckled. "I've stayed for *you*, preacher." More dry chuckles, echoing and ominous, and then: "I am so glad you still live. I have wanted since our last meeting to deal with you more appropriately—and I know you want *me*. Perhaps you even crave my mouth around your tasty cock again. Yes . . . you *do*. You want that and you want me . . . in your hungry mouth and up your juicy ass."

The hissing, unnatural voice made Warren cringe and he struggled to locate its source, peering through black shadows and gritty metal dust that floated all around him. It burned his watering eyes. He lost his sense of direction and forced himself to stand immobile against the antagonistic aura.

Then the crash of a breaking bottle pulled his eyes to the right, and he felt the oozing cold of fear crawl into his heart.

"You son of a bitch," Dixon finally gasped with a voice close to and yet beyond trembling.

The tall, gaunt figure stepped from behind a stack of weathered brooms, its red eyes flashing terribly, berserkly. It smiled horridly, hiding its fearsome secret behind tight lips. "I am every name you could call me," it growled, its voice fading to near softness as the monster passed back behind a stack of ancient crates, "but I am so much more! "You want me, preacher . . .

you want me. Only your sniveling God frightens you away. The need in your body is mine as well. I can and *will* meet that need your God impels you to deny. I will hold you close . . . *and listen to you moan as you moaned when your friend Jack broke the cherry of your asshole. I can give you what you want"*— the tone grew shrill—*"or perhaps you would rather receive it from your wife?"*

Dry, enticing laughter filled the air. "We can give you anything and make you free from the guilt you hold so tight. Carolynn—she waits for you at your son's grave. You've taken him from her, and she longs for your consoling touch." The wheedling voice turned into a harsh salesman's bluster. "She is hungry for you, too, Ben Dixon."

"No!" Dixon was shaking, the tendons and veins standing out on his neck and forehead. "My wife is dead!" he shouted. "I saw her buried. The marks on her breast disappeared when I destroyed Todd. She in a better place than you can even dream of."

"She is *undead,"* hissed the voice. "I fucked that dead elk the way you wanted me in you, and I saw her rise. You did not see the mark I made, tender as I was"—he snorted another laugh—"on her fair pussy."

The vehemence and dismay on Dixon's face was terrible as he flashed the dusty beam of light through the warehouse. His feet slapped the floor loudly as he moved, kicking paper vacuum bags out of his path. "You damned bastard." He lit the filthy walls wildly. "You son of a bitch!"

"Are these words your only weapon now? Go to your wife, little minister," taunted the disembodied voice. "I will be waiting within this city for some time. My thirst is great and there is much to be done—there are many who long for my touch. Who long to be free as I am."

"You bastard!" Ben raised the flashlight to search the rusted girders that crossed the ceiling. "You goddamn bastard!"

A sinister chuckle replied. "I certainly am, and if she doesn't get you, preacher-dick, I will." Then the voice was suddenly behind them. "And you will love it. You will become the man you are . . . and I will give you your friend as well." Warren wheeled and gaped at the gaunt figure that appeared only a few feet from him, its searing eyes feverish with hate. They forced electric pain into him, dripping green pus and clotted blood over his thoughts. "Be sure," the vampire intoned darkly, "to tell everyone the one about the traveling salesman."

In a second it was gone, and the warehouse door slammed shut. Freed from the eyes, Warren shot toward the door even as the loud reverberation crashed through the stillness. He slammed into the barrier and threw it open with his shoulder. Just outside he stopped, remembering what he was chasing. His guts tingled, and he backed against the outside wall warily to look around the deserted street and sidewalk. He searched for even a flying bat, remembering the movies, but there was nothing, nothing at all. It raised a chill in him more piercing than the freezing wind and he finally doubled back breathlessly to Ben Dixon.

"Damn him," Dixon bellowed as Warren stepped back inside the warehouse. *"God damn him."* The light came to rest on the floor and Ben spoke in exhausted humiliation. "You . . . heard it?"

"I saw it." Warren gasped, regaining his petrified vocal cords. *"I saw it."* He tried to overcome the terror squeezing his heart. "My Lord . . . Carmen. Where is she?"

Dixon stared without comprehension at the exit. His face was red, as it had been when he appeared pounding at Warren's door earlier. "We've got to go after it."

"We've got to help Carmen!" shouted Warren, grabbing Ben's sweater. "You brought her here!"

Dixon wiped his wet forehead. "She *came* here. I only followed her, MacDonald!"

Warren pushed him away, grabbing the flashlight from his hands. "You're as big a monster as that thing is," he spat. "Chuck trusted us."

"I had to!" Dixon cried. "I—*we have to stop it, MacDonald.*"

Hearing the scurry of rats as he peered around the boxes and piles of stinking garbage, Warren hated Ben Dixon as much as he hated the vampire they both chased. He knew the twisted fire in the man's eyes was only a mild version of their quarry's hate.

"We've got to go after it!"

Pushing aside a brittle sheet of plastic, Warren heard a soft moan.

"MacDonald! We *have* to—"

He wheeled to shine the bright beam into Ben's blinking face. "Shut up. You're as bad as it is! Shut up!"

Dixon shook his head wildly. "You don't—"

A moan floated from the farthest corner, and Warren turned the flashlight until he saw a white bundle on the floor.

Warren ran, stumbling when something sharp ripped through his slacks and slashed across his thigh. Huddling amid bottles, cans, and shredded paper, was the shaking, naked body of Carmen Richison.

Warren stretched his hands out, bent down, and gasped at the pasty, death-shadowed face. Her eyes stared blindly and her limbs were limp, twitching with her shallow and raspy breaths. He grabbed her wrist and found a pulse that was thready and terribly weak. Hurriedly, he took off his coat and began to wrap it around her cold body, cringing at the blood streaming from the reopened wounds between her legs. He cursed the creature that had done this, and Dixon, who had helped. He picked her up, leaning into the wall to keep his balance, and said nothing, not trusting himself to speak with Dixon so near.

Taking the flashlight once more, Dixon huffed, lighting their way. "Did you see it out there?"

"See what?" he muttered, his eyes on Carmen.

"The vampire."

"Forget the damned thing until we take care of Carmen. She's suffered enough."

"I . . ." Dixon fell back when Warren stepped through the door with her, then walked quickly to keep up.

Warren ignored him, hurrying to his car down the street.

Carmen moaned pitiably when Warren laid her in the backseat, then he climbed into the driver's seat as Dixon got in. Warren slammed his door angrily.

"I'm taking her to the hospital," he panted, starting the car. "This is your fault, Dixon. If you hadn't—"

"We should have gone after it." Dixon stared at him dully.

"It's time to let Chuck in on this," Warren went on.

"Who?"

"Her husband."

Dixon snorted. "Tell him the one about the traveling sales-man?" He shook his head. "Go ahead and try. Look what it's taken to convince you."

Warren followed the street ahead. "I'm going to tell him."

4

"You're crazy," Chuck told Warren.

Meeting Dixon's disdain with his own, Warren sat rigidly in the plastic chair. Carmen lay sedated on the hospital bed. Though her wounds had reopened, she'd lost very little blood. He didn't understand why she wasn't hurt worse, and Dixon couldn't explain it.

"Do you think," Warren had asked when they'd checked her in, overcoming his rage enough to speak, "that we can still save her?"

"Maybe she's been left for just that purpose," Dixon had surmised, "as something to tie us down and divide our strength. Watching Carmen will keep one or the other of us occupied."

Dixon viewed even life in terms of whether it helped or hindered his obsessive quest.

"With what I've been going through," Chuck burst out, "I don't see how—"

"At least your wife is still alive," growled Dixon.

"All I'm asking you to do is keep watch over Carmen," Warren told him, "and to be ready if something happens. I'm still not sure what to make of this myself, but you'll be better prepared from hearing this, Chuck. I *have* to do something, or others will be hurt. We can't stay here and guard Carmen with you."

Chuck stared disbelievingly, chewing a plug of tobacco. His eyes switched from Warren to Ben Dixon, then back, and back again. His hands scraped together noisily.

"If we're wrong, nothing's lost, Chuck. But if we're right . . . Don't you see we've got to do something?"

Reaching down to hold Carmen's limp right hand, Chuck closed his eyes and leaned his head against the plain white wall. "Warren, I've known you a long time. . . ." He reopened his eyes.

"Then how do you explain what's happened?"

Chuck shook his head. "The *police* are out looking for that guy. They said there's been a rash of these attacks lately. Hell, look at that place downstate—that Freeport place. It's probably one of those psychos. Maybe the son of a bitch thinks he's some kind of vampire, but I bet a forty-four magnum will blow him down."

"I don't blame you." Warren sighed.

"It's a joke, right? Some kind of therapy to take my mind off what's happened?"

Warren looked at him steadily. "I—"

"Mr. Richison," Ben Dixon broke in suddenly, rising from his chair beside Warren's and staring down at him, "there are many others in danger besides just your wife. I have put myself in danger every day for nearly a month, and I can guarantee you that your wife's soul *is* damned *right now.* If she is to have any chance at all, and if you care enough to give her that chance, you'll watch her every second." He turned and prodded Warren to follow him.

For a long moment Warren didn't move. Finally he clasped Chuck's hand. "Please?" he pleaded. "Just watch her and don't let anyone you don't know in here. I'll be at my house if you need to call."

Warren followed Dixon out and did not look back at the perplexed irritation he knew he would see on Chuck's face.

"I told you how he'd react," Dixon murmured, speaking clinically. "Like all of us he'll have to see to believe."

"Yes, you told me." They walked down the smudged hallway to the elevators several yards down. "What are you going to do?"

Dixon looked straight ahead, then sighed. "Sleep, I hope. I'm exhausted." The edginess Warren had noticed in him seemed more and more pronounced in his flushed face. "I'm not sure myself what to do now." He gulped loudly. "It said my wife, Carolynn—"

Despite Warren's aggravation he felt pity for Ben Dixon at the reminder. "Don't you think it was lying?"

"I don't know. Someone was killed in Freeport tonight, Mac-Donald, remember? People are dying *there.*" He pushed the bottom elevator button. "He said . . ." Dixon closed his eyes as his voice faltered and broke off.

They got into the empty cubicle and dropped to the ground floor, then walked blindly out of the building to Warren's car. The night had become eternal, so dark and damp that it fit Warren's bleak thoughts exactly. It made the previous hours seem so endless that Warren was surprised as he looked at his watch and saw that it still counted the seconds. It was four forty-nine. Trying with discomfort to hang on to his pity, he managed to smile faintly at Dixon. "My house?"

Dixon stared back at the tall stone hospital. "If you will put me up for the night."

He didn't want to. The mystery surrounding Ben Dixon had grown, and it was nearly as dark as the evil he was tracking. Despite the new pity Warren didn't want to be near him. "You can stay if you want," he finally managed, swallowing sticky saliva. He tried hard to identify with the pressure of this man's fear after the vampire's entreaty and revelation, tried hard to make even his annoyance fade in that compassion. "I guess I don't really look forward to being alone, anyhow." The car revved evenly as he turned the key, and he pulled out of the nearly vacant lot.

Dixon laid his head back on the seat, unwrapping another cigar. He lit up and allowed silence to enclose them again, unsuccessfully masking his dark moodiness.

More time went by and they finally passed by the warehouse from which they'd taken Carmen short hours ago. Warren turned the corner, glancing in his rearview mirror. When at last the deserted building was out of sight, he breathed more easily.

But he knew the vampire was there, or somewhere near, and that with its strange powers, it might very well know where they were.

It did know where Carmen was.

IX

1

"Hi, Emily."

Turning in the narrow library passage, Emily looked up from the books lining the scarred shelves. She was face-to-face with Randy Clagget and smiled at him unenthusiastically. "Hi, Randy."

He nodded in silence and worked his jaw.

"How's it going?" She moved her eyes over his almost muscular body to his round face, then to the tiny gold pin on her blouse. Sudden irritation grew at him for having given it to her, and at herself for wearing it. Was she really so insecure that she had to prove someone liked her enough to claim her? Pin the tail on the donkey. It was more a mark of his possession than an offering of love.

"I tried to call you last night." He blushed, then stared down at the checkered floor. "I'm sorry."

She touched the pin absently, restraining the urge to tear it off and give it back to him. Everything seemed different to her now . . . and its representation of ownership bothered her. It stunted her.

"Is there anything I can do?"

Emily twisted a strand of hair nervously around her finger. "No—nothing, Randy. I just need more time." She wondered what he would say if she told him what had really happened. She knew he wouldn't believe her. Even so, he might tell someone else and then they would be watching her.

She forced the thought out of her brain and looked around. With what she had to do, it wouldn't be good to have people notice her. They would try to stop her.

". . . and a lot of the kids have left school," Randy was saying.

She looked at him sharply.

Randy shrugged. "With all the stuff on TV about these weird murders, I'm surprised my parents don't pack up and move us out of here too. Four people are dead now, Emily. Seven if you count that preacher's family last month."

"They weren't murdered," she said curtly. "I *know* who's been murdered."

"Hey, I didn't mean—" He touched her arm and stepped closer to her. "Damn it, I'm sorry about your folks, Emily. I really am. It's just so crazy. Everybody's kind of worked up, you know? Hell, at least you're not the only one."

"You think it makes me feel any better?" she shot back.

He shook his head. "I didn't mean it that way, I—" Randy took a breath and touched her arm gently. "Look, it makes me worry about you. They're talking about calling in more police and the FBI, maybe even the National Guard—you know, to patrol the area."

Emily looked back at the books.

"I just didn't think you'd be back at school so soon, Emily. Especially not at night. They say we should stay in after dark. One of the students was chased by some creep the other night."

"I just wanted to get out and think, Randy." She avoided his eyes carefully.

"Yeah." He moved against her and held her with his powerful arms. "Hey, I said I'm sorry."

"Randy . . . I want to be alone right *now.*" She repressed a sudden urge to push him away, raise her knee into his balls with unladylike precision, then toss his pin at him. But the notion made her smile, imagining him squatting there as he soothed his most cherished possession. She giggled, disentangling herself from his arms.

"Look, I only wanted to know how you were doing. I want to

make sure you're okay." He flushed as his raised voice broke the stillness.

Emily stared at him uncharitably. He always got loud when he didn't get his way. It was one of the many things she found she didn't like about him, and those reasons had kept her from seeking him out. She had come to the school when she knew he'd be in class, to avoid running into him. She would be safe here, the very last place she expected Randy to find her. His being in the school library had to be a first. Her face twisted sarcastically. "How'd you know I was here?"

"It's all over the damn campus, Emily. Almost a bigger deal than the murders." Taking a comb from his jeans, Randy ran it through his short blond hair and made a face. "Shit, everybody was coming to me asking what you were doing here. No one expected you to show after the other night, especially after what happened to your mother."

"Cut it, Randy."

"Well, damn it, Emily, how do you think I feel? I've hardly talked to you since—since what happened to your mother. All I know about you is what I see on the TV news!"

"I said to stop," she whispered icily, then smiled at its effect on him.

"Shit." He peered up and down the book-lined aisle and took a step toward her. "What're you doing in here, anyway? Your evening class isn't over."

"I didn't go to class." She pulled away from his puffy face and all the sudden imperfections she found there. The pin was hot against her breast and she wondered why she'd ever gone out with him. The memories of his hands all over her in the backseat of his car revolted her. *He* revolted her. The day after that first time, everyone in school had seemed to know they'd made it together, that he could add her to his list of conquests.

"What the hell are you doing here, then?" He moved his finger with aggravation along the books she'd been studying. "Why are you looking at this witchcraft crap?"

"I was looking something up."

"Great. Your parents die and you withdraw from the world to read bullshit." He shook his head. "Look, Emily, it isn't good for you to show up here after something like this and with all this other stuff going on and not even tell me about it. I don't even know where you were last night."

"I don't care what it looks like," she replied with rising temper. "You're not my damn keeper, Randy. What happened happened to me, not you—okay? I can deal with it without you."

Their eyes were locked together for a long time. "You mean you don't need me," he spat out.

"No. I don't need you." She touched the pin's cold shape.

Randy's face bulged, warping his cheeks into fat red apples, and he raised a clenched fist, then slapped it hard against his palm. "Then I don't need you, either, bitch."

Twisting the pin off, she knew she hadn't done this right. She'd meant to dump him flat to his surprise, but it wasn't coming off that way. He was dumping *her*. She held the pin out with distaste. "And I don't need *this*."

Without warning Randy grabbed it and stuffed it in his pocket. "Your social life is dead," he told her coldly. "After I get through talking about you, not even fucking freshmen'll take you out. I'll tell 'em why I dumped you and they'll think you're some kind of a witch. Some kind of a witch-bitch. A witch-bitch that hates men."

Emily laughed bitterly, but could feel the blood leaving her face. "I could care less what you say."

"Yeah. You fucking witch-bitch-dyke!" He growled it loudly, then grinned. "Yeah," he went on viciously, "that's it. You've gone dyke. Only another witch-bitch is good enough for you."

The words made her cold and she gasped, fighting a panicked perverse laughter that struggled to come out with it. "St-stop it, Randy. You—you sound like Elmer Fudd."

Wascally witch-bitch. She saw it on his lips, but instead he shook his head. "Dyke," he whispered, then shouted it through the library's still aisles. "Butch-dyke!"

The fact that it was a lie didn't help. The words tore a deep hole into Emily despite it. She hated him as he stalked lewdly away, and hoped that a library attendant would catch him for his loud, crude behavior. The words hurt bad—worse than the sticks and stones that broke your bones, because she had been raised with their harsh discipline. Mom and Dad's name-calling rebuked her even on the verge of adulthood, and she knew the physical torment of their infrequent spankings was a luxury she would have cherished growing up.

Spoil the rod and spare the child, Dad said, and Mom had nodded. *We won't spank you, Emily. If you do something wrong, though, you will know it.*

The words hurt worse than anyone would ever know, but she didn't dare to dwell on them—not now. She had to put Randy out of her mind. She could not afford to let him fill her brain with anything that wasn't in her purpose! It had been her idea to break up, anyway, and she knew he would try to get with her tomorrow as he always did after these blowups.

But he'd never been so angry.

Forget him. Emily tried to concentrate on the book titles. There wasn't time to think about him. There was too much to do. The night before last she'd seen the impossible.

Officially, her parents were dead from attacks by "a person or persons unknown." But she *knew.* Emily knew. The berserk killings turning the whole college and town on end were being fruitlessly investigated. Tonight someone else would die the same death.

But she knew. *She could stop it.* No matter how many there were, she would hunt them down and destroy them. Most especially, she'd find her mother and father—*and kill them again.*

Her hand closed around an old book and she took it from the shelf: *The Vampire: His Kith and Kin,* by Montague Summers, a Catholic priest. She put it under her arm and chose another, similar title. Yes, she'd stop them, no matter their number. She'd destroy Mom and Dad, no matter how long it took. She hated them, even more than Randy, and she would beat them. She would beat them all.

She'd be free of Mom and Dad forever.

2

It was already dark outside when Warren woke up. He pushed aside the stale blankets and wiped his greasy hair, and then, against the knowledge he shouldn't waste the time, took a hot shower. He hurried through, dried, and put on new clothes. Ben was seated on the couch, staring at the broken window. They didn't speak, and Warren wished he hadn't allowed Dixon to stay here last night.

Trying to put aside the hostility Dixon's callousness infected him with, Warren went into the kitchen and made their very late breakfast and a pot of coffee. When the hot water began to sputter through the maker and brown refreshment drooled like blood into the carafe, Dixon came in and sat down at the table. Warren sensed that Dixon wanted to break the silence but didn't know how. He placed a plate of bacon and eggs in front of Dixon and a steaming mug in his hands.

"I'm not adapting to this schedule," moaned Warren, breaking their discomfort as he sat with his own plate.

Dixon scooted closer to the shiny oak table, scowling. "It's difficult at first." He pushed the egg white onto his fork, lifted it to his mouth. "But I've gotten used to it." He chewed. "I've come to enjoy waiting just before dawn as the first light breaks evil's pall. I've almost felt like a watchman at times"—he swallowed and made a dry chuckle—"a night watchman, trying to hold out the elements of evil. 'I will take my stand to watch, and station myself on the tower. . . .'"

Warren fidgeted, not liking the fluctuating changes in Dixon. "What happens to them in the daylight?"

Dixon peered at the dark coffee inside his cup. "They certainly don't dissolve as they do in the films, MacDonald. I only know their supernatural strengths leave them under the sun's rays, except for that power that keeps them 'alive,' or undead. That's why they return to their coffins or whatever they stay in.

It's safer for them. *I only want to destroy the things!"* Dixon's voice rose, regaining a shadow of its previous intensity.

"It might help if we learned more about them," suggested Warren.

"If we know one way to destroy them, I think it's enough."

Warren eyed him with dissatisfaction. He wanted a rational basis for all this. His reason had been insulted and proved fragile, and he wanted to make up for it by finding meanings. He listened to his unchosen companion chew, disgusted by the sound, by the taste of the food, by its smell. The clock on the wall ticked surely.

"I know you hate me for what I did," Dixon whispered as he laid down his fork, finished.

Warren flushed at the truth of the accusation.

"I can't apologize," he continued. "I'm not sure I would, even if I could. A lot has happened, and I'm just doing what I have to do."

"I don't want to talk about it. Please?"

"It is hard, MacDonald." He sighed.

"I appreciate what you've been through."

The words made Dixon smile briefly. "Then perhaps I could offer you an after-breakfast cigar?" Dixon took two from his shirt pocket.

"Smoking's supposed to be bad for you."

He held the cigar out insistently. "At least it doesn't bite you in the throat and send your soul to hell."

Doubtfully, Warren took it and inhaled the aroma. "Why not?" Biting off the end, he lit the tobacco and tasted its almost forgotten richness.

Dixon puffed speculatively. "I have to go back, you know."

Warren raised an eyebrow.

"If my wife's become one of those *things* . . ." He rested his elbows on the shiny tabletop. "I owe it to her, MacDonald. Those things tried to trick me. I know they tricked *her* by using Todd—they use our feelings and love against us. That's the worst thing about it all. They know what to use against us, and they do." He rapped his fingers violently on the wood, then did it again. "I owe it to what she was to me and what I tried to be to her. I owe it to her potential victims to save them from her

. . . from *it.*" He breathed deeply. "I owe it to God. This is my mission."

Silence followed, and they smoked. Warren felt a nagging responsibility. "I'll . . . go with you," he offered at last.

Dixon shook his head. "I don't trust your friend enough to leave that woman in his care. He didn't believe a word we said, and won't until he sees. It'll be too late then." Ben stared at the smoke for a long minute. "I'll go alone. I have to go. People are dying—someone died last night." He gulped. "It means that *another* will be out there, and then another. They have to be stopped, just as surely as the originator must be stopped."

Warren put down the cigar, its taste becoming bitter in his mouth. "Can you do it alone?"

Dixon didn't reply

"How long ago did your wife die?"

"Almost three weeks ago." His eyes narrowed with understanding. "You saw the news, too, MacDonald. There aren't that many there yet."

"Are you sure? How many have been dying back in Freeport?"

"The newscaster said only four or five, didn't he?" Dixon's broad shoulders seemed to slump to the floor. "I wasn't checking that paper very often. I was trying to catch up with—"

"That's why it said those things and told you about your wife! The authorities may be keeping a lid on the facts!" Warren exclaimed. "There's no telling how many of those things are crawling around down there."

"It doesn't matter." Dixon was shaken but spoke firmly. "If I don't go, it will be due to fear. Because I doubt I can master them."

"That many—"

"Numbers don't matter." His face seemed more lined now, and he covered it with his hands, proving the fear he denied. "If I doubt that with a dozen, how can I believe it with one?" He looked back up with a face that demanded to be challenged. "I've destroyed two with faith. With *faith.*"

Warren thought of Carmen and the way Dixon had used her, but felt his anger softening. Something had happened to Dixon last night in that confrontation, and even before that as they'd watched the news. He knew the man was afraid and heard the growing uncertainty of his actions behind every word, no matter how he tried to hide it. With a deep breath Warren smiled at the resurrecting humanity he saw and clasped Dixon's hand briefly before the man jerked it away. "I'll go with you, Ben."

"No." His eyes flashed with his old firmness. "You will not. You can't. You've got to stay with Carmen. You said it's my fault she's the way she is." He coughed, inhaling some of his smoke. "I could live with that, if we had killed it, but you've got to stay with her." He looked up, as if at God. "Our plans have been laid down for us from the beginning, and we cannot thwart His will. If we don't succeed, we'll become what they are. If I don't go, I've failed without trying."

"You're really going?" Warren hesitated, awed by Dixon's guts and will. The feeling came close to burying his misgivings about everything that had already transpired. "God. After last night it's more than I could do."

"It's because of last night that I have to go," he said. "But I ask one thing of you. . . ."

Warren clenched the cigar in his mouth with dread anticipation.

"Could—could I borrow that car in your garage? I think it would be more convenient than taking the bus, and faster."

Warren nodded with relief. The Chevrolet had been Susan's. Loaning it to Dixon was a small way he could help. It was the least respect he could pay to this man's lunatic courage, though it felt like compliance with a condemned man's last request.

"Thanks," Dixon said. His face wrinkled. "Thank you."

"When do you plan to go?"

Dixon sighed. "I'd like to get there just before daybreak tomorrow. As close to daybreak as possible." He picked up his smoldering cigar from the ashtray.

Warren reached out and touched his hand compassionately.

Dixon pulled away once more, standing up. "I think we should go to the hospital and relieve your friend now. He needs to rest so you and he can keep watch tonight." Squaring his shoulders, Dixon led the way to the door.

3

"Where are you going, Emily?" Karen asked with surprise.

Slipping into her knee-length coat, Emily pulled her long black hair out to lay over its back. She smiled at Karen, already in her nightgown. "Just out."

Karen bent forward from her place on the floor and turned down the tiny TV. She looked worried. "Out where?"

"God, stop it. You're starting to sound like my mother."

Karen was stunned at her emotionless voice. "I'm just—I just want you to be careful, Emily. You've had a—you're not yourself. You really need to stay here and rest."

"So you can keep an eye on me?" Emily glanced in the mirror at her slender face and the deep circles under her eyes. Karen was trying to possess her now, wasn't she? Like Randy and her parents. "I went to school by myself, remember?"

"You have to go to school," said Karen, pushing up from the faded green carpet and walking toward her.

Emily buttoned the thick leather jacket. "You told me I shouldn't go back so soon." She picked at a stain on her worn jeans and looked Karen in the eye. "I'm okay, aren't I?"

"Yeah, but you shouldn't have gone yet." She held her hand out to the garage-sale chair and the mismatched sofa and sighed. "Don't you want to watch TV?"

Emily clenched her teeth.

"Look, then, where do you want to go and I'll get something on and go with you, okay?"

"Karen . . ."

"Emily, you're my best friend. I know you're upset. I can tell. You won't even talk about it to me—you're keeping it all inside." She stepped back to the sofa to pick up her discarded jeans, then searched for her sweater. "I don't want you to hurt yourself, Emily."

Hurt yourself. Emily tried to ignore the lump in her throat and giggled lamely. "Karen, I'm not going to 'hurt myself.' I just want to get out for a while."

Karen looked at her watch. "At nine-thirty? Look, you know better than anyone else what's been happening around here." She found the sweater on the floor and shook her head. "Who're you kidding?"

"I'm not going to kill myself or anything, Karen, and I'm not going to let some psycho get me." She sighed uselessly. Why did everyone think she was so overcome with grief? Yes, she missed Mom and Dad, though she wasn't sure why. She hadn't loved them any more than they'd loved her. She could handle this. Especially because of how they'd died. She had to handle it. She had to or they'd come after her now, just as they had in life. They'd come after her to make her just like them. She had decided. She *had* to stop them.

"Then where are you going?" Karen pulled off her sheer top and shook out the sweater. "They want people to stay inside, you know. They might even enforce a curfew."

Emily didn't want company. She knew Karen wouldn't believe her and would ridicule her. She would try to stop Emily and might even try to get her put into the hospital mental ward . . . and Karen might get hurt. Emily understood the danger and didn't want the added responsibility of Karen to distract her. Her own safety worried her enough, even with police swarming all over the place. This whole idea was terrifying and she knew that most people would run from it if they had known what she knew.

But she wasn't like most people. She prided herself on that. She was afraid, yes, but she saw what had to be done. Simple logic told her that the way to destroy fear was to destroy its source, and that source was Mom and Dad, as it had been for most of her life. Emily wanted badly to be free of the fear, and at last there was a way to do it.

"Emily, where are you going?"

Mom and Dad had always frightened Emily in their little ways. Their nastiness and callousness had hurt her, and now that they were dead, they wanted to hurt her still more. She never could've killed them in life. But in death she might be able to remove them forever. She felt no sickening twinge at the notion of killing them, because they were dead already. And once she had killed their spirits, then she could begin to live, remembering the good times, forgetting the bad, and planning for tomorrow without their interference.

"Emily." Karen started putting on the sweater.

"I—I saw Randy tonight," she said quickly.

Karen stopped and frowned, waiting.

"He wanted me to come over to his apartment, but I said no." She stretched out her fingers and drew them into a fist, then stretched them out again. "I haven't said two words to him since Mom"—she pretended faint sorrow for effect—"since Mom di—passed on. I want to see him," she lied. "I want him to hold me."

"Oh." Karen at last looked understanding and smiled easily.

Emily shrugged, hating herself for the pretense, but knowing there was no other way. "I'm just going over there to be with him. To talk to him."

Taking her sweater back off, Karen probed her with relieved eyes. "I think that's a good idea. You need to talk to someone. Want me to drive you over?"

"I can drive," she said.

"Keep your doors locked and be careful, then. It's what they told people to do on the TV." She pursed her lips. "You going to stay all night?"

Emily bit her tongue and nodded. "Yeah. It'll give you a chance to have Ken come over."

Giggling brightly, Karen moved close and hugged her. "I think I will." She flushed. "But thank God. I've been so worried. . . . I hope this helps you, Emily." Her arms squeezed tight. "Remember when we were in high school and we both agreed we'd always tell each other everything first?"

"Uh, yeah. It seems like a long time ago."

"And several boys ago. Don't worry, I understand, Emily."

"Thanks." She picked up her lumpy bag and slung it over her shoulder.

"Change of clothes?"

"Yeah." Emily walked to the door and turned the knob, then faced Karen seriously. "You never met my parents, Karen."

The young woman showed surprise. "No. No, I never did."

The smile on her lips fluttered uneasily. "That's strange, isn't it? We've been friends for years—"

"That's why." Emily's mouth was crooked. "They never liked my friends. I kept anyone I liked a secret. They didn't want me associating with anyone they didn't select first." She opened the door and shivered in the cold air. "They would've hated you, Karen."

Karen's mouth dropped open. "Emily, I—"

"I'll see you tomorrow, Karen." She stepped onto the concrete walk and pulled the door closed, remembering only the bad things about her parents. She hurried to the stairs.

A door opened behind her. "Emily!"

She turned and saw Karen at the apartment's doorway.

"Emily?"

"I'm okay, Karen. I'll see you tomorrow."

"Be careful," Karen called.

Making herself reject the offered warmth, she merely nodded and went on, hearing the door finally close. She refused even thoughts of Karen, or the compassion she'd tried to show.

Hate was the only thing that would see her through tonight. Hate for her parents. She needed to dwell on the bad things they'd done to her. She needed to fight the growing reluctance that made that hard. Even if Mom and Dad hadn't loved or cared for her, she had cared for them. A little bit. But she didn't dare think of that. She had to hate them, and kill them again, or they'd take her in death as they had in life. As those books said and the movies had shown her: The same movies Mom and Dad didn't like her to watch.

If she didn't get them, they'd get her, and hold her to them forever. She'd be under their thumbs, a plaything to mold.

The metal steps slapped under her feet and she slid her hand down the cold iron rail of the stairs. She got in her dented Pinto wagon and closed the door. Opening her clothes bag, she checked the short pointy pieces of wood she'd pried from the garden fence in her backyard. She'd gotten them this afternoon while the sun was still high, then taken the heavy mallet from Dad's workshop. Her hand slipped into the bag and touched the weapons reassuringly.

Vampires. She locked the door and started the car. Vampires.

It was nearly impossible to believe, but she'd seen it with her own eyes and knew insanity wasn't the answer. She'd gone over it time and again before she'd even called the police.

Vampires. Mom and Dad. Through their uncaring parenthood in her youngest years to the resulting guilty overprotection they showed as she grew older, they had sucked her strength from her in life.

She wasn't about to let them do the same to her in death.

4

It was ten P.M. Warren looked from his watch to see Ben Dixon asleep in the plastic chair beside him. His heart was cold with what lay before the worn man, and he hesitated to wake him. But if Dixon didn't go tonight, he would be sure to leave tomorrow night, and that might mean more of *them* to face. Making the unwanted decision, Warren shook him gently.

"What?" he shot out, then became quiet as he saw Warren and the cold sterility of the hospital room. He sat up and peered haggardly past the adjustable table at Carmen's pale face. The blanket rose and fell faintly with her steady breaths.

"The nurse checked her a little while ago," Warren told him. "She's holding her own."

He blinked and yawned, scooting his body back into the chair. "Where's your friend?"

"He went downstairs for coffee. He's still tired; the strain has really taken it out of him."

"Yes."

Warren felt the heat in his cheeks. The irony of Dixon waiting with Carmen here had made him uneasy again as the man slept. "Yeah." He cleared his throat. "Feel any better? You slept almost an hour."

"I needed it," he acknowledged. "What's the time?"

"A little past ten."

"I need to get going. Freeport's several hours southwest of here." Dixon stood up and stretched, yawning again, then his eyes turned briefly to Carmen. "Don't try to do anything on your own tonight, MacDonald," Dixon warned. "Just stay with her tonight and we'll make other plans when I get back."

Although he had no intention of continuing the search alone, Warren was surprised at Dixon's laxness. What he said hardly fit in with the passion he'd shown against their target, proving again the way last night had affected him. "I thought," he said, unable to contain a certain resentment, "that we had to hurry." Warren scowled. "I thought that was why you made Carmen your bait."

"You aren't ready to try to do what I've done, MacDonald, so it's better you don't even try. You'll be safer here, and at least you know enough to protect this woman if *it* comes to her. But I'm trusting it won't even be able to get in. In their studies scholars have noted that the vampire must have permission to enter any house other than its own." He touched a finger idly to his lips. "Still, in a public place like this it may be that if a door is unlocked, the vampire may enter, even as it can enter a body not wary of its evil."

Warren thought carefully. "Your wife was in the hospital, wasn't she?"

Dixon swallowed hard, and Warren could see how this new lapse bothered him. But he knew why. The holes in the man's knowledge had already changed the scope of the plans he'd created so hastily. Miscalculation, disbelief, and the hot insanity of the inner turmoil the vampire brought were the flaws it was using to defend itself.

The door opened then and Chuck walked quietly inside. He nodded at Dixon. "Coffee?" he asked, offering one of the cups on the tray he was carrying.

"Thank you, sir." Dixon made his voice strong and reached to take one. He blew on it, then took a sip, and Warren followed suit.

Chuck drifted to Carmen's bedside, began to stroke her arm.

"Ben's going to go now, Chuck," said Warren when he finished his drink. "I'm going to walk out with him. I won't be long, but remember what I told you, whether you believe it or not . . . *please.*"

Chuck's hand went still. "Warren, I told you—"

"Never mind, Mr. Richison." Dixon dropped his cup into the wastebasket and picked up his heavy coat. "But if we're right and you're wrong . . ." He shook his head and managed to force some of his prior smugness. "Just remember she's your wife. If you love her, you will deny yourself for her sake. If you love her." He left.

"Who the hell do you think you are?" Chuck yelled. "What did he mean by that?"

"I'll be right back," Warren said. "I'm sorry. He didn't mean it." He hurried after Dixon. "Why'd you say that to him?" Warren whispered. His see-sawing emotions toward Dixon tipped hard toward anger. "He looked as though he wanted to kill you, and I don't blame him. I can't believe you said that."

"The anger will set him on edge and make him more watchful in our absence, just so he can prove me wrong. It's a natural reaction. Ministers must often use psychology, you know." They entered the elevator, and Dixon's mouth twisted into a grim wrinkle. "Just like vampires."

"I don't see how using the methods of vampires can help us defeat them," Warren shot back, his eyebrows raised.

"You will when you know what they can do to you. You will when you know how they can use you and make you betray yourself."

The doors slid open and they stepped into the midst of nurses and visitors headed for the exit. "What if you don't come back?" Warren spoke in anger, but when Dixon stopped and turned to him, his mouth set, Warren's anger crumbled.

"Then you will learn it all on your own, and there will be no one to save you from your mistakes."

"But—" A tired family pushed past them. Warren swallowed and stared down at his feet. "I don't see how you can face so many of them alone."

"I hope to put them all to rest," he said anxiously, continuing toward the glass doors at the front of the lobby. "There are safe ways to deal with those monsters if you know their resting places. If I don't call, though, or if I'm not back late tomorrow afternoon, you'll have to learn to harden yourself, as I have, to know any hope at all." Dixon took his hand with pressure, then released it and pushed open the door.

Warren started after him, Dixon's drive drawing him with the same indisputable magnetic charge the vampire had used against them in the warehouse. But it made the man detestable just as often as it forced Warren's admiration.

Warren stopped at the glass doors, following Dixon's determined progress across the parking lot. That unrelenting drive made Ben overlook things, as he had only minutes ago in Carmen's room. The incident had shown Warren how vulnerable Dixon really was, and that vulnerability was the only thing that allowed him to see past Dixon's inflexible near-psychosis.

Ben Dixon contained secrets he would not tell; those secrets scared him and that scared Warren.

He would pray hard tonight. He'd pray more fervently than he ever had. The prospect of being alone against this insanity was more frightening than anything he'd ever faced, for even though his heart was convinced, his mind still struggled in doubt. Alone, that battle would distort his judgment as Dixon's bitter violence twisted his, and could make his actions fatal. Not only for himself, but for all the others he was now responsible for by his knowledge.

In the parking lot, Ben got into Susan's car. Warren wanted to run out after him and make him stay, but his concern was another emotion that was turned against them. He was afraid for them both, and wanted Dixon to stay, but knew if they didn't split up, then—as Dixon had said—they'd probably already lost.

X

The air in the room was close with the scent of antiseptic, and Warren finally coughed from its incessant tickle. Under the dim light of the bedside lamp Carmen twisted in the throes of yet another nightmare, her cheeks drawn and forehead lined grimly in the room's shadows. He coughed again, and Chuck glanced at him, then laid his meaty hand protectively on Carmen's shoulder.

"You don't have to stay here, Warren. You're tired and you've been through more than enough yourself. I'll be okay if you get some sleep."

The thought of Ben Dixon made Warren shake his head.

"You don't really believe that crap, do you?" The bags under Carmen's eyes had turned purple, and seemed darker against the paste of her cheeks. She looked worse. "I—I don't know," he answered. It was even harder to be committed in the crazed man's absence. He began to doubt what he had seen. "I don't know," he said again.

"I think you're paying too much attention to that friend of yours."

"I don't think I'm paying Ben too much attention, Chuck." The lamp's light emphasized Chuck's tight lips, the irritation showing in every muscle. "I hate to admit it, but . . . I've seen things . . . myself."

"Like what?"

Warren took a breath. "I saw Susan."

Chuck leaned forward, stroking his round chin disdainfully.

"I saw Susan . . . *come back from the grave.*" Warren's hand found the small cross he'd brought with him.

"You what?" Chuck's eyes were wide as he laughed nervously.

Warren looked away, his tongue turning to lead. The ridicule he was inviting already embarrassed him. "She came back"—he forced out the words—"and tried to seduce me."

"I think you had a hell of a bad dream, Warren."

"It wasn't a dream." The room was quiet in the aftermath of his confession, and he was surprised at the confidence his statement brought him. It was as if saying it had cracked a mental block, that he'd overcome his intellectual's logic at last by admitting what he'd seen—terrible sights that he wouldn't forget. "It wasn't a dream," he breathed again.

Chuck's face had gone loose.

"Ben saved me from her, Chuck. He *knew,* and was waiting. I —he brought me to Susan's grave and we waited there. We waited and—she came *back.* She was naked, and"—he put a damp hand on his forehead, quivering—"God, she had all her fingers. Every one of them! I couldn't believe what I was seeing. She—there were *fangs* in her mouth. She dragged me into her eyes and made me see *things.*" He remembered the unrepentant evil in her smile. "Ben Dixon destroyed her, Chuck. He destroyed her, and I saw her turn to dust."

Chuck hesitated, his uncertain eyes turning to the buzzer button that would summon a nurse. "You need help, Warren. You have no idea how crazy you sound. Vampires are legends."

Warren chuckled stupidly, hearing himself in Chuck's words. "I know."

"You're kidding," he asked hopefully, "right?"

"If I was, I'd go home and go to bed. I'm dead tired. I don't really even want to know what is and isn't real anymore—I just want to go back to the way things were." He stood up and walked to the window. On the street below an ambulance drove by, its emergency lights dark. "But too damn much has happened. Too damn much." He turned back. "I've suddenly realized that I don't know as much as I thought I did, Chuck. I thought I had all the answers. Some of them are right, but God . . . I'm no longer sure of them *all*." He shuffled back to the bed and formed a gentle smile, then laid his hand over Carmen's with love—a love strangely devoid of personal gratification. "I don't think I'm crazy, Chuck." Tenderness poured out, and he felt the same love for Chuck, and for Ben Dixon, despite his unthinking hostility. In his earlier darkness he'd never felt it for Susan, and now it was too late.

"I'm sure of love, Chuck. *Love*. Real compassion. I never truly loved when I was thinking of myself and how bloody smart I was. Love is thinking of others—to *do* unto others . . ." He felt a tear and thought of Ben Dixon, seeing where the man had lost his way.

"What?" Chuck's face was furrowed with lines.

Warren grinned. "I understand it now." He clasped Chuck's arm, his other hand still on Carmen's. "Without love—without *Love*—we're all *vampires*. . . ."

Chuck pulled away. "It's sick, Warren. *Sick*. And you're a minister. . . .Good God, one minute you're talking of nasty fantasies as though they're real, and the next you're practically praying. You were always so reasonable, Warren. You taught us there was no hell, no true evil. How can you believe in vampires?"

Warren's ears were hot. "It's what I'm trying to tell you, Chuck. I don't know. I can't explain what I saw—"

"*If* you saw it." Chuck came to the window beside him. "Warren, I've known you a long time, and your sermons helped me a lot when I needed it. You've done a lot for me." He rubbed his hand across his nose wearily. "Most of the time you've got yourself in gear, but this time, well, this time I think you're way off base. You've been through a hell of a lot. I know you and Susan were having your problems, God rest her soul, and it's made this rougher on you. What you need to do is take a vacation and relieve the pressure, maybe even get counseling for yourself."

Warren laughed without humor. "I'm a counselor."

"I'm serious, Warren. Don't be offended. I really think the best thing you could do would be to take some time off and get your head together."

He lowered his eyes. "I think it'd be best for Carmen too."
The mistrust stabbed him. "How's that?"

"When she's conscious again, I mean." Chuck went back to
the bed. "All this kind of talk won't do anything but upset her. I
mean, God, it would upset anyone, right? And if you tell her that
a—a *vampire* put his . . . *mark* on her . . ."

"Hold it." Warren looked at the assured man and hated his
own knowledge. "I know what you're thinking—I know how all
this sounds. For a while I thought I was crazy." He paused,
wanting to get it across. "I . . . but I'm *not*. Please believe me,
Chuck. I know I'm not insane. Look at Ben Dixon, he believes."

"What is it with you and that guy?" Chuck asked coldly.
"Where the hell did you find him?"

"He," Warren said, "found me."

Chuck's forehead furrowed. "Yeah—when he saved you from
Susan, right?"

Trying to ignore the sarcasm, Warren nodded.

"Damn it, Warren, I just don't like him. I don't trust him.
When you two found Carmen, he said he was following her. I
know he had something to do with this." Chuck walked back to
his wife and looked at her with a mixture of sorrow and rage. "I
know it was him. He made her scream when you two were
talking with her . . . and I'm going to tell the police if he does
anything to her again, Warren." Chuck's face was red. "I'm just
not going to tolerate any more of this shit—you hear me, Warren? I don't care if he's a minister or not, he's not coming back
in this room and seeing Carmen!"

"Chuck—"

"And neither are you if you don't cut it out."

"Uhhh . . ."

Carmen's lips twitched feebly. Warren turned quickly and the
blast died in Chuck's throat as he jerked around too. The sudden
anger crumbled unwillingly, his mouth became a circle. He bent
down as her arms began to quiver—he tried to hold her still, but
comedically, her legs were trembling now. He stretched to stop
them with one arm but she wouldn't quit. Her entire body was
trembling uncontrollably.

"Uhhhh . . ."

Warren hurried to the bedside and grabbed the plastic box that would bring a nurse. He punched the sluggish button—

"Warren, call the doctor!"

The light on the device wouldn't come on, and Warren pushed the button harder still. No light. "I don't think this thing works." He put it down frantically. "I'll go get someone." Nervous excitement was moving his legs fast as they could go, and Warren grabbed open the door and rushed into the hall, looking quickly up and down. He couldn't see anyone in the dimmed night lighting and aimed his feet toward the chest-high counter that enclosed the nearest nurse's station, fighting the oppressive feeling that strangled him.

"Room 416!" he cried, slamming into the counter.

No one was there.

Throwing back panic, Warren peered down over the Formica top. Two nurses lay crumpled one on top of the other. He saw them but could not comprehend. "Hey," he shouted. *"Hey!"* He pushed though the swinging half door into the station and saw the bloody gashes on their heads with empty, sick squeamishness and dropped to his knees. After a timeless, soundless instant he saw that they were still breathing. "My—my—" He saw the stained metal cane inches from his knees and touched its red smear dizzily, knowing what had happened as his mind began to clear. He reached for the desk, knocking over a pencil holder as he grabbed at the interhospital phone.

"Hello, I—" He recognized immediately the empty echo that proved the system's death. Warren dropped the receiver.

"Help!" he cried in a voice cracked by fear. He knew he must get up. He *must.* Slowly, but faster than he wanted, Warren's fingers found the countertop and pulled him to his feet, and he was staring down the way he'd come—through the empty dark to the half-open door of Carmen's room. Sweat was cold on his back, and he longed to crawl under the varnished plywood desk to hide, but knew he could not. He could not when he knew that Ben Dixon was nearing Freeport and would face greater horrors not far from this hour, and he bit into his lips as he regained his heavy feet, then began running toward the next nurse's station far, far down the hall.

"Warren!"

The terrible shriek made his heart stop and he wheeled on rubbery legs, staring at the distant room but unable to move one way or the other. He didn't want to move. The raw silence hurt his ears and he tensely waited for another scream.

A minute passed and the horrible quiet was not broken again in the long, vacant hallway.

Silence.

"Chuck?" Warren forced his voice weakly.

Silence.

What would *Ben* do?

With an effort Warren took the cross from his coat. He gulped. *Right foot forward, then left foot.* He gulped again, forcing himself to obey those orders. Very slowly, he marched down the dead corridor, past the dark rooms, his steps flat and disconnected.

It took an eternity. At the door he realized he was biting on his fist. He forced his bloody hand from his mouth and, through sheer unthinking will, made himself enter the room.

Carmen lay twisted and gory on the linoleum floor, the torn pink hospital gown barely hanging on her body. One arm had buckled behind her at a sickening angle and he knew it was broken. Her face was sheet white. Warren gagged and looked away, and saw the chair he'd been sitting in fallen over Chuck, who was crumpled on the floor, his pallid face stark. Chuck coughed raggedly, stretching out a trembling arm. The sight made bitter vomit rise in Warren's throat. His friend's legs were spread wide—the pants stained and shredded—torn by the dark fiend who bent there. It turned, revealing a thin, cruel face reeking of evil and death.

Its eyes found Warren. It cackled slowly with malice, shaking the shiny blood from its moustache and dribbling lips.

"You have become a lot of trouble," the evil thing intoned gutturally, provoking new shivers in Warren. *"Like your friend you fight me needlessly. I offered him the lust for men he has craved since boyhood, and I can offer you the same. Any experience that you may imagine! I offer you an amusement park that is everything you ever wanted: women . . . even the abilities you seek so blindly."* It stood with awesome height and opened its mouth to expose evil, blackened teeth. "Your life is so *short*, Warren. Too

short to learn all you search for or to help those you strive to. You don't understand them; you only hurt. I can give it to you: *life eternal and knowledge, and the strength to find the peace you seek and bring it to those around you! I will free you even from your inhibitions that chain you from pleasure!*"

Warm fog bathed Warren's brain.

"*You are so much like me, and without the guilt of your vile God, you will love whom you wish—true Love—and you will bring others into the truth I offer you! You will be a preacher for the truth of the nature you uselessly hide.*"

Warren flinched as it held him still with hard eyes, showing him wonders that could never be reached from books and study; the social skills he so lacked and wanted to acquire, the ability to love as he'd never been able to love Susan. Warren swallowed, his face hot, seeing even the promise of a guiltless coupling with Carmen—and the vampire chuckled, crossing the distance between them in seconds—

He wanted it all more than he'd ever wanted anything! He wanted the life he was promised, but as he saw it open before him with the vampire's closing steps, he thought of Susan, her feverish countenance proving the emptiness of her impulsive needs . . . and he saw himself in far different pursuits, but with that same maniacal glare.

The vampire was beside him then, its long fingers stretching to him, making him ache with those needs, impelling him with a sudden lust for the ecstasy in its touch.

Like his lust for Carmen that it promised to fulfill.

Shuddering, Warren focused on her broken body. "D-damn you," he mouthed hotly, shaking and backing away. Then, as hard, cold fingers pressed into the soft flesh of his arm, he screamed.

Sick pain surged through him, wrenching his already feeble stomach until he threw up willingly, covering himself with sour gagging vomit. "N-no! In—in the name of Christ!" he moaned without thinking—but Ben Dixon had said you must *think,* and *believe* in the invocation. The vampire crushed harder and Warren felt his flesh give . . . heard the wet sound of it tearing, and the bone cracked. "In the name of . . . *Christ*"—he gasped, grueling needles driving into his belief—"in the name of

Christ, *leave me!*" He brought the cross up with his unhurt arm, panting when the incredible grip weakened, and screaming when it resumed. In agony Warren detected his still present doubt and sought to conquer it: "In the name of Jesus Christ, Lord and Savior—*My Lord and Savior*—leave me!" The crippling talons lodged deep in his flesh shrank back hesitantly, and he concentrated on those words, repeating them in his mind. " *'Greater is . . . He that is in me . . . than he that is in the— world!'* "

The vampire jerked away as though Warren were a burning ember and snarled, spitting a putrid stench into the air. It backed off, picking up the fallen chair and holding it out with warning.

"In Christ's merciful name—*begone!*" The slimy warm blood flowed from the flesh of his crushed arm and his eyes blurred. Something silver and black was hurtling through the air—the chair—but he couldn't act. He was too enervated to do anything but fall and gurgle, trying to breathe through the bile filling his mouth. *But the cross in his hand gleamed.*

Hideous, inhuman laughter tormented the air as the chair smashed into Warren's already dropping body, and he winced in its echo as his face slapped heavily onto the cool floor. Through white flashes he saw the creature standing over him, and raised the cross weakly.

With a howl the vampire danced back, wincing as though blinded. It bared gory fangs and positioned itself to spring on him. "You will *beg* for what you refuse, preacher. Your own heart is dark with me already. *What you have coveted will find you!*" It howled once more, then retreated into the hall, growling with the hate of a mad dog.

In the fire of his throbbing arm Warren did not feel the cross slipping through his hand to fall onto Chuck's bare leg as his own dribbling vomit puddled around his head. The terrible stink was all he knew as his eyes finally closed and he entered welcome darkness.

XI

1

Emily shivered and looked at her watch in the streetlight. She'd put this off long enough. It was time.

Yes, it was time. The sun would be coming up within the hour. She'd fortified herself with the sour beer and cigarettes her parents had forbidden her in Ernie's truck stop until her mouth felt like shit and her tongue like cotton, but it was time to go now and meet Mom as she returned to her grave. Emily was on the graveyard shift tonight and would be again tomorrow; she was done putting it off, as she had the date for Dad's funeral, which was finally taking place tomorrow. He would be after her, too, then; she couldn't put it off anymore because not meeting Mom tonight would mean facing her and Dad at once.

Emily looked at the flickering Budweiser sign in the window and twisted her keys, making the engine cough. The taste of beer, stale coffee, and tobacco tainted her mouth triumphantly and she basked in the hate she needed, exchanging it for the fears of her mission, contemplating its soothing intent until the motor smoothed out.

This is it.

People had tried to mold, shape, and possess her all her life. But in spite of Mom, Dad, her teachers, the church, and now Randy, she was still her own person. She alone could claim the right to herself.

It was why she had to destroy them. If she'd been terrified

before, she was petrified of them now. If they made her like them, her opportunity to be what she wanted, and not what others wanted for her—*her choices*—would be lost forever.

Her right to be herself.

"My right," she whispered, looking at the darkened street as she swallowed and touched the pedal. The groping glimpses of shadows grew and twisted in the corners of her eyes, forcing her tense hands to shiver on the cold steering wheel. It was all she could do to keep driving through the badly lit, pitted streets.

The houses dropped behind her, and Emily slowed down as another black-and-white police car passed. It was the fourth since the truck stop. Cops were everywhere tonight, trying to stop the flux of mayhem that had come to town. Emily gritted her teeth: How many had been killed by vampires?

She watched the police car's taillights in her rearview mirror —yes . . . *how many vampires were there?*

But even a hundred of would be easier to face than Mom *and* Dad. She was scared, but not of the unknown, not of any of the others or how many must be out there. She knew exactly what she was afraid of . . . and everything else would be okay if she could only get rid of Mom first.

But how many were there? The uncertainty made her sweat cold, and she felt the unfathomable hypnotic frenzy of Mom's stare. She could go back to Karen's, get her stuff together, take her money out of the bank, *then get the hell out of Dodge.*

She pushed her foot down squarely, stopping the car. *Mom and Dad.* Then she stared through the smudged windshield at the tall bare trees swaying their skeletal branches, inviting her into the cemetery they danced for. *Come in, come in,* they rattled, reaching out and pulling back, leering with secrets. *Come in, Emily, we hide nothing you haven't already seen.*

The wintry creaks cackled past her, surrounding her with that promise. The jagged holes in Dad's throat shaped her dread . . . and the slimy dripping knives that had risen up to press against the window glass.

But she had faced that. She jerked her head and shoved her foot down hard, forcing her clumsy hands to steer to the side of the road. The branches shivered again, and she stared at the pale gray tombstones and scraggly bushes across the street, rising out of dead leaves that carpeted the slumbering grass in yellow and brown. Her heart thudded heavily as she licked dry lips.

"What the hell am I doing?" she muttered to herself uneasily. No one was out here. No one. Maybe she'd been wrong about what she saw. Maybe she was insane and had hallucinated the way Dad died. Maybe . . . She touched the cold keys. *What if I just start the car, turn around, and get the hell out of here?*

She sat still, feeling the drops of cold sweat drip down her nose.

Headlights were suddenly behind her then, freezing her when they illuminated the cab. Before she could duck down to hide, the unknown car's engine rattled close and she slid down at last, peering over the door to see it park across from her. The lights went off, and a big overcoated man got out. Emily stiffened when he turned. Even in the shadow his gritty face was so familiar, she wanted to scream. It was the preacher who had died in the fire last month—his picture had covered the paper and TV screen for days.

She held in her breath while he walked to the cemetery, crunching the leaves so loudly, it seemed he was right beside her. He stopped at the low stone fence, looking at something in his hand, then stepped over the masonry and crept among the tombstones. Dry mouthed, Emily reached up and turned off the car's overhead light. She gripped her clothes bag tight, pulling it over her shoulder as she took her chance and opened the door. Her hands closed rigidly around the hammer and a stake, and she knew there *were* vampires. Mom and Dad were *vampires.*

Leaving the door ajar, she slipped out of the car's safety and tiptoed cautiously to the fence, then scrambled over it, scraping her jeans on the rough stones. A giddiness rose in her and she worked herself silently into a thorny bush and peered from behind it . . . looked at the man in the middle of the lawn now, waiting at one of the graves.

Vampire. The word's menace crawled through her gut and she remembered there might still be others . . . and Mom. She tore her eyes away and searched . . . peering through the mist of her own breath.

Yes. Down the winding empty road a dark figure hobbled with

the jaded contentment of a fat man finishing the dinner most only dreamed of. She dared not breathe as his eyes floated lazily in grim sockets, searching for yet more—as a bear just fed will track a castoff bone beyond his own consumption. But the inhumanity of the man's gait was truest in its chilling silence. Not even the satisfied slurp and cackle of a vulture passed his greasy lips . . . and she crouched down as far as she could, feeling the warm set of cement tighten around her muscles when his gluttonous stagger shifted to reveal another . . . and yet another. Her chill heart pounded feverishly and she tightened her fingers about her weapons. And another . . . and two more—*God, how many were there?* She slipped deeper into the bush.

The preacher man saw them too. The moonlight bathed him brightly as he stood over the grave and watched their progress without expression.

She looked back quickly, into the dead white faces of the seven creatures coming closer and closer, clutching obesely and scratching their long fingernails as they groped the wall and slid over it to drift toward the graves. She tasted curdling saliva as it dripped to her chin, and closed her eyes as the first creatures shuffled loudly through the leaves to her right. Her lungs shrank and she fought the gurgling scream that left them dry.

The first light of dawn from the hidden sun colored the sky. *Day.* It provoked her to action. Mom—she had to get to Mom before it was too late. She didn't dare think of the others now— she didn't dare look at the others. There were too many. She would only destroy the thing that had been her Mom and get out of here. *There were too many of them!*

She listened to the steps crunch farther and farther away and grabbed her way blindly out of the bush, terrified of groping hands waiting to stop her. But the others were spread out now, and she panted, knowing she had to go to Mom's grave, hoping the others, in their haste to return to the coffins, wouldn't have time to regroup and attack her. Seeing the movies at Karen's showed her enough. Even without the books she'd scanned, she knew the sun would kill them if they didn't get back, and the sky was getting brighter.

Emily sucked a breath as quietly as she could and hurried across the brittle, frozen grass. Her feet crashed harder and harder, their steps strong once more as she put her will into them alone. She was running fast now, and Mom was in her eyes, her features slack in that hideous satisfaction. Charging to meet her, Emily passed behind the vampire preacher, waiting at that grave, and prayed that none of the others noticed her.

But they did. She felt their eyes bore into her and forced her legs faster, faster, until at last she was gasping at Mom's marker, the mallet and stake slick in her clammy hands. Mom, only fifteen feet away, saw her too.

"Emily, my sweet," came her harsh voice, *"I looked for you tonight—"*

A louder voice boomed out, cutting the sentence short: "In the grace of God and the blood Christ shed, you damned have no more power over me!"

The preacher. He repeated the words into the vile atmosphere, and the things around him cringed from the cross he held. At a barking snarl from her side she whirled back. Mom.

The terrifying figure was running with its arms raised high, terrible fingernails cracked, and calling to her. The distance between them disappeared, and Emily was barely able to bring the stake between them to protect herself. It was knocked back when Mom's icy arms clamped over her. She shoved the wood forward with faltering strength, into the dry white flesh. They fell, Emily's eyes frozen on the vulgar, lusting countenance inches away. Death was screaming in the obscene eyes, and she squealed, forcing the stake into its flimsy body again, tearing deep into the flabby dead flesh. She swung the mallet against the stake and felt it sink farther . . . and screamed at the cold ooze of brown-purple slime that spilled out with fetid odor.

Mom's screech shattered her own and the cold night as her body fell onto Emily's. The gore streamed everywhere, and Emily bit her tongue to hold back more screams, faint with the raw acid breath that touched her. She rolled awkwardly from under the writhing blows, then grabbed another stake from the clothes bag—but as she stood her howling heart steadied. She didn't need it. Mother's graphic contortions and livid agony were final, and filled her with the sweetest pleasure she had ever known. The lips shriveled against the dark teeth, and the thin, skeletal

arms splintered as they stretched into the morning air . . .
oozing and boiling into steamy white smoke that covered her.

The smoke drifted away.

Mom was gone . . . and only a mound of dust remained.

Emily sighed, and when she at last looked away the sky was
lighter. Three of the vampires had gone to crouch at graves on
the far end, and the remaining three now surrounded the
preacher in a semicircle, swaying back and forth like the trees,
their poking gestures almost playful. He faltered as she
watched, mesmerized by the two naked vampires nearest him.
A small bottle dropped from his flaccid right hand and a dull
metal cross from his left.

He wasn't a vampire. The knowledge struck Emily suddenly,
and she felt a rare kinship toward him. He'd come here, as she
had, to kill them.

He staggered backward and tried with his useless, frantic
arms to stop the first vampire, a man, from moving closer. The
thing reached out in dark confidence, stilling him and pressing
him to his pale white flesh. The other, a woman, cackled and
snarled, her voice thinned by the distance: *"Is this what you
wanted all those nights, Ben? Did you want a man? Did you
want that?"*

Without thinking Emily ran toward them.

The grating voice bit the air louder as Emily ran: *"Won't I do,
Ben? Can't I take you into the oblivion you gave me . . . ?"*

Closer . . . closer. The creatures began to disappear. Even
the man holding the preacher fled quickly to his grave and became vapor, his mist disappearing into the earth. The fantastic
sight startled her as she ran, but she didn't let it slow her down.

At last she was there—the vampire woman's back scant
inches away. In the force of her momentum Emily pointed her
stake high, unthinking as she began ramming it into the cold
papery skin, throwing them both to the ground. The thing
screamed with spraying red saliva, and Emily felt the same cold
wet stuff pouring onto her hands. She raised her mallet and
hammered with all her strength to drive the stake deep into the
convulsing body, and even the freedom brought by her mother's
destruction didn't help her nerves in this unknown creature's

horrible spasms. Her stomach turned as the woman's thrashing ended—and the flesh began to bubble and decay.

"Oh, my God. . . ."

The preacher was lying on the brown dirt, his neck slick and shiny.

"Are—are you okay?" Emily choked, somehow finding her voice inside the self she had salvaged tonight.

Tears rolled down his cheeks, and he touched his neck with a trembling hand. "Oh. Oh, God. I've failed. I—I didn't believe. *I —I wanted to be like them.*" He stared at his wet fingers and shut his eyes.

She scooted back from the wrenching sobs. Her eyes crawled the grounds to the mist still rising from Mother's dusty corpse, and back to the ground at her feet where boiling ooze was turning to gray powder with the stench of an acid fart. Her triumph made her smile. It was over. She'd done what she'd set out to do and more, and she could leave. In the aftermath of her adrenaline, exhaustion was setting in. She wanted to go.

But she couldn't leave this man out here.

No, she couldn't. Emily had grown hard to many things, but if she left him, she'd be doing as her parents always had. She couldn't ignore him.

"Get up," she ordered him. "I'm going to see if you're all right."

He winced, his hand returning to his sticky neck. "I'm—I'm sick," he whispered. "But . . . the mark is gone." He stared at the ground where his fingertips trailed the faint lines of a cross, then wiped it away. "Its evil was destroyed with it."

The new sun's rays bathed them both brightly. Emily faced the foreign warmth, then looked down at the bones that had themselves crumbled into dust and vapor. She stretched out her hand. "Come on. I'll take you back to my house and get you fixed up."

Submitting, he let her help him to his feet and limped beside her uncertainly. When they were in her Pinto, she gunned the engine, smiling once more.

She felt good. Proud of herself, and very, very good.

2

The water kettle whistled. Emily poured its steaming contents into two cups without missing a drop, relaxing in the new exhilaration of acting just how she pleased. She felt a dawning maturity not even approached when she'd moved to the dorm. The house was hers. Her life was *hers*.

I can do whatever I want after I get rid of Dad. . . . She could even have Randy spend the night.

Wascally witch-bitch! Butch-dyke!

Seeing his puffy, angry face again, she dismissed him quickly. No. Not Randy—not after last night. But still, she could invite someone else over; someone who wouldn't try to make her his property.

After tomorrow's dawn.

"How do you like your coffee?" Emily stirred the freeze-dried particles into the water until it was muddy brown, then tried a sip.

Ben Dixon glanced up from his seat at the dining room table. "Uh . . . strong. Strong . . . with lots of sugar, please."

His voice was still weak. Emily added three spoonfuls of sugar to his cup. After she'd helped the big man wash his neck, he'd explained to her why the marks that should have been there had disappeared, and then, bit by bit, some of the events that had led to his being in the graveyard.

"How do you feel?" She put the cup on the table and sat across from him with her own.

"Tired—and *dirty*." He shuddered and sipped the hot brew thirstily. "Thank you, Emily."

"You can take a bath or shower if you'd like," she offered, glad he was here, even in his bedraggled emotional condition. The opportunity to help him kept her from thinking. It kept her from thinking of that last-minute stunned betrayal showing in the eyes of the thing that had borne her. Emily bent her head back. . . . Yes, but it made her feel grown up and capable, too, and she was proving the worth of her freedom by helping him all by herself and of her own choice, and strangely, that peace was even better than what she'd felt when she'd destroyed Mom.

"Not that kind of dirty," Ben told her quietly. "I came here to stop those things . . . to stop my wife. To prove myself. To prove I am worthy."

Emily nodded. She'd already heard this once.

"But I'm not," he whined. "God gave me this mission, and I failed. I failed again!" Tears dripped onto his streaked cheeks. "God. Her *eyes* . . . and that *man*. God, I saw her hate for me, and how he wanted me! He promised . . . and I wanted it! They destroyed my will."

"I thought you said to refer to them as things," she reminded him. "You said they weren't human anymore."

"They're not." His forehead wrinkled. "She—*it*—they *both* lied to me, and somehow made me believe the lies! *Like before!*"

The emphasis in his voice made Emily turn from the bluebirds outside the window. *Like before.* She studied his tormented grimace. "What do you mean?"

His eyes narrowed. "Before," he repeated, "*it* offered me . . . whatever I wanted. *It knew what I wanted.* It knew I just couldn't help myself." He buried his wet face in his hands. "I knew better! I knew what would happen. I shouldn't have come alone."

She tried to piece together what he was telling her, and his weakness irritated her. "It was good that I was there, wasn't it?"

The uncertainty in his eyes showed through the pain of his defeat. "I . . . Yes, it was. I thank you, Emily. You saved me. Yes, you did that. I came to destroy . . ." He shook his head. "I only came to destroy myself. I came to destroy my past."

Emily could only think of how she'd barely conquered her own fears, and allowed her irritation to pass. "That's all right, Ben. I killed her okay."

"Yes." He bit his lip. "In a way. At least the body is destroyed." He scowled at his hands for a long moment. "But that demon will seek another habitat. Another body. Only God can imprison the devils within them—within her."

"How do you know that?"

"Books." He wiped his cheeks, then scrubbed his left hand across his right, hard. His expression flickered.

"They might be wrong."

Ben took his glasses out of his shirt pocket and put them on, not smiling at all. "I hope so."

Emily looked at the clock. It was eight-thirty. She yawned. "Uh—Ben? I've got to go to Dad's funeral this afternoon. I'm going to have to get some sleep." She suddenly felt the impulse to be alone—she wanted him to leave. *Now.*

Or did she? The opposing desires clashed: Her aunt—Dad's sister—had made the funeral arrangements from out of state and would certainly be there today. She was irritated with Emily's delay of the ceremony's date, and might even plan to stay *here* tonight. That would be just like having Mom and Dad back.

The very idea made Emily draw up into herself, and she shook her head: though Ben's repetitive ramblings were aggravating, his presence just might keep Aunt Joanie away. Ben was annoying, but not at all like Aunt Joanie; though she had never been a parent, she said she'd known so many bad ones that it certainly made her quite an authority. She always remembered the failures she'd seen so many times, and simply advised the opposite.

Emily frowned. More important, how could she allow herself to throw this man out just as Mom and Dad would? He was pale, as he'd been in the graveyard, and his schizophrenic babblings exposed the similar battle in Emily's own soul. She reached for his hand, stopped, then went ahead. "Are you okay?"

He squeezed her fingers very tightly. From her studies and what they'd both been through it was easy to see that he was enduring a great emotional shock, a trauma he was uselessly trying to hide now. "You can stay here, Ben. You don't have to leave. You can stay here and I'll go to the funeral, then come back."

"Can't." He shook and she could feel the tremor running through his body. "I've got to go. Warren's alone and he can't stop any of this without me." But he lowered his eyes. "I can't even do what I came to. But he's so obsessed with protecting Carmen that he can't fight that thing by himself!"

"Who's Carmen?" He'd told her about Warren and Warren's

wife, and about the vampire who began all this and was still spreading its disease, but that was all.

But she knew there was far more.

Ben clenched her fingers tightly. "Carmen. She's an infected woman I tried to help—and Warren says I failed her. Warren says I led her into danger. That if she dies her soul will be on *my* head."

Emily shrank back, feeling the shadow of Mom and Dad in the unknown Warren's accusations.

Ben sighed. "Warren just doesn't know what he's doing. He doesn't know how to cope with this kind of thing." His voice dropped low. "I've got to go back."

Emily shook her head. "You're in no shape to."

"I must."

His shaken manner proved his frailty, and the condemnation he told her of made Emily understand Ben better. Somehow she wanted to assist him. But she had to get rid of Dad first. She *had* to. Then she would be completely free.

"I have to do it," Ben repeated.

"We both need to rest." Emily finished her coffee and got up to take the cup to the sink. "After the funeral I'll come back and we'll talk, Ben. You can't drive that far alone, anyhow." She wondered once more how her aunt would react to Ben Dixon. "Maybe I can take you back tomorrow, myself. Maybe I can help you."

"Maybe you can," he whispered, his voice a mixture of exhaustion and gratitude. He rubbed his neck gingerly, his lips tight with distaste. "I'll have that bath now, if you don't mind."

She smiled. "I'll show you the way."

3

The next hours were slow. Emily couldn't get much sleep, and the little she managed was full of uneasy excitement and dread. Finally she gave up, pushed her awkward limbs out of bed, and put on a robe.

Ben managed to smile at her when he saw her coming down the stairs, and she returned it. She drank another cup of coffee with him and hoped he was better. It was hard to be sure, since he hardly spoke, but something about him seemed less withdrawn. It made her glad, especially when he promised to wait for her to return.

Leaving him in an armchair as he started a cigar, Emily hurried back upstairs to put on the indigo tweed suit she'd bought for Mom's funeral. Didn't waste any money on this, she thought. Two funerals for the price of one. That humor seemed strained even to her, though, and she kept it to herself, then hurried back down the stairway and left the vinyl-sided house to drive onto the rocky, unkempt road she'd traveled twice today already. She thought only of the bad things again, knowing she had to stay strong for tonight, then passed through the open gates and the low wall over which the vampires had slipped, finding the bush she'd shrunk behind.

"God," she breathed, and followed the winding path to the graveside ceremony. She parked and sighed as her father's friends and business associates took her hand to help her from the car.

The ritual was far too long, and the minister said a lot of good things about Dad that weren't true, just as he had for Mom, but it was finally over. Emily kept her attention and was silent, afflicted by an unexpected remorse that tugged at her for several seconds. She suppressed it; there would be time for that someday. But now she only wanted to feel the anticipation of an impending finish to a long wait. She was a short walk from being free.

When everyone crowded around her to press her hand, express their sympathy, and offer their help in the coming days, Emily thanked them briefly. Inside, she could barely hide the secret joy for her future . . . until Aunt Joanie came to hold her hand.

The flesh of Emily's palm crawled. She avoided the belittling green eyes squeezed too close together on Joanie's triangle of a face. They made her tiny nose even smaller.

"Hello, dear," Joanie said in her clipped Eastern voice. "I'm glad to see you bearing up to all this so well. I'm sure Adam— your father—would be proud of you."

Emily nodded agreeably, as expected of her.

"It was such a shock," Joanie went on, "such a terrible shock. You must feel very much alone, Emily."

She nodded again. Joanie was Dad's younger sister. She had married a well-to-do man several years ago, divorced him only months later, and was set for life with the alimony payments. Her main concerns since then seemed to be looking young and impressing others, which she generally did with surprising ease. To Emily she combined the worst of Dad and Mom into one personality.

"Poor dear, too upset to even talk." Joanie took her arm and led her away from the open rectangle in the ground right next to Mom's small marker and hideous final resting place. There was no trace of the thing that had worn Mom's body—the thing she'd destroyed an eon ago. But Ben had said there wouldn't be.

"There's nothing to say," Emily cracked impulsively, trying some of her new independence.

Aunt Joanie frowned. "No. No. I guess you're right, dear."

Emily looked at the sun, still high in the sky, then at her watch. She'd called Karen earlier and told her she wouldn't be coming back to spend the night tonight. Karen guessed she was staying with Randy and that was fine with her. It wouldn't be long before she knew differently. Randy had never managed the grip over her that Mom and Dad had crafted. She was finished with him. She was her own person.

"Shall I take you home, dear?"

"I brought my own car."

Aunt Joanie's frown was more pronounced. "Every bit the

unaffected Miss Independence, aren't we?" She stopped, grabbing her wrist painfully, and held Emily back as the last mourners got into their vehicles on the winding drive.

"What do you want, Aunt Joanie?"

The cold wind picked up and Joanie shivered, glancing abruptly at her brother's tombstone. She crossed her arms. "You are my niece after all, Emily. I want to help you. God knows, from what Adam said, you don't deserve it, but you *are* family. You're awfully young to be out on your own, dear, especially in such tragic circumstances. . . ."

Emily stared with unconcealed disgust. Her own opinion was that anything Joanie did was for appearance's sake or money. Just like coming to this funeral. She'd taken time out from her busy, busy life to arrange and attend her brother's funeral and prove her remorse. The black slitted dress Joanie wore was so typical of her style. *I didn't have time to get anything else, she would say, and it is a nice dress. I paid three hundred dollars for it—*

". . . and I thought you might like to come live with me, dear. I don't pay much attention to the news, of course, but I've heard something about the trouble in this dreadful little place. These small towns just aren't safe, Emily. There's not even a police force to speak of. We can sell the house and furniture, and the cars, too, and you can live with me. I'll keep the money in savings for you until you're older."

"I don't want to sell—"

"Emily, we have so much to do in New York, and it's so dangerous here. If we can sell the house and invest the money wisely, you'll be able to find your own little apartment after you've settled." She smiled secretively. "I can introduce you to some of the men I know, and you'll forget this horrid experience in no time."

"I want to go to school," Emily broke in sharply.

"Oh." Joanie batted her long eyelashes and looked forgiving. "Well, you could get some classes there if you really wanted. They're better schools, anyway."

"I want to go to school here in Freeport."

The silence between them was strained, but Joanie let it pass with an exaggerated shrug. "You can always come back, you know, Emily, after you're feeling better."

"I'm fine," she whispered through clenched teeth. "And I don't want to sell the house."

"Don't be hateful, dear. I just want what's best for you. What does a young lady need a house for, especially out here in the middle of nowhere? And it has all those memories." Joanie leaned close and draped a thin spider arm around her. "It will take time, Emily, but you'll get over this."

Emily started to butt in again, and Joanie shook her head, leading the way to their cars. "Death is such a tragic thing. It's hard to think clearly when something like this happens. I'll just stay with you a few days until you're better, and we can plan your future then."

Plan your future. The words gnawed at her. They were her mother's and father's words. Terrible words. *But they were dead.* Dad and Mom were dead, and so weren't the words dead as well? They couldn't cause the fear Emily dreaded anymore, could they? They couldn't cause her to regress to her former self. Aunt Joanie wasn't enough of a parental figure to use words like those, anyway. At best she was the parody of a parent: her self-righteous demands were *funny.* Emily laughed.

Joanie sniffed. "I didn't realize you would find your father's death so amusing."

They stepped onto the broken brick road and Emily tried to stop. "No"—she gasped—"it's you, Aunt Joanie. I can't believe you really think I'd let you help me plan my future."

"And why not?" she asked sharply. "A girl your age needs guidance."

"I'm nineteen!"

"Hrumph." Joanie pulled her coat tight in the rising wind. "Your father said you had the maturity and abilities of a much younger girl. I see he was right."

"I . . ." Emily blushed. Those words held a strange power over her even from Joanie, because she knew that Dad had said them—*and he could still come after her.* Her will crumbled, and she knew she wouldn't be really free until he was destroyed too. Now even the invocation of his name stifled her.

"You're upset," Aunt Joanie told her, walking her to the

rented Buick. "The horrible things that have been happening here." She opened the passenger door and tried to look compassionate. "Get in and I'll take you home."

Sneezing at the potency of her aunt's perfume, Emily tried to stay calm. She fought desperately to retain the last vestiges of her own desires. "I don't want to go with you. I'll drive *my* car." Foul curses formed on her tongue, and she barely swallowed them. "You can follow . . . if you have to."

They stared at each other for a long time, then Joanie shut the door and sighed. "Very well, Emily. I'll follow you home. But if you have an accident in the shape you're in, don't blame me." She stepped around the car and opened the door on the other side. "Your father would be ashamed if he could see you now, young lady."

Emily winced. The old fear was trying to control her again and she tightened her lips to keep from apologizing, turned away guiltily, hearing the cold upholstery squeak and the door slam shut. It was so hard—

But she was so close. Emily forced her legs to the Pinto a few yards down. After tonight she would be free.

After tonight.

4

"It was very kind of you to come and stay here with Emily"— Joanie gave Ben a false smile and sipped from the glass of wine she'd asked Emily to bring her—"especially with all the other trouble here, but I'm sure that since *I'm* here, she'll manage fine now."

Ben's mouth was crooked and his eyes dull with strain. "Yes . . . yes. I, uh—"

"I asked Ben to stay until morning, Aunt Joanie," Emily said.

Joanie raised her eyebrows. "I see. Well . . . do you really think it's proper that a minister like yourself should be alone in

the same house with an attractive young woman like Emily?"
She poised two fingers on Emily's shoulder and let them slide
down to her hip.

Ben Dixon frowned at her.

"He's here for the same reason you are, Aunt Joanie," Emily
explained. "With the murders and—"

"I see." She grinned at Dixon slyly. "Don't the police take
care of those things here?" She chuckled to herself. "It's good I
decided to stay on with you, Emily. People do gossip. A young
lady must be careful with her reputation."

You should talk. Seeing Ben's annoyance with Joanie pleased
her and made her feel more sorry for him at the same time. At
least *she* was used to being criticized like this.

But she thought of the man Warren, whom Ben had mentioned earlier. Maybe Ben was used to it *too.*

"Yes, people *do* talk. A woman must keep up appearances
even if totally innocent." She giggled at her own wit. "Oh, my."
Smiling, she put down her glass and stood up. "Pardon me,
please."

Emily watched her aunt swagger out of the front room to the
stairway and glanced at Ben.

"I think I should go now," he said quietly. "I feel . . . better. And I called Warren." Ben gulped without strength. "He's in
pretty bad shape. Something terrible happened last night. I need
to go back."

He didn't talk down to her. Ben talked to her as an equal,
possibly even looking on her as a leader after she'd killed those
two things and saved him. She liked the feeling it gave her. "You
might need help," she suggested.

"I've got to go back *now*," he said again.

Emily peered at him, admiring the unrelenting single-minded-
ness of his thoughts. "You should at least eat something first."

A silent moment passed before he nodded, and she went past
him through the den and into the kitchen, opening the refrigera-
tor as he sat down at the table behind her.

Emily chewed her ham sandwich and turned from Ben to look
out at the rapidly darkening sky. "It's sunset now."

"I know."

"You're too late," she said matter-of-factly.

Ben's face screwed up.

She stood, putting down her food, and walked with tiny steps to his side. She touched his shoulder gently. "Last night?"

"Y-yes."

The single word held the totality of the disintegration he had displayed when she brought him home, and she felt the tremendous pleasure of being needed. *"I'll take you back, Ben. I think I can help you."*

"No." He seemed even more tormented now, more lost.

"I saved you." The familiar resentment rose to the surface. "I killed two of those things last night—*by myself.*" She made herself as tall as she could. "By *myself.* I'm going to kill another tonight."

Ben twitched, putting down his sandwich. "I can't allow that. You saw all of—how many there were! You can't do it alone."

"I did last night."

"Not alone." Ben's face contorted, and he became very quiet. The muscles in his cheek were taut. "I'll have to come with you, Emily. You can't face all of them by yourself."

"Do you people have HBO, Emily?"

Emily looked up at her aunt as she entered the kitchen, her black dress unbuttoned almost to mid-thigh. "Yes, we—"

A quiet knock came from the front door.

"I'll get it," Emily volunteered, then stopped when she heard Ben's gasp. She gulped, facing him, and followed his gaze out the darkened window.

Oh, God. The sun was down. She saw Ben's terror at the shared realization and knew his fear. She hadn't considered what staying at her own home tonight might mean. But she did now. The sun was down. Her father would come here first to find her. She'd destroyed his wife—her mother—and he would be looking for *her!* He *had* come looking for her. *He had found her.* She searched wildly for the clothes bag.

"Well, aren't you going to answer it, Emily?"

The dusty bag was still in the den where she'd dropped it this morning. Emily stared at it, feeling Aunt Joanie's angry eyes at her back. She *wasn't* ready.

"Emily, you've got to learn to keep up appearances."

She wasn't ready.

"Do you really think one of your crazy little town psychos is going to knock if he wants in, Emily Knox?"

Another knock, louder and stronger.

"Get in there and open that door now, Emily!" Joanie snapped, stumbling forward to grab her. Emily backed away, staying out of reach until Joanie threw up her hands. When the knock hammered again, Emily dropped her eyes, scooting back to the sink.

"You are a very immature girl." Joanie's eyes hated her with belittling force, and she huffed, walking into the hall to go to the door herself.

"I . . ." Emily tried to warn her, and looked to Ben anxiously. He stared back and she saw the sweat on his face. He knew.

Silence. Then Emily heard Joanie throwing the dead bolt. "Emily, you are going to have to grow up one day!"

The words faded in the front door's creak and Ben stood up, holding the back of his chair tight. Emily saw the panic boiling against his resolve, and finally, the need to do something broke through the ice surrounding her and she darted to the doorway and bent to retrieve her nylon bag. She heard a deep voice, and Aunt Joanie's panicked laughter. As she pulled open the nylon bag, she clutched a stake and held it close.

Ben was biting his lips, and his wide eyes enveloped her.

The house was silent.

Emily heard Joanie's awful giggle again.

A minute passed, and then another; the giggles grew louder and louder, but Joanie didn't scream.

Ben blinked intently with each new sound.

"Maybe," Emily breathed hopefully, "maybe it *is* someone else."

But Ben didn't answer. He cringed when more laughter echoed down the hall from the front room: *Joanie's and a deep hiccuping gurgle that sent chills spreading into her soul.*

"My dear sister . . ."

It was Dad's voice and Dad's horrid laugh. Dad.

Dad.

Emily forgot Ben, clenched her fists around the stake, and

stood, looking around the corner into the den, and into the dark hall.

She couldn't see anyone. Her mouth filled with stickiness. Her feet moved soundlessly forward, ready to turn and run back. She crept nearer and nearer the entrance to the front room, and heard the mumbles of a strange, excited pleasure growing louder.

"I have so *longed* for you, my lovely Joanie," said the voice that was unmistakably Dad's, though its undertone was greedy, and far more lifeless than Emily could recall. "I used to hide in your closet all those years ago as you undressed for bed, watching. *I watched you take off your dresses and bras and your little lace panties and wanted to fuck you until you screamed. . . ."*

Terrified and disbelieving her own ears, Emily sank to her knees, waiting for Aunt Joanie to break down in hysterics.

But Joanie only laughed louder.

Emily slowly poked her head past the doorway molding.

It *was* Dad. The sound of his chuckles and of Joanie's ignorant giggles was like two files scraping together, and Joanie licked his bloated biceps as he stripped off his shirt and pushed her down on the couch.

Joanie's eyes were glazed, and she stared, awed and surprised at the sight of the body he made naked for her.

"I *always* wanted you, Joanie," whispered Dad, filling her mouth with his tongue and reaching down to tug at her black dress. He pushed it up to her navel, bending to nuzzle into the black bikini panties that scarcely covered her crotch, then licking her cheek again.

She kissed him back earnestly for long seconds while he clawed her, then she pulled back and frowned briefly, pushing his hands away. She snickered and sat up, reaching back to unzip the dress herself, then gave him a strange smile. *"I'll* take it off, okay? You're going to rip it."

His chuckle rose.

Joanie's smile grew larger too. "I *knew* you were watching me back then, Adam. I could see you in the dresser mirror. *I could see you pull out your cock and masturbate."*

Emily flinched with sick fascination as Joanie pulled the dress over her head and dropped it on the floor, and then did the same with her slip. She mashed her hips into his and pulled her brother's face back into hers. "I stripped so slowly for *you*. I wanted you, *too*, Adam."

Emily felt weak, forgetting the stake that was slick in her fingers.

Joanie's braless breasts quivered with excitement, and when she tugged her panties at last down her toned legs, Dad clamped his fingers around her arms and lifted her up, bringing her to the mirror on the wall. "Sister," he whispered, "watch me in the mirror *now*."

Joanie's eyes grew large, and Emily thought she saw a spark of shock and sanity as she dropped her jaw.

Dad had no reflection.

"I have come back for *you*, little sister; would you believe that my lust for you surpasses even *death*?"

Joanie finally gasped. *"Adam?"*

With his bulging arms he raised her sleek, naked body off the floor and thrust himself forward to part her legs, then lowered her onto the huge, stiff pole that poked up between his thighs. *"I will fuck you until you scream!"*

His back was to Emily, but she cowered anyway, hardly comprehending the spectacle of the incredible, shared lust. It turned her stomach inside out . . . and as he pushed into Joanie, the molasses coating her limbs slipped away.

Vomit surged up into Emily's mouth, but she staggered to her feet, holding the wall with one shaking hand and the pointed wood tight in her other.

It was worse than anything she had ever imagined—worse even than when Mother had come after her last night. Trembling, Emily tried to gather her strength and remaining will together, struggling against the wrenching gasps that tried to warp her brain into hysterical insanity.

The thing that had been Dad bobbed Joanie up and down as he impaled her, making her grip his lanky hair tighter with each moan. She blinked eyes that were crazed with excited lust—but tried to push him away when he pumped so hard that blood began to run down her thighs. Then her mouth opened, but no sounds came out, and she shuddered.

Dad braced Aunt Joanie against the wall and continued to

thrust into her silently, his motion jerky and unnatural. He cupped her firm buttocks with his pasty hands. *"Now you are mine, sister!"*

He pounded her forcefully, dashing her head into the mirror that jiggled and then crashed onto the floor . . . again and again, pummeling her skull repeatedly with the violence of his strokes. Loud cracks splintered the air and the wall ran with the dark gooey redness splattering up from Joanie's sweat-drenched hair. She was struggling at last, forcing a sudden, whining pitch from her throat.

Emily ran her thumb across the splintery wood. Inching forward, she smelled the essence of death spilling through the air. Something solid clamped over her shoulder and she jumped and screamed.

"No!"

Ben released Emily and dashed past her, grabbing his coat from the divan. His hands thrust into the pockets and pulled out the small bottle from the graveyard. Overcoming a shudder, he forced his shaking knees until he was within two feet of the ghastly, frantic rape.

The vampire tossed his head back with a gloating smile, then bared his deadly teeth and bent to one of Joanie's breasts. His tongue flicked the nipple as she finally began to scream, and he shoved her viciously again, driving his mouth around her soft, untouched motherhood.

Emily flinched at the grisly liquid rip and gasped at the blood suddenly spilling down her aunt's stomach.

"You . . . *cannot!*" Ben screamed with panic, reaching out with halting intensity. "In Christ's h-holy name, I—I *forbid* you!" He raised the tiny bottle, looking like a depraved David against Goliath, and shook it wildly.

The tiny container sprayed its mist onto the stinking thing that had been her father. The droplets streamed down its hate-filled face as it slurped thirstily at Aunt Joanie's nipple, spilling what it couldn't catch in its mouth all over the brick-tiled floor.

Ben shrank back when the sinister thing only cackled, and dropped the useless vial from trembling fingers.

The fiend laughed louder, swinging around with his feast to

glare at Emily. His eyes shone, and he smiled with his drooling promise. . . .

Dad wanted her too . . . to possess and own her again.

Screaming at the onslaught of horrible uselessness that those eyes injected into her, Emily charged at the monster with the stake, enduring the thick waves of lust it emanated, and stared again into the fiery deep eyes, sank into them unwillingly, and saw her father as he'd been before—taunting her, laughing at her punishments—making her a prisoner. *Emily, you cunning little bitch,* snapped his eyes, *you thought you could put it over on us again, didn't you? You thought you could live without us? You thought we would let you?*

Her hated father.

"Damn you!" she screamed, lunging, and shoved the sharp stick into his chest with all her might, knocking Joanie out of his grasping arms. Her torn breast spurted blood that drenched the air and dripped from his chiseled pale skin.

Emily cried out as its sticky warmth spilled onto *her.*

The vampire gasped, the stake protruding from his chest, but didn't fall. His bony hands groped for Emily and the sharp nails bit into her elbow, pulling her nearer. His frozen breath, reeking in foulness, moved to her throat.

"I want to fuck and lick you, too, my darling daughter!"

"No!"

Strong arms dragged her back, and Ben pushed ahead of her. She heard the vampire snarl and felt the swipe of his nails graze her cheek as her legs gave out.

"Damn you, you sucking shit of hell!" Ben screamed, and his vicious hatred and violence made her gasp as he grappled with her resurrected father, sweating his hostile fear and at last throwing the flailing creature onto the coffee table. But it merely dripped its smile and snarled vile chuckles.

"Preacher man. *Preacher-dick.* I know your lusts. We *all* know it. You stare at my prick and want to eat me up—*but I must eat you first."*

Ben sucked in a breath as if he'd been slapped, but dropped to his knees beside Dad and began to pound the stake Emily had fixed in his chest with his bare hands—hitting, bellowing, and snarling himself. The vampire choked against the horrible, unexpected fury, trying to grab Ben's face with its groping, powerful hands. Then Dad whined as Ben slammed his meaty fists harder and harder, until Dad's arms dropped and blood bubbled from his mouth. Ben glared insanely and pounded the stake again and again with bleeding hands, plowing the stained plywood completely through the body.

Until Dad's incredible grimace grew slack.

Free. Emily saw the horrid scene and felt the ballooning relief of her escape in the steaming gaunt shape—and then anger. *She had only watched!* She hadn't gotten to destroy her father and tear his hold from her at long last! *Ben had done it.*

He dropped his arms and stared at her vacantly. "We're even now, Emily." His voice shook with receding hate. "You saved me, and I saved you from—*it.*" He scooted away, breathless in the gagging stink of the decaying body.

They were even. *Freedom.* It drove through her, but not as last night. It was quieter now, but more real—more vivid. She turned to her aunt on the floor beside her, covered in blood from a wound that no longer existed. She wasn't breathing.

"Thank you, Ben," Emily said at last. "We're even."

XII

1

Dad's body turned to dust, and after a muddled hour Emily managed to take a broom and sweep it out of the front room, over the threshold, and out of her life. It made her smile, but it was a bleak smile. The horrors were far from over. She was careful to watch the darkened street and the silent houses, wondering where the other vampires were. She trembled with exhaustion and hoped they wouldn't pick her house tonight.

"What about Aunt Joanie?" she asked Ben hoarsely. Stained gauze bound his torn hands loosely. She'd done it herself and had been glad to be doing something. Now, as last night in the cemetery, she only wanted to get away from the penetrating stench that yet lingered in tonight's motionless air.

"The marks are gone." He frowned at his hands and bent to pick up the empty bottle clumsily. "It didn't take enough blood to kill—"

"She's dead."

"I know." Ben touched the woman's shadowed face, which was gaunt and frozen. "She must have had a heart attack. She *could* become one."

"When will we know?"

He drew his lips together and moved back. "Not until it's too late. They can't come back until they're returned to the earth, or until a funeral prayer is said for them."

Setting the broom down and locking the door, Emily picked up the mallet and another stake.

"I came here to destroy my wife," Ben said, speaking more to himself than to her. "I came to consecrate all the graves in the cemetery." His gaze met hers, seeking absolution. "I was going to consecrate them so those vile bastards would be trapped and unable to get out. They'd be trapped *forever*. But dear Jesus, I don't think I can now. I've failed somewhere, and God has turned His back on me. I tried to stop that damn, sucking *shit* and I *failed*. I doubted, and only faith can bring out the holy water's power—only faith can consecrate the graves." Tears were in his eyes. "I can't. I've failed."

"You killed my father."

"I hated him—I hate them all." He shook his head. "But that's all I have left. Sweet fucking God, that's the most I have left."

Emily stared blankly. "Ben . . . it was enough."

"Like hell it was!" His eyes were violent but hollow of threat. "You don't know what I've done, even before any of this started. Sweet fucking God." He pointed at Joanie's silent sprawled body, a pornographic snuff shot on the tile. "But all I can do now is put a stake through her and go on. I must try." He touched his neck and made a face.

"Does it still hurt?" Emily asked.

"Inside." He gritted his teeth. "Goddammit, give me that stake and hammer." He took them from her, then knelt beside her aunt.

"Ben, your hands! You'll hurt them worse." She got down beside him and tried to take back the wooden picket he held over Joanie's breast.

"It doesn't matter." Ben pushed her away and lifted the hammer, bringing it down heavily as he forced the wood into her body. Thick, dark blood seeped up slowly as the stake sank deep, making the air's pungence harsher. At last he stopped, in considerable pain.

"She'll dissolve as well, I think. The infection is in her." He got to his feet. "We'll have to go to the cemetery and get MacDonald's car to drive back. Get your things together."

Emily hesitated at the idea of leaving her own car, or of even going to the graveyard after having seen the growing army last night. She no longer wanted to take them on, and never all at once. Her furious drive was spent with Dad's destruction. "Wouldn't it be better to wait until morning?"

Ben shook his head. "MacDonald may need me now. Enough time's been wasted already. The bastard who started all of this must be destroyed *first*. It—it tempted me here to get rid of me and almost succeeded." He touched her hand. "It must be destroyed first. The others will wait. Their destruction will be much easier."

Emily felt herself nod as she stared at the faintly perceptible fog enveloping Aunt Joanie's body. The sight gave her an indisputable loneliness. Her family was dead, leaving her with memories much worse than ever before. It took a great effort to hold back the forming tears. "I'm glad you're going to take me with you," she said.

Ben smiled tiredly. "I'm glad you're going to go."

Then she could no longer hold back the sobs, and they burst out of her in an unexpected torrent. Finally, Ben bent back down and pulled her into his uncertain arms, stroking her hair with his bandaged hands.

2

"How's the arm this morning?"

Warren opened his eyes and raised the ponderous cast gently. With the prescription he'd been given he could barely feel his arm inside. "Okay, I guess."

The doctor put down his chart and smiled cheerfully. "I think you'll live, Reverend. You've got what we call a green-stick fracture, all right. The break the X rays showed is nasty, but no major vessels or tendons were torn when that bone went through your skin. We should be able to let you out of here by noon."

Warren nodded. "How's Carmen Richison today?"

The young intern didn't answer for a moment, then shrugged. "You'll have to call intensive care, Rev. At least nothing happened here last night, right? Especially since the newspaper this morning said there weren't even any leads on whoever creamed this place. Still, I bet they'll find them before long—not even an honest man can hide in a world of credit cards and news-center-watch cameras." He picked a nail absently. "Want me to get you a copy of that paper? They mentioned you on page one. You're a celebrity now."

"Just what I've always wanted."

"At least it wasn't the obituary," he cracked, then reddened. "Sorry. I—"

Warren shook his head.

"Well, I'll try to bring one in before you leave. Go ahead and have breakfast here first, okay? Then you can call anyone you want to come get you." He touched his good arm. "And take it easy. That prescription should prevent an infection, but I want you to call me immediately if you have any problems, okay?"

"I will." Warren smiled as best he could, anxious to find out about Carmen. And Ben. "Thanks for everything."

"That's what we're here for. Just remember you were appreciative when you get the bill."

He managed a grim laugh. "I'll try."

The young medic grinned smoothly and glanced at his clipboard again. "I think you'll do just fine, Rev."

Warren watched him to the door, then rubbed his heavy eyes and returned to the memory he'd replayed a dozen times already. The drab whitewashed room reflected his fatigue, lowering his spirits even more. Despite having saved himself and finally driven away the vampire, he'd been too late to help Chuck or the three hospital employees. Too late to help Carmen. She was breathing only because of the fiend's demonic, unknown plan. It could have killed her.

It *should* have killed her. He remembered with wonder all the prayers he'd said on her behalf. Had they made a difference? Considering everything else, it didn't seem impossible.

But it made him all the more anxious for Ben Dixon to get

back. When Ben had called yesterday, his voice had been strained and halting, proving something had happened.

Something *bad*.

As gently as he was able, Warren rolled back the sheets and got out of the bed, working against the heavy immobility of his arm. His bare feet touched the cool tile and he waited there to find his balance, then shuffled awkwardly to the small closet and slid open the door. His shirt was missing and he knew it had been disposed of. He'd have to make do with his coat.

"Good morning, Mr. MacDonald."

The woman's high voice colored his face hotly. He knew the open hospital gown didn't even try to cover his naked backside. Quickly grabbing his pants off their hanger, he turned.

The nurse met his eyes and turned away politely, then pushed the breakfast cart to the adjustable table. She slid his tray onto it without comment.

"Thank you," he said.

"You're very welcome," she replied, and squeaked her cart back out the door.

Warren sighed at the stupidity of his embarrassment, swaying dangerously to the nightstand. He pulled out his cotton briefs, glad he never wore those bikinis Susan had bought him, then bent over and managed to get each foot through the leg holes. He tried clumsily to pull them up with his left hand, losing his balance and only just catching himself by falling against the bed. "Darn it."

"MacDonald?" There was a tap from the partially open door.

"Ben?" He looked up. "Come in, Ben." He smiled as the worn man shuffled inside, then quickly averted his eyes. Warren felt a sorrow for him, and it increased when he noticed Ben's bandaged hands. "Are you—"

Another movement from the door made him look back, and he choked when he saw the young woman.

Dixon glanced up unwillingly, then managed to smirk, muffling a laugh. "What are you doing?" He hurried to Warren, holding him steady. "You didn't tell me your arm was broken."

The young woman stared in curiously as Warren tried to get himself into a less revealing position. "Who—who's *she*?"

Ben seemed to remember Emily and nodded her back. "Could you wait outside for a minute?"

She turned away and took a step back through the doorway as Ben bit his lip. Then he bent down to pull Warren's undershorts up his legs for him and helped him get on his pants. "Are you okay?"

"I was. I just—I just didn't expect you to bring a girl."

"Yeah. Sorry." Ben snapped the pants for him and zipped them up. "That's Emily. She's going to help us." He stood back with twitching lips.

Warren raised his eyebrows.

"Sorry," he said again, following Warren's gaze to the door. "It's a long story." He helped Warren to a chair and pushed the table and food in front of him. "They said you could go when you finished your chow."

"I can get something later."

"Go ahead and eat. Emily and I had breakfast in the cafeteria —we've been waiting down there forever. They wouldn't let us up before visiting hours."

Warren took the lid off the plate of eggs and bacon. "I am kind of hungry." He took a fork in his left hand and began to cut the egg clumsily. "Have you seen Carmen?"

"She's doing as well as can be expected. I didn't see her but I talked to a doctor there." He paused. "I'm sorry about your friend."

Warren didn't let his thoughts stray to Chuck. He tried to get the piece of mushy egg to his mouth. It proved more difficult and less tasty than he had imagined and he wished uselessly that he were ambidextrous. "Why don't you call your friend back in and let me meet her?"

Ben turned. "Emily?" he called.

She peeked into the room, then entered.

"Emily, this is Warren MacDonald. Warren . . ." He raised a hand and dropped it again.

Emily pointed to his cast. "Ouch—that must *hurt.*"

"Yeah. Whatever happened to 'pleased to meet you'?"

Her face tightened. "Sorry. Pleased to meet you, Warren." She exchanged looks with Ben, seemed to make an effort to continue. "Does it hurt much?"

He cracked a smile. "Only when I eat." He attempted to cut a slice of bacon. It was harder than the egg.

Emily walked to his side and their eyes met uncomfortably. She finally put her warm hand on his, observing his struggle with a tight smile. "I—I think you need some help with that."

Warren fidgeted at her soft touch. "Do you propose to feed me?"

She blushed, but without feeling. "You need help," she said softly. "I'd like . . . to help you."

"Thank you," he said. "I think you'll be the first person to feed me since my mother."

She smiled apprehensively as Ben Dixon pushed up a chair for her, then sat on the bed to watch the progress. Warren leaned back lazily with his mouth open but kept his gaze on Dixon. The man was strained and his voice unsteady—his face pale. It made Warren chew each bite slowly. "So what's wrong, Ben?"

Dixon glanced at him from the corner of his eyes but kept his jaw clamped shut. He shook his head. "If you don't mind, I'd like a drink before we get into it." Dixon sighed.

Warren swallowed. He felt a depth in the man's words he didn't like.

XIII

1

Not wearing a shirt under his coat made Warren shiver, but he was glad to be out of the hospital, and sighed in the sunshine streaking into Susan's car. They'd left his Mercedes at the hospital. Ben managed the wheel with his bandaged hands.

Disturbed by his continued silence, Warren eyed Emily in the rear seat. She returned his stare steadily.

Long minutes passed before the older man finally pulled Susan's car jerkily into Warren's drive.

Emily got out quickly and set her bags on the concrete, then opened Warren's door.

"Thanks," he said, but she was staring at Ben.

Ben was preoccupied. "Help Warren to the door, okay?"

Emily obeyed, careful of his arm. Warren heard Ben close up the car, then saw him carrying Emily's things in his arms, keeping his hurt hands free, his face wrinkled in concentration over something far away. Heightened curiosity beat Warren endlessly and he was barely able to fight back the questions on his tongue.

"It's locked," said Emily, trying the door.

Warren nodded, and tried to put his left hand into his right pocket to get the keys.

"I'll do it," she offered.

Trying to relax, he blushed as she slipped her hand in to take them. She spread them out in her palm.

"This one." He pointed.

She fitted it in the lock, turned it, and pushed the door open, then stepped back so he could enter first.

He nodded at her, not daring to speak, and walked into the unlit hall, groaning at his heavy arm as he tried to lift it high enough to turn on the lights. Giving up, he flipped the switch with his left hand. "I'm afraid I'm not much of a host," he breathed.

Dixon came in next with the luggage and set it down on the carpet. Emily shut the door behind them. Warren felt their dark secrets.

"If you don't mind, I'll help myself to that drink," Dixon said, taking his coat off moodily. "I want you to tell me what happened to you, Warren."

"I want you to tell me what happened to *you*." Warren looked into his ungiving, deep-set eyes, then at Emily. Dixon disappeared down the hall.

"If you'll tell me where to find a shirt, I'll get you one," she offered, helping him remove the coat.

"I . . ." He shook his head. "Wait. Is he okay? What happened? Why the hell won't you talk to me?"

"He wants to tell you himself." She hung the coat in the closet. "Where are your shirts?" she asked again.

He told her, then balanced himself and hobbled into the living room to sit down, very confused.

2

Warren's throat seemed to shrink as he looked at Emily, and then at Ben. Ben Dixon did tell him everything. He told him his weaknesses, affirming Warren's suspicions as to his bisexual tendencies. It was something Ben held tremendous guilt for in the faith he'd grown up and ministered in, and he told of how the vampires used the very desires he'd made himself deny. They seized on the memories of those occasions when he'd given in, as Susan had seized on Warren's own guilts and memories. Instead of the disdain Ben feared, though, Warren sympathized and inwardly pardoned him for all the miscalculations he had made. It made Ben more human.

What really frightened Warren was that they were talking so matter-of-factly about the things that had happened. But at least Ben spoke more readily now, reassured by Warren's understanding. His hands were wrapped in clean bandages and he slouched tiredly in the chair beside the unlit fireplace, swirling his half glass of brandy. His eyes were far away, and Warren understood at last. He had been through an experience that had shaken his faith—not only in himself, but in the God he trusted and in his own purpose.

Contemplating the horrible stories they both had told, Warren calculated the implications of the circles under Emily's eyes and the dark maturity that was rooted in her. She was still hiding something. He could feel it in her reluctant words.

"Is that all?" he asked her.

"I . . ." Her eyes were wary. "What do you mean?"

"You're a very strong young lady to have handled yourself so well in such a situation, Emily."

"She's got guts," Ben said flatly.

"Yes, she does," he agreed, wondering how she'd been able to do it. Even after he'd known Susan's true nature, her promises had still nearly paralyzed him. Ben had buckled during an even more ghastly experience. But Emily . . .

"What are we going to do now?" she asked, ignoring his stare.

Ben sipped his drink and yawned. "We've talked the whole afternoon. I need to rest. I—I don't want to face that thing . . . *tired.*"

Looking back at Ben's wretched face, Warren nodded quickly. "Go ahead. You can sleep in the master bedroom. It's the door at the end of the hall."

Ben put the glass down gently with wrapped hands and stood. "Thanks. Sorry. I'm all in." He turned to the cardboard still covering the broken window. "Make sure the doors and windows are locked, okay?"

"Yes."

The ashen-faced man walked by him to the hall. A moment later the bedroom door closed, leaving the house in the silence of the past echoes that only spoke in Warren's thoughts.

"Strange bedfellows." Emily smiled, but like everything else she'd said, her words were ambiguous.

He felt the awkwardness of their proximity. "Worse than politics," he returned.

"Are you sure?"

"I . . ." He trailed off in discomfort. "Uh, are you ready to sleep, too, or . . ."

Her eyes relaxed a bit. "I'm still to keyed up—I wouldn't be able to shut my eyes." She paused and brushed the black hair from her forehead. "Talking to Ben hasn't helped much. He just kept saying things over and over. He told me about the vampire. He told me . . . about his past. He told me about you." She stopped again and looked at the dark hall, frowning.

"About me?"

She picked at her jeans. "I don't think you've been fair to Ben."

Warren crossed his arms. "What does that mean?"

Emily glanced up. "He told me everything, Warren, and he told me what you said to him about some of the things he's done."

Warren pressed his lips together.

"You just don't understand that he's suffering. I *can* understand. I understand that at least he's trying, even after he's been kicked so many times that it would be easier to just *give up.*" A potent fire flickered behind her calm features, then ebbed. "But he needs you to try to understand him—that he's doing the best he can." She scowled, moving her head up and down. "At least he's doing *something.*"

The cardboard behind them flapped in a rising wind.

"He's afraid to tell *you* everything."

"How's that?"

"He doesn't want you to know how badly he's been beaten. He told you everything that happened, Warren, but he didn't tell you what he felt when his wife—*that thing*—bit him."

Warren leaned back into the divan and grimaced as the shift caused a sharp stab. He moved again and relaxed his arm in a better position, then laid his other hand on the rough cast. "And he told you?"

"He knew I understood." She made a strange sound in her throat. "It paralyzed him. Part of him tried to fight it, but he wanted her . . . just like 'Aunt Joanie'"—she shivered—*"wanted Dad.* I saw Ben get bitten, but I didn't know what he was feeling. I didn't *know.* I only saw it suck his blood." She shuddered, tightening her fists. "He said it was as though she was sucking out his soul. But he didn't even try to stop it!" Long moments passed, and Warren held the silence, thinking of the vampire's offer of the power of understanding, of the power to help.

"I think," Emily finally continued, "that the only reason he came back is because he feels like he owes it to you. He's been trying to prove himself to God and feels like he's failed at it, so he at least wants to prove himself to *you.* You don't appreciate him enough. Your opinion means a lot to him." She sat very still, then inhaled deeply.

The defensive words forming in Warren's head tasted bitter as he let them rest on his tongue, so he held them back. "That's . . . some pretty good surmising on your part, Emily," Warren said. "You'd make a darned good psychiatrist."

She smiled reluctantly. "Oh, yeah? I was going to major in psychology back at school."

"Was?"

"Yeah. Before all this happened."

"Aren't you going to go back?" he asked, less from curiosity than just to be saying the words. To be thinking of something other than her unexpected accusations and the other terrors looming so near.

"I might." She looked at her nails. "I don't know. Everything's changed now." She closed her eyes, softening to him. "I . . . everything's changed."

Feeling her mystery increase, he faced Emily cautiously. Though she was hardly beautiful, the soft feminine lines of her face were warm and she seemed to welcome his being with her. He tried to return the feeling with a grin. "Why did you come back with Ben?" he asked softly.

"Because he needed me. Because I didn't want to be alone

after last night." The glow of sunlight behind the cardboard window was fading. "I don't know anymore. I don't know what I want to do."

"I know what you mean," he agreed.

"No, you don't."

Warren got up to check the door, swinging the bulky cast slightly to keep steady. He was getting better at moving around now. The dead bolt was unturned and he fixed that, switched out the lights, and came back. He passed her to go to the windows and adjust the slipping cardboard. "Why?" he asked.

"How do you mean that?"

"Why don't I know?"

"You wouldn't understand. You didn't even try to understand Ben."

"I try," he said. "I am a minister, you know." He recalled her broken sentences earlier. "This has affected us all, Emily, not just Ben—we're all hurt by it in some way."

"No," she whispered bitterly, "I don't think *hurt* is the right word."

"What would you call it?"

"My parents. I killed my parents."

The pent-up pain of her voice jarred him. "They were vampires. You had to kill them." He sat back down beside her, his leg touching hers.

Solemn features appraised him. "They *always* were vampires. But Ben helped me, Warren. He helped free me from them. No matter what else he's done, he did that for *me.* I watched my mother die . . . and I was happy. I *thought* I was free. But Dad . . ." Emily rubbed her small nose frantically. "I just froze, and then Ben came in . . . and I saw him kill *Dad.*"

Leaning closer, Warren reached to her, wanting to comfort her.

Emily's eyes shrank into tiny embers as she pushed his hand away. "No—I wanted to do it. *I wanted him and Mom to suffer and to die before it ever happened!*" She sucked in a harsh breath. "Ben saved me from that hatred, Warren—I owe him for *that."* Tears bubbled in her eyes but she didn't let them fall. "I *hated* them. I killed Mom, and I wanted to kill Dad so bad—but after

Ben killed him and tore up his hands, I don't know, I just felt the hate, and I didn't want it. God, I didn't want to be *like* them!"

"It's okay," he soothed quietly.

"He tore up his hands for me." Emily turned her dark eyes to his with open wonder. "He put that stake through Aunt Joanie for *me*. I was afraid, and he helped me, Warren. I was *afraid*. I've already killed two of them and seen two others killed, *but I'm afraid.*"

Warren let her lay her head on his shoulder; squeezed her hand tighter. "So am I, but you can't blame yourself for fear."

"But that's what I don't understand!" Emily cried suddenly. "I wasn't afraid to kill Mom or Dad because it was *them—I hated them!*"

This new burden was heavy and he let it sink in silently, feeling the responsibility for her and Ben Dixon weigh against the threats to humanity itself. As a minister he had preached that one soul was as important as a thousand, and that thousand as important as the one. But his enthusiasm to help as many as he could had driven him to ignore the problems of individuals.

"I thought they hated me, and I hated them back, Warren. But . . . I might have been *wrong*. I don't know. I came with Ben because I don't know. I don't even know where to go now—I'm alone." She watched him steadily for a few seconds, finally shut her eyes. "I'm tired of it all. I don't want to be alone anymore."

A tight sting bit him as Warren put his left arm around her. "You're not alone," he said.

"I can't even find myself, Warren. How can you?" Her face was flushed. "They may have even loved me . . . but I didn't see. I didn't understand—*I don't understand.*" A tear slid down her cheek, and she quickly brushed it away. "Ben said we should destroy them because of what they are. I did it because of what they *were!*"

There was nothing he could think of to say—nothing that didn't sound condescending or false. Words weren't strong enough, anyway. He could only try to guide her, and be there if she needed him.

As he had with Susan? And now she was dead.

No. He would have to *be* there, ready to *help*.

"I'm exhausted," Emily whispered, wiping her eyes. "God,

I'm tired." She managed a hollow smile. "Thanks for listening, Warren. I needed to talk."

Her eyes became Susan's, full of need. But what if *he* needed help? He agreed with Emily's diagnosis that Ben couldn't rise to that occasion, and wondered if she was as strong as she seemed, or if the dark guilts in her soul would distort her as Ben's had ruined him.

She giggled unexpectedly. "God, I've been calling you 'Warren'—is that okay? Do you mind?"

"Not at all."

"I hadn't thought about it. It's just so strange that I'm talking to two ministers and using their first names." But she smiled as though it pleased her, breaking through their dark mood of gloom.

"You don't mind us calling *you* by your first name, do you?" he asked, trying to figure out her emotions.

She giggled again, her face turning pink.

"I guess we're all equals here. We all need each other," Warren said carefully.

She yawned, but turned up her lips to finish it as a smile. "Do you mean that?"

"I mean it."

Their eyes held each other's and she relaxed. "Thanks, Warren," she said softly, and yawned again. "I'm *really* sleepy now."

The trust her statement offered him encouraged his smile, and he took her warm hand. "Me too. Go on to bed if you want to. Last door on the right. I've just got to call my associate pastor before it gets too late."

She got up and looked at him for a few moments, then touched his shoulder gently. "Is your arm okay?"

"Hurts like the dickens, but I'm getting used to it."

"I'm sorry," she told him. "Can I do anything?"

He shook his head and picked the telephone up from the coffee table, setting it on the divan. "I'm fine, Emily. Thanks, though."

"Good night, Warren," She picked up her bags and went down the hall. Warren waited until the door closed to dial. As the line rang, her door opened again, then the nearer bathroom door opened and closed. He sighed and moved into a more comfortable pose for his arm.

3

They were all up and sipping from a fresh pot of coffee at three A.M. Warren served himself another cup with his left hand, hoping it wouldn't be long before he became more accustomed to using it.

Emily put down her cup. "Are we going to drink coffee all night, or what?" she blurted.

Warren looked out the window into the dark. "I talked to Bill Findley, my associate, and I think I know the area we ought to keep our eyes on. He told me who in the congregation had been taken sick. Some of them sound like they're having the same problems as the other victims." He saw Emily's expression. "Their families called to ask for guidance," he explained.

"Did he give them any?" Dixon asked, but his sarcasm proved it wasn't a question.

Warren frowned seriously: "I looked up the names he gave me in the church directory. All of them live in this area within two to three miles." He turned to Dixon. "He—*it*—could still be in the warehouse."

"A warehouse?" Emily asked. "Where is that?"

"A few blocks from here," Warren said.

Dixon crossed his arms, his attention on Warren. "Have there been any deaths?"

"Not that he knew of. Except for Chuck."

The older man rubbed his face and looked relieved. "You know we'll have to do something about *him,* MacDonald. When will he be buried?"

Warren took a deep breath. "Tomorrow."

"Thank God. It gives us tonight, at least. It's still contained *here.*"

Ben's emphasis bore on Warren, and it grew more forceful as the older man grimaced and choked, looking away from him and Emily. Ben turned pale and stood up. "Excuse me." He stumbled from the room, one hand on the wall.

Emily shook her head. "I don't think he'll be able to help us at all."

"I won't make him." Warren drained his mug and set it down, then pushed back his chair with a squeak. "But *I* still have to do it. That thing's infected at least twenty people in my church already. If any of them die before it's destroyed, they'll become vampires." He wondered at the ease with which the word rolled off his tongue. "He's right about taking care of Chuck. We've been lucky. God know how many others here are under the curse, and as they die . . ."

Warren felt faint. *The sick members of his congregation.* What did that mean or prove? How could he be sure their nemesis wasn't finding victims elsewhere? St. Louis was a large city, and people died here every day.

Emily shivered. "It's like a bunch of time bombs . . . and we don't know where they all are. It's too scary to imagine. And there's still Freeport."

"Yeah." Warren heard the toilet flush. Ben Dixon had said the plague was still contained here, but how did he know? He frowned as the older man walked back into the kitchen morosely.

"Are you all right?"

Dixon shook his head. "I—I'm afraid, Warren. I—" He shook with a spasm—"I didn't tell you, I—" He stood blankly, then finally shook his head. "God. Maybe we should just leave it be for now and protect *ourselves.* We should regain our strength." He lowered his eyes heavily. "Maybe . . . we *should* protect your friend, Carmen."

Refusing to give in to the sick drop in his stomach, Warren faced him. "You were the one who told me we had to go after—"

"And you told me we had to *protect* her," Ben shot back bitterly. "You said her soul was upon my head!"

"Ben—you said it's still contained here, but how do you know?" Warren asked. A soft warmth covered his hand—Emily's warning fingers. But he felt as well the urgency Ben had tried so hard to force into him before. "We *have* to find it! You told me yourself that the only way to save Carmen—that the only way to save anyone—was by doing *that*!"

"Warren," Emily said, "he's been through enough."

Enough. Warren remembered having said that word to Ben as he was questioning Carmen. He sighed, almost wishing for the berserk resolve Ben seemed to have lost. "Okay. If you want to take Emily and watch over Carmen, I can go to the warehouse."

Ben clenched his fists at his sides. "Alone?" His voice rose with the ragged remnant of his strength. "You'll need *me.*"

"I turned it back before," Warren said, shoring up a courage that grew increasingly more reluctant.

"You'll need me," Ben insisted, then lowered his voice and turned to Emily. "Will—will you come with us?"

She chewed a nail as she turned from him to Warren, then back. "Why can't we just look for it in the daylight? Couldn't we find it then?"

"If we knew where it might be," Ben said. "But we don't. This city is just too big. And it will be very cautious where it goes in daylight, when its powers are reduced."

Warren nodded. "That's what I'm saying, Ben. We've got to find out if it's still in this area tonight. And if it is, we've got to stop it before it moves on, or else we'll waste a lot more time looking for it."

Emily glared at him. "We're wasting time *now.*"

Warren nodded and felt the undertone of heat erupting. "She's right, Ben. You said that yourself—that time is this vampire's greatest ally." But as he looked at Emily, he thought of Carmen. Ben had reawakened his fear for her defenselessness.

But when the vampire had divided them before . . . "We'll go after it . . . and offer a prayer for Carmen's protection," he whispered.

"You think *that* will be enough?" Emily said.

"It will have to be." Warren touched Ben's arm. "What do we need to do?"

The man stood without moving for a long moment, then led

Warren to the sink. "I can't do more than tell you . . . you need to consecrate some water first. Just fill a container with tap water and bless it like communion wine. I . . . can't—" But the apology in his face held a remnant of the spirit Warren had first seen in it. "Bless the water and the stakes Emily brought, and we'll go."

Warren stared at the man wordlessly, then reached out and hugged him close. Ben stood impassively, then bent down to pull an empty brandy bottle from the trash.

"I am too far from God for Him to listen to me," Dixon said. The strange gleam suddenly flashed more violently in his eyes: "This undead tool of damnation has confused us and tricked us from its track before and almost destroyed us. Warren, you must pray and see to it it does not do so again."

Once more, Warren felt an incredible burden, but he took the man's hand as strongly as he could, then reached for Emily's. "God be with us," he murmured.

They bowed in prayer.

XIV

1

It was the darkest night Warren could remember, and the coldest. Fighting apprehension at their frailties, he led his companions to the ominous warehouse where he and Dixon had met the vampire before. The streets were unnervingly silent, and the lights at the corners threw eerie shadows over the area. A chilling breeze sent litter flying through the street.

He touched the container of blessed water in his coat, the metal cross beside it.

Ben and Emily walked together, and her arm held him in a way that seemed as much to support him as to support her. "Not much of a place to live," Warren heard her quip nervously.

That black humor that had seemed so antagonizing when Ben first entered Warren's life suddenly flickered in his voice: "But not a bad place to be undead." Then, even as Warren felt a faint grin tug at his lips, Ben's tone dropped into futility. "We'll be lucky if we don't die here."

They hesitated at the front of the building and Emily stepped closer to Warren. "Couldn't we just burn this place down? Won't that destroy it?"

Ben Dixon shook his head. "The body would be destroyed as your parents were, Emily, when we used the unblessed stakes." He shuddered and his mouth trembled silently. "Destruction of the body without a blessing would only leave the demon within free to seek another body."

The words rang true in the night, and she reluctantly followed them into the abandoned warehouse. Ben lit their way with a flashlight and they began their search of the damp structure warily, staying close together.

"It stinks in here," complained Emily.

Ben ran the flashlight's beam around the big enclosure, from rusting pipes to ruined, discarded vacuum cleaners, to crates stacked high.

"Let's check those boxes," Dixon suggested hoarsely, leading the way toward the back of the building. They followed and began to pry open the rotted crates, one at a time.

"Oh, my God!" Emily cried.

Ben jerked the light toward her, exposing several huge rats darting back and forth in the nearest corner. They scattered quickly among glass bottles of green cleanser. "Are you okay?" Warren whispered shakily.

She nodded. "Yeah—just five years older. When I saw all those eyes, I thought . . ."

The lurking fright that there might be any number of vampires hiding in the darkness tugged at Warren too. Despite Ben Dixon's apparent certainty, there was no way of knowing how many outside of his church congregation the vampire had attacked.

"Rats," Ben Dixon said. "Creatures of the night."

"What?"

Dixon's words broke out of the darkness: "The vampire is Lord over the night creatures: the bat, the lizard and snake, the rat, spiders . . . If the vampire is here, it can make them attack an intruder."

Warren's blood tingled at the words. "Let's hurry up and finish," he muttered, trying to keep the tremor out of his voice.

"I hope it's *not* here," Emily whispered behind him.

He glanced back but didn't answer her. He didn't want the vampire to be here, either, but knew at the same time that they must find it. They *had* to find it. Only the vampire's dissolution would mean an end to the nightmare. He stepped to the next box, Ben following with the light. A board was missing and he peered into the opening. He jerked back, his heart pounding.

The blood drained out of his face and he wanted badly to run from this building . . . and just keep running.

"What is it?"

"Spiders," he said, shivering as a hairy black one crawled toward him. Clenching a fist, he smashed it.

"They should be hibernating," Emily said.

Dixon glanced at the spider and moved to the next box without a word.

Half an hour later they opened the last crate big enough to hide anything the size of their opponent and gave up. When they stepped back into the cold but fresh-smelling air, Warren breathed in deeply. His disappointment at not finding their quarry was almost dissolved by his relief at being out of there.

Emily smiled weakly.

"Do you think it's even in this area, now?" Warren asked.

"I think it has a definite purpose." Ben paused, standing tall in the lonely breeze. "I know it has a definite purpose. It is a minister of damnation. It steals our thoughts, our spirits, and then our souls. It is a missionary of hell, come to bring us the evil we try to escape each day."

"But where can we find it?"

Dixon brought his hand to his mouth. "I think," he said, his voice barely a whisper, "that it will come for *us.*"

"Ben . . ." Emily walked ahead toward the streetlight, her shadow shrinking up against her. "Before we went in you said—" She looked back at the deserted building uneasily— "what did you mean about using the unblessed stakes on Mom and Dad? Will they come back," she breathed, *"again?"*

The wind pushed at them, creaking through the ancient warehouse. "The demons that possessed them may," he told her. "They aren't imprisoned by this physical plane and can enter other diseased bodies unless they are stopped by opposite supernatural means." He frowned. "Faith is the only protection against them."

She pulled her coat close. "But—will they *remember*? Will they come after *me*?"

"I . . . don't know," he said slowly. "If the memory is retained, they may." He shook his head. "But that traveling salesman from hell will come after us *all*. Its plan is secrecy, and we know that secret. It knows we know."

"Then the others will come too," Emily said. "They'll know, too!"

"But they can't enter a body unless it dies from a vampire's bite," Warren said, "Correct?"

Dixon nodded. "The infection invigorates the acceptance of evil in the human soul. It makes evil openly desirable." He coughed bitterly. "It's why I'm so afraid now and why I *know* these things! It's why I couldn't consecrate the graves," whined Dixon. "My wife was killed without sacrament and faith. Her taint remains in me." Tears glistened in his eyes at the admission. "It is still in me!"

"Then we *have* to stop this," Emily said in a stronger tone. "I can't go through all that again."

Warren felt his jaw grow slack and put his arm around her. "Come on," he said to Dixon, walking them back to Susan's Chevrolet across the street. "We've got to find a way to disinfect you before we go on."

Dixon chuckled dismally. "Do you have that strength, MacDonald? And if you do, how do you know there'll be anything left?"

Warren stopped in the middle of the shadowed street, clutching the young woman, and stared at the complete listlessness of Ben's walk. "You . . ." The weight of solitude stabbed into him as sharply as his arm's steady throb and he bit his lip. "I can *try*," he managed at last.

A hollow gratitude showed in Ben Dixon's face. "I think we should go check on Carmen first," he said, his voice shallow. "There is nothing else we can do until our enemy reveals itself."

"All right," Warren agreed.

They all got into the car, Dixon in the driver's seat. Warren positioned his arm carefully, now realizing how valuable an opportunity an encounter with the vampire was. Unless the vampire *wanted* to meet them, the chances were small that they would ever find it.

2

Sirens filled the air as they got close to the hospital, cutting deep into the edge of Warren's nerves. He and Emily struggled to hold the city map still.

"I don't know what I'm looking for," she breathed. "There's too much."

"It's a needle in a haystack," agreed Warren. It was, and he believed Ben that finding their nemesis would be impossible unless they could catch sight of it.

"You don't know what this mission involves," muttered Dixon. He squinted through the windshield as the sirens became louder. Revolving red lights flashed into the car. Three police cars were stopped in front of the hospital. Dixon pulled up behind the last one, opening his door even as the engine died and getting out with a mechanical speed. It was almost as though he gained strength from the confusion of a new crisis. Warren hurried after him, praying silently for Carmen and for *him.*

Pushing past others huddling in the frigid night, they trailed Dixon to the front doors and the policeman who was standing there.

"Excuse me," said Dixon gruffly, stepping through to the officer.

The big policeman was uninterested. "The hospital's closed right now," he grunted.

"He . . . we're ministers. We're supposed to see one of the patients."

"The hospital's closed off right now," the cop said again. "You can't go in."

Warren looked through the closed glass doors and into the lobby. Patients, doctors, nurses, and orderlies filled that room, and two other uniformed men stood between them and the first visible hallway.

A hand touched Warren's arm. "Some maniac was loose in there," explained a high whine beside him. "I didn't see it, but they said he was awful—that he was like a crazy man! I—I heard him screaming."

Warren glanced at the bleary-eyed woman, his heart pounding unevenly at her stressed voice. "We're concerned about a patient." He moved closer to the policeman. "We're concerned about a patient inside," he repeated.

"Step back, please. I'm sorry. I can't let anyone through." The cop stiffened as another police car pulled up at the curb and two men got out.

"What happened? Has anyone been hurt?" Dixon asked.

"I can't let anyone inside."

There were murmurs from the others as a man in an overcoat pushed through them with another young uniformed officer at his heels. "Who're these people?"

The cop at the door saluted. "They're recovery-room visitors, sir. The staff and the patients are still inside."

"Carmen," Ben Dixon whispered, his voice mixing hate and strong depression.

"They won't let us in, Ben."

"It's here! We've got to get in there."

"They won't let us *in,"* Warren hissed, taking his arm and pulling him away. "Let's wait out here and be sure!"

Emily tried to take Ben's hand, but he refused it and stood wheezing—staring at Warren through eyes that were empty and dead.

Emily pushed against Warren, making him look at her. "Warren, Ben's right. Shouldn't we help them? They don't know . . ."

The overcoated man huffed and turned away from the guarding policeman. Warren recognized him as the plainclothes detective he'd talked to the night Susan and Carmen were attacked, and again after Chuck was killed. Warren tried to remember his name.

"Detective Mishkin!" He touched the man's arm.

"Yes?" he asked briskly, not even turning.

"I met you the—"

The jowly man pushed a finger into his nose and his eyes narrowed with a slow reciprocation. "I haven't got any time right now."

"Please—we came by to check on the woman who was attacked the night my wife was killed—Carmen Richison."

Mishkin signaled a policeman inside the hospital to unlock the front door. He looked back at Warren as he stepped inside. "I understand your interest and you have my word that we're doing everything we can. Everyone—*please go back home.*"

Warren turned back to Emily, and looked sharply at the unknown faces on either side of her. "Where's Ben?"

Emily gasped, tossing her head as she searched the slowly dispersing group surrounding them. She squeezed his fingers tight. "God, Warren, he was right *here.*" She craned her neck from side to side wildly. *"We've got to find him."*

3

Ben Dixon's pallid face trembled and his lips formed soundless words. "I'm all right," he managed to grumble, but wished Emily were there to help him.

He wished—

But there was no time for that anymore. He slipped through the bushes surrounding the hospital's wall, barely hearing the sound of the people he'd left, trying each door he came to.

Upon his head. His stomach lurched in hot futility. His own soul was already stolen from him, and he had delivered Carmen's as well. Perhaps he had even delivered his own wife and son's.

His only redemption was in the destruction of this vile creature who had destroyed him.

Evergreen branches slapped his face, stinging in the chilly night, but he ignored them, concentrating on the inner pains that proved his defilement. He had to find a way in and face down the nemesis who had dragged him into hell.

But every door was locked.

Dixon pushed out heavy breaths with an effort, sliding his

thumb along the smooth concrete wall, then stopped and listened as a policeman at the next entrance stopped his melancholy whistle, lit a cigarette, and peered around. Ben waited with clenched fists. The man went back inside, and Ben heard the lock click as it shut.

Every damn door was *locked*.

Walking faster, Ben reached the walkway the policeman had left and watched him through the glass window of the door, waiting until his back was turned to hurry past to the other side. He *had* to find a way in!

The crunch of his steps was loud on the white gravel and he moved faster, feeling time's burden. More branches dashed him, but he was running now.

He tripped on something hard.

Ben grabbed for stability, and his fingers closed around a metal rail. He grunted. A darkened concrete stairway led into the hospital's basement. He checked to see he was unobserved, then hurried downward, praying it would lead him to a new moment of truth as well.

The door opened easily. Ben leaned in, examining the room that was filled with the hospital's supplies and janitor's tools. He swept his eyes through the dim lighting of fluorescent tubes, from the shelves of uniforms and bed linens to the high-tech equipment gathering dust. The mustiness tickled his nose and he reached up to hold back a sneeze, but only muffled it. Licking his dry lips and wishing again that Emily were with him—even Warren—he walked soundlessly inside and pulled the door closed.

Where to start? His heart thumped hard. Quietly, he walked to the end of the first row of shelves, then past the ends of two more. He saw the door that led into the rest of the hospital and, listening cautiously, walked slowly toward it.

"What do you search for now, high priest of cocksucking? Another man?"

Dixon stopped dead. Behind a box of disposable syringes he saw *it,* and was struck cold by the consuming potency of its presence.

The salesman grinned, showing stained teeth, and leaned against the box companionably. "There are ten men as dead as you above us . . . and six women, but they are nothing. I wanted you more than them all, and I knew you would come." He straightened and walked slowly, inching closer. "I have waited for you as I promised and I knew you would not let me down. I even knew you would *come in the back door."* The smile became larger, and it licked its lips. *"That is how you've always liked it best, isn't it?"*

Dixon faced it with a shiver, feeling exposed. He slipped a hand into his pocket and brought out his cross.

"You didn't even bring a gun," cackled the drooling cruelty. The tall figure stepped another foot closer. "I told you I would enjoy your suffering—and now, suffer more in knowing that every fear you have is *true:* Your Carmen's precious soul is mine, and her loss is upon your head . . . *or to your credit."* The vampire reached out a long slender hand, its nails brown with dried blood. "You are so helpful to me that you may as well be on my side."

Ben held up the dull cross, knowing it was useless to him. His throat was dry, and he wanted to run back to Warren's car to find one of the stakes and plunge it into this dread beast's heart.

But the vampire held him in its eyes, filling him with wet, slogging cement, and he had to fight to keep moving back.

"You know you're already damned, dicksucker, so why fight it? Suck my dick now, and let me suck you—*grab all the gusto you can from life*—"

Something solid pushed into Dixon's back, and he stopped, then felt the shelf blocking his way.

"—while you still can."

He was trapped, inside and out. *"Damn you!"* Dixon screamed, and waited for the fire of hell to consume him at last.

4

"He can't have gone far," Emily said, dragging Warren behind her. She looked up at the tall hospital and its darkened windows. "He was right beside me."

They walked quickly, bypassing each guarded entrance. So far, the others were all locked.

"God, where could he have gone?" Warren peered back at the parking lot. "Where—"

Emily pulled him past another door, hardly glancing at the policeman gazing out its window. "Maybe," she said quietly, "he *knows* where *it* is."

"What?"

She gripped his fingers harder as they walked. "I mean *exactly* where it is, Warren. Back at the warehouse, he said that the evil was *in* him; *that he knew things*! That's how Carmen knew to go there, right?"

The idea pushed past his other thoughts. "But . . . he said he can't fight it."

"Look over here," she urged him suddenly, pushing him up a narrow sidewalk. *"Look."* She took him almost up to the building, and pointed down a stairwell cut into the earth. At the bottom waited a solid door.

Warren sucked in cold air, staring into that darkness with her. He could almost feel Dixon standing here and looking down too. "Come on." Warren clutched her icy hand and went down the steps. He touched the door's handle, testing it.

It opened.

Emily squeezed his fingers, then nudged him forward into the dimly lit storeroom . . . and the low murmur of voices came toward them.

"Ben?"

"Come on," said Emily, leading Warren past stacks of paper towels and toilet paper. They moved more slowly now, trying to keep quiet, creeping close to the folded linens until they became spotless white uniforms. The opposite wall came closer, and Warren could nearly read the numbers on each of the lockers lining it.

"Damn you!"

The sudden scream exploded from the other side of the shelves, and Warren jumped, releasing Emily. He ran to the end of the row, his feet scraping on the concrete floor, and he grabbed one of the stored mechanical beds to bring himself to a halt.

A penetrating chill cut into the small of his back. Ben stood facing the vampire, who advanced on him slowly, hatefully. Dixon's own panicked hate sounded in a harsh gasp as he struggled to break his stare from the sickening, cruel visage.

"You bastard!"

Dixon lunged forward with sudden energy and Warren crept closer, digging his hand into his pocket, raising the cross. *"Stop!"* he cried out, colliding with the vampire in an insane fury. The undead thing glared with evil triumph. It grinned at Warren and grabbed Dixon's arm with a long white hand that tore effortlessly through his bulky clothing into flesh, discoloring it . . . ripping.

Ben screamed.

The hideous sound made Warren wince and he tried despondently to charge the cross with power, to believe.

"Oh, God," Emily said from behind him.

His responsibility for Emily, for Ben, beat into him, clouding the vampire's evil pall. He gripped the cross with slow, rousing strength.

Ben Dixon cursed, sinking to his knees as blood dripped from his cracking arm.

"No." Emily moved to his side. "He helped me! We've got to do something." She looked back at the door quickly. "The stakes are in the car!"

Warren felt the pressure increase. *Faith.* He walked into the vampire's piercing aura, its stink covering him. He shook as the hot cruelty spread into his very soul.

"You have been a great difficulty, preacher." The vile thing snarled, turning his vicious gaze to Warren. "You both—" He squeezed Dixon's arm with relish, the wet snapping of the bones

overpowering the hoarse howl it provoked and sending shivers
up Warren's own useless limb. He stopped indecisively as the
undead thing chuckled.

"You could have had anything. All of you could have had anything at all! Sex beyond your imagination. You could have had
knowledge! All but for your feeble ideas! *Your pitiful fucking
faith,*" the vampire spat, looking only at Warren. "And you don't
even have enough of that to save *yourselves*! Your pitiful faith
has been enough trouble, preacher. Drop your cross." Its dark
eyes burned Warren, and it smiled. "Drop the cross and I will let
him go. I will give you another chance."

Warren moved closer, trembling, silently repeating the
prayers he'd used to bolster himself before.

"Is your faith the only symbol you hold?" it cackled, reaching
out confidently. "Is it as dead as you are, preacher?"

Symbol. Warren remembered Ben's explanation and his throat
ran dry. He forced himself close to the clutching fingers and
swallowed through the dread of his doubt. *Only a symbol.*

He held it out, forced his stiffening fingers to open, quivering
in the terror of offering the creature this cross—

But if he didn't, then he didn't believe in his own faith, the
cross would cease to have any power.

The strong thin hand reached close, nearly touched it.
Closer . . .

Warren felt the scaly brush as the dryness touched his thumb,
but somehow did not jerk back. His eyes watered in the putrid
odor that dragged the very air from his nostrils, and he felt the
hand circle his like a slithering snake.

"Your fucking faith!" shrieked the vampire, hissing its slimy
spit and jerking away without warning. Its slender talons yanked
Ben Dixon to his feet, filling the room with the man's agonized
cry, and its long yellow teeth sank deep into his throat, spraying
the air with blood. Utter horror ripped from Ben's lungs and his
neck ran wet and red.

Warren gasped, icy with the terrible sucking sound. In desper-
ation he pulled back his arm and threw the cross at the grisly
monster.

The small metal ornament spun like a knife, hurtling endlessly, shining as it caught the fluorescent glimmers of the ceil-

ing. Then it slapped the vampire's drawn face, forcing a hellish bellow as the stench of dead flesh smoldered from the creature's livid cheek. The hypnotic wreath binding Warren vanished and his leaden feet slogged forward again. *To stop it. To kill it— to make it burn as Susan had burned!* "In Christ's name!" he shouted.

The vampire flinched and staggered back, withdrawing its hands to clutch at the seared mark on its skin, and in that moment Warren saw it as it really was: a dead and decayed thing of damnation, slimy, festering flesh hanging from brittle bones.

"In Christ's name!" he shouted louder, reaching into his far pocket and clutching the bottle of blessed water.

The vampire cowered back, Dixon dropping to the floor, while Warren struggled to unscrew the bottlecap with one hand.

"Preacher . . ."

Warren looked up as the vampire leapt at him, and threw himself to the side. It bared its stained teeth and darted, slamming Emily to the floor. Warren gulped hard, dropping the unopened brandy bottle to the hard floor.

It bounced, and Emily caught it, shrinking back as the vampire snarled and bent to her. She scooted along the concrete back toward Warren, unscrewing the cap as fast as she could.

The vampire growled at her again, letting its eyes graze her before bringing them back to Warren. He laughed pitilessly, then backed along the linen-filled shelves, reaching behind to pull the door open.

Warren could not move, frozen in the grip of its power.

Fingers tugged at his elbow as Emily stood beside him. She tried to push the opened bottle into his palm.

The vampire knocked over a dusty microscope, backed out into the night, and slammed the door shut.

"Warren?"

He coughed, coming out of the evil paralysis, shook his head at her, hurried past the broken microscope. He threw the door open and saw the vampire standing midway up the stairs.

"Warren—*don't!*" Emily grabbed his coat sleeve.

"You're a fucking, cocksucking hypocrite like your comrade!" the thing spewed across the distance between them. "The shadows in your shitting heart match my evil—anything I have done

or will do. He craves my dick in his mouth . . . your dick . . . *anyone's* dick!" The vampire laughed gratingly. "And you crave as well—but you want only the altruistic abilities and forbidden knowledge you desperately seek . . . *and the body of your best friend's wife to use as you used your own wife! You hypocrite! You preach your sermons of God, but your heart is truer than those words—your cold, fucking heart!*"

Warren felt a shudder in his soul, and his eyes were engulfed with the temptations the vampire offered. He stared into its invitation with a fearsome yearning.

"I offer you joys of the flesh—*the ultimate joy of your flesh!*" wheedled the sallow voice. "*The fellowship of other souls and a greater quenching of your desires than you dare dream.* I offer immortality of the flesh through the fulfillment of your dark needs . . . *not through the impossible obedience and denial of self the one you call on requires.*"

Warren saw the offering of even Susan in the creatures' compelling eyes. "I *am* the traveling salesman!" it howled. "I sell you your *self*! I sell you freedom from your guilt and the dreams you fear to follow. I will make you the master of knowledge beyond you now! Beyond you *ever*!" The vampire hissed. "You will be my new harvester—a new *real* saver of souls—*saving them from the hell they live on earth in hopeless self-denial.*"

"Warren!"

Emily's voice broke through the mist of forbidden cravings stifling his mind, and he tore his eyes from the vampire with an agony of self-rejection. "Damn you!" he gasped. "You—*you're barred from our bodies and spirits . . . in the name of the Father, the Son, and the Holy Ghost!*"

The vampire stepped back. "*You filthy shit of God!* The hypocrisy in your heart will make you mine. Yes, I will suck the life out of you, but you will yet live, to suck my hard cock, as my fucking slave, before we are done."

"*Away in God's name!*" Warren screamed.

The vampire did not move.

"Ben *needs* us!" Emily cried. "Warren!"

But Warren was staring back into those eyes that had held him in weakness, understanding how and why Ben Dixon had gone over the edge . . . comprehending the incredible hatred in Ben's own eyes.

"He needs us!" screamed Emily.

The vampire laughed. "Yes. Go and see the fruits of your faith's victories, evangelist. I do not damn. The damnation in your comrade is from your own God. *He damns us all.*"

The twisting blasphemy stung him, but Warren slammed the door shut and let Emily take him back into the storeroom. He could not let Ben Dixon die and come back as Susan had—he couldn't.

Dixon was sprawled motionlessly beside the shelves. Blood trickled from the savage wound in his throat. Warren went to him with the cold, pale visage of the vampire imprinted on his thoughts. He knelt at Dixon's head, Emily beside him, and thanked God as he saw Ben's chest move. Warren reached to Ben's sunken cheeks and touched his face with the gentleness he had to struggle to regain. "Ben?"

"I'm . . . dying." The thin words broke over him. Dixon's ashen face screwed up in the shudder of unfathomable distaste and torment.

"We'll get you to a hospital," promised Warren.

"We're . . . in a hospital," Ben croaked, biting his lips hard enough to split the skin. "I won't make it. I don't want to make it."

The hollow emptiness of the words tore at Warren. "You're infected, Ben. If you die . . ."

"I can't go through it anymore. The evil . . . oh, God, *I'm* the fucking evil. That fucking bastard salesman showed me my true self. I've been damned for years, I've damned myself. And I'm tired." He gurgled. "God, the *sucking.* My soul is decaying. I can feel it crumble."

"Ben!" Warren shook him. *"Ben."* What could he do?

"Damn you, MacDonald, let me die. I'm part of it now. I . . . *am part of it.*"

"Ben," Emily whimpered, bending closer to his strained face. "You're a good person. You are."

The bottle of holy water in her hands caught Warren's attention. "Emily, give it to me—give me the bottle."

"I—I opened it," she said absently.

He took it, and fire shot up through his straining shoulder. He brought the container to Dixon's lips and tried to push it between his teeth. "Open your mouth, Ben. You're not evil. My God, you're as worthy as any of us. Ben, you tried—you've tried harder than I ever did! Try to pray—try that *too*. Accept forgiveness."

"I—" He gurgled and spasmed.

Warren tipped the bottle and water spilled onto Ben's ashen face and into his mouth. Ben swallowed.

A high whine exploded from his throat. Ben's face blanched anew and he shook violently. He vomited all over himself, then drooled bile over his lips. Warren pushed his throbbing broken arm under Ben's head, then spilled more of the water into his mouth and the open wound. It hissed and boiled, steaming over the parched lips and making them bleed. The squealing man thrashed and tried to raise himself weakly, tears streaming from his wide eyes.

Warren poured the water into his mouth until most was gone, then sprinkled the last on the man's shredded neck, its flesh as pale as his face.

Ben's cries stopped.

The mark on his neck glimmered, then the flesh seeped together until it disappeared. Warren felt Ben's chest for a heartbeat.

"He's still alive," Emily whispered. Her fingers were pressed to Ben's wrist.

Warren smiled. It brought him needed joy as Ben's agony melted into quiet peace, even as his heart became erratic . . . and stopped.

A minute passed.

"He's . . . dead." Emily said hoarsely. She bent and kissed Ben's cheek, then his bloody neck where the wound had been. She wiped the stickiness from her lips and squeezed Warren's hand. "He's dead."

Warren returned the pressure silently and heard footsteps at the door from the room's inner side. He scooted back, remembering where they were, and eyed the door on the other side of the shelf of linens.

Emily took a deep breath. "Will—will he come back?"

"No." Ben's pale face was full of peace. Warren faced her, still on his knees, then pulled her close and hugged her—needing her. "I don't think so. He won't come back."

"If he does, he'll know how to find us, Warren."

Warren pulled back. "We haven't even got one of the stakes. But I don't think we need one. We can—"

The footsteps from the hallway stopped outside the door, and they both looked at each other. "Can what?" asked Emily, pushing herself to her feet.

"We can trust in God's salvation," he replied, standing with her as the door clicked open.

Emily regarded him hesitantly. "This time . . . I guess we don't have any choice." She held his arm, and they both crept back the way they had come.

XV

1

With pleasant warmth, Warren's consciousness crawled from heavy sleep to the sweet familiarity of Susan's body curled against his side. He rested a hand on her hip, trying to turn over.

Hot knives sliced effortlessly through his nerves to the bone. He gasped, shutting his eyes against the bright sun and the truth of his life. He turned to the young woman beside him, knowing she was not Susan.

Emily. He stared at her sleeping figure guiltily. In the exhaustion of last night he said a stuttered prayer for Ben while they drove back, and then he and Emily had staggered here tiredly to rest. Neither of them wanted to be alone, and they'd clung together, dropping quickly to sleep.

But Ben was dead.

Warren squinted to hold back tears, thanking God he still had Emily. His fist squeezed the sheet uselessly. Ben was gone, his body soon to return to the dust of the earth.

The phone rang.

The jangling bell startled him, and Emily sat up. She showed him a tiny smile, pressing close in an awkward hug, bringing a heat of embarrassment to his cheeks. The phone rang again as Warren hugged her back, and he propped himself up slowly with his left arm to swing his legs over the bed. Emily got up and stepped easily to the phone across the room.

"No," Warren said. "Let me."

She stood still, frowning.

The harsh ring broke through the silence twice more before he put the receiver to his ear. "Hello?" he answered.

"Warren MacDonald?"

"Yes?"

"This is Dr. Wentworth. Officer Mishkin asked me to call you."

"Yes?" he asked with a low voice, surprised the detective had remembered his concern and shamed that he'd forgotten Carmen. He turned away from Emily, embarrassment burning his cheeks.

"Carmen Richison was unhurt last night. It seems that she's doing a little better this morning. Her vital signs remain steady and she's stronger. Indications are that she may soon pull out of her coma." Emily went into the bathroom and drew the door shut behind her.

"Thank you." He felt the relief and leaned against the wall with it. "She wasn't attacked, then."

The voice hesitated. "You're a friend?"

"Her minister."

"Well, It's funny," he relented. "They say her room is where that psycho turned up first. I heard that he went crazy when he broke into the room and saw her. He started screaming and attacking everyone he saw and—" He stopped and Warren heard a distant criticism.

"That's all I can say," he resumed after a moment. "Uh, Mrs. Richison is doing well, Mr. MacDonald. They told me you can come to see her if you like."

"Thank you."

"Certainly, Mr. MacDonald."

"Thanks for calling," he replied. The line clicked dead, and Warren bit a knuckle.

Emily came out of the bathroom. "Carmen's okay?" she asked.

He nodded, running his eyes over her wrinkled clothing. "She's alive. How are you feeling?"

Emily grinned back, trying unsuccessfully to hide her discomfort. "I haven't ever slept with a minister before."

He reddened, but crossed the room to put his arm around her. He let out his joy in a bright laugh. "Carmen wasn't even touched!"

Emily tugged at her sweater self-consciously. "You mean—you mean she wasn't hurt at *all* last night?"

"She was under protection," Warren said.

Emily started to open her mouth again, then shook her head. "Prayer?"

He hugged her again.

"Great." Her tone was unconvinced. "Why don't you pray that damn vampire back into the ground?" She brushed dust off her sweater with distaste. "God, I'm filthy. So are you, Warren."

Warren went back to the bed and sat on the giving mattress. His eyes moved over the mess the room had become since Susan's death. "You . . . could put on some of Susan's clothes," he offered.

"Susan? Was that your wife's name?"

"Yes." *Susan.* But he couldn't let those memories in now. Not now.

"I appreciate it, Warren, but I won't need them. I brought some of my own things with me. What I really want to know is how the two of us are going to track down and kill the vampire. Shouldn't we call the police into this now?" She walked over to him.

"What good would it do to tell the police?"

"It . . ." She creased her face and sat down beside him. "We might make them believe about the killer being a vampire."

"No, I don't think so, and they would detain us for hours. Nobody's going to believe something like this. You don't know how much it took to convince me."

"Isn't it worth a try?"

Her face pleaded with him, and he knew she was as afraid, as he was, of taking on the evil by themselves. "They wouldn't even have listened to us if we told them they were chasing a vampire at the hospital last night." Her face fell. "It has to be stopped, Emily."

She traced a cross on her jeans.

"You don't have to go with me."

Her hand seized his, and she stared back furiously. "I do. I *do* have to. I *have* to help you, Warren. You couldn't even unscrew that bottlecap last night! You're just like Ben sometimes. You were standing there so close to that—that bastard and . . ." Her face screwed up with frustration. "You need me, Warren. I can't just leave you!"

Ben had fallen into the vampire's traps repeatedly. Warren prayed that he was stronger than Ben and held tight to that hope.

"I don't want to go home, either, Warren. There's a lot of those things there."

Ben hadn't consecrated the graves. That menace would be growing dangerously night by night. "You're right," he said.

"And if I did go—" Her fair brown eyes searched his with a terrible need. "If I go, we'll both be alone. Your wife is dead . . . and I told you, *I killed my parents.*"

Warren stroked her damp cheek, recalling his analysis of her problem.

"I want to be with you, Warren. I can't be alone until all this is over. *I have to know it's over.*" She sniffed. "I'm afraid of them, Warren."

"Yes," he agreed, holding her tight and feeling the assurance he sought come back with the bond they were making. He didn't want to do this alone. She was right that his fledgling faith would fail him without support, as Ben's had.

She pressed her lips to his cheek. "Just promise not to leave me alone, Warren. Promise."

"I promise." He smiled gratefully. "Thank you, Emily."

"Are you afraid, Warren?"

He was. Ben said that only absolute purity would be safe from the dark threat. It did frighten him. "Yes."

"Well, you did pretty well last night."

He smiled. Her appreciation and warmth would help him remember that this mission wasn't of revenge, but salvation. "You're right, Emily—I do need you." He pulled away from her reluctantly and got up from the bed. "Come on. Let's get cleaned up. We'll need to make some plans and find out everything we can. And"—he paused, feeling the joy of the earlier phone call—"I want to go see Carmen."

Emily laughed weakly. "We need to get something to eat, too, Warren. If nothing else, I guess you need me to remind you of that."

2

With their late start it was near two that afternoon when they left the hospital. Carmen was doing better, but Warren had to fight himself to leave her alone again. Though she wasn't touched, a nagging doubt still tried to persuade him it was all part of the undead demon's strategy.

But there was no other way.

They *had* to go.

Emily sat behind the wheel. "Where to?" she asked Warren.

He shut his door and tried to pick out Carmen's window, his fingers laced together. "The library," he said gruffly. "Follow the road out of the parking lot to the right." The car pulled away, and he sank into the seat.

"What's at the library?" she asked.

"Newspaper obituaries. That's how Ben was keeping tabs on where the vampire was."

She drove carefully, scooting up close to the steering wheel. "You've got a newspaper at home."

"Yes. I want to find more out about this vampire too."

"I've already done that," she replied. "Warren, you said we shouldn't waste time."

He eyed her with surprise. "Maybe I can find out something that you missed," Warren insisted. "We can't find it in the daylight, anyway, Emily. We don't know where to look. Ben said—"

Emily didn't look at him and he saw her fingers press the wheel harder. "Ben's dead. We need to go to the cemetery and take care of that man—Carmen's husband. You said they were burying him today."

Warren stared at the other cars around them and at the men

and women walking on the sidewalks. He looked into the normal, preoccupied faces all around—none of them had any idea of what was happening in the city they lived in.

Or maybe some of them had been bitten already.

"Please, Emily," Warren said in a low voice, "I won't take long."

But two hours later Warren knew he *had* taken too long and that they *were* wasting their time. Most of the books contained only what he already knew or could guess. The methods described to ward off the undead were numerous and all equally problematic: the pagan protection of garlic would keep the vampire at a distance but would not destroy it, and to honestly believe the odorous plant would protect anyone would take more faith than he presently had. Cremation would consume the vampire but leave the impelling force within it free to enter another victim, as would a stake through the heart unless it were accompanied by faithful prayer.

A stake of hawthorn or aspen, though, required faith but not prayer with its use: ". . . one of the most approved methods to render him harmless was to transfix the corpse through the region of the heart with a stake which may be of aspen or maple as in Russia, or more usually of hawthorn or whitethorn. The aspen tree is held to be particularly sacred, as according to one account this was the wood of the cross. '. . . the aspen tree shivers mystically in sympathy with the horror of that mother-tree in Palestine, which was compelled to furnish material for the Cross.' Of whitethorn Sir John Mandeville says: 'Then was our Lord led into a garden, and there the Jews scorned Him and made Him a crown of the branches of the Whitethorn that grew in the garden, and set it upon His head. And therefore has the Whitethorn many virtues. . . .'"

Warren closed the book, leaving it on the table with the others, to find Emily. All in all, there was little recorded that Ben hadn't already told him. The only method of permanent annihilation was through faith in God, no matter the means, and one seemed as difficult as another.

There was no easy way out.

As Warren reached the stairs, he saw Emily coming down and stopped.

"Are you finished?" she asked briskly.

"Definitely." He dropped his voice at the sight of two tow-headed children clutching a Dr. Seuss book. "We're just going to have to patrol the area where we know the thing's been. Maybe if we spread out from there, sooner or later we'll find it."

Emily looked at him without enthusiasm, and they walked past the table Warren had used. "I lost track of time up there, Warren. I was searching the obituaries, and then I saw the Freeport newspaper. . . ."

Warren frowned, stopping with her.

"Where Ben and I lived—there were five unexplained murders there last night. They've had the highway patrol and extra police working a whole week. The story said they might quarantine the entire place and call in the National Guard."

"Oh, God," groaned Warren, "as if that will do any good." A lump grew in his heart as he thought of five more souls damned while they chased the fiend who'd begun it all. Indecision swept through him.

"There were only a few the night I killed . . . my mother," Emily went on. An old man sat at a nearby table and rubbed an age spot on his forehead. He smiled at her, then opened a book. "Warren, it must've started going crazy the night Ben and I left. There's no telling how many there are now, and Freeport's not that big. Pretty soon they'll start going somewhere else." She buried her fingers in Warren's wrist. "That means there's at least a dozen more vampires to stop now, and after tonight there'll be more. We can't count on someone else figuring it out and trying to stop them."

Warren nodded and felt intensity mount, spreading into him from her grip and words. He put his hand over her fingers and rubbed gently. "We've got to do something before there are so many that we *can't* do something," he said. "We've got to go there."

Emily was pale. "But with five more last night—Warren, there's already too many."

"If we can't stop them now we may as well give up," he replied bitterly. "We've got to get our things and go there now." Disheartened, he held her hand, walking toward the exit.

"Sir?"

Warren turned automatically, meeting the eyes of a tall woman dressed in black. She stopped at the table he'd left and looked at him as though she were a schoolteacher chastising a student.

"Please keep your voices down. This is a library."

Blushing, he nodded and started to turn away.

"Sir?" the middle-aged lady icily addressed him again. "Did you forget to return your books to the desk?" She stared reprovingly, drumming her fingers on the pile.

He felt his jaw tighten in the anger of frustration and noticed Emily's equal annoyance. "Sorry," he muttered.

"Rules must be obeyed," she told him haughtily, and waited until he began picking the texts up. "Coming to the library is a privilege." As the librarian walked away Emily began to help. She dumped the books loudly on the counter and took Warren's hand. "She makes me think that Dracula's been to the library."

Looking back, Warren realized that following the dictates of society would only work against them. Rules must be obeyed, the librarian had said.

But what were the rules now?

He forced it from his thoughts, and they hurried outside to the car. The sun was already low in the sky.

XVI

1

Sirens grew loud on their way and Emily pulled over to let a fire truck by. Smoke billowed over Warren's neighborhood.

When they pulled onto his street they saw the two fire trucks far down the way. A cold paralysis gripped him. His house was burning.

"Oh, shit," Emily gasped.

Warren didn't reply, and they continued slowly until they saw the flames covering his home. He tightened his hold on the dashboard, the inferno consuming all his valued possessions: the rare books, the papers and memorabilia . . .

And all the stakes and holy water he'd prepared.

Even with the windows closed, hot air pressed into the car.

"Shit," said Emily again.

"Ben said it tried this on him—tried to burn him alive."

Emily cruised down the block slowly, watching the dying house in the rearview mirror.

Warren didn't want to look, and only glanced up as they passed Carmen's dark home. He prayed for her again. And a shadowed figure stood from a chair on the porch.

"Chuck," he whispered, his heart pounding at his panicked lapse.

Emily gasped again. "Shit, Warren."

"We've got to do something." Ben had said a vampire went after the people it knew best; Chuck might have tried to go after him, and maybe he'd tried to force him out of his house by setting it afire.

"Pull over," he told Emily.

"Goddammit, Warren, he's coming after us!"

Chuck was limping toward the car, smiling, his white teeth flashing in the fire's brightness.

The walking corpse came at a slug's pace, but the sight of the stiff shuffle dragged bony fingers of terror into Warren's tingling scalp. Chuck walked as if his legs were in casts, and when his arms began to writhe, it was as though he were being filmed with stop-motion photography—one frame at a time.

His jaws chewed nonexistent tobacco, or perhaps they moved in anticipation of his first meal of blood.

"Warren!" Emily shrieked as Chuck smashed his dead white face against her window. "Damn it, we can't leave without getting him first!"

She reached to unlock her door, but Warren pushed his open first. "Stay in and lock up," he ordered her, getting out on legs that didn't want to hold him.

Chuck was charging around the car at Warren, baring vicious fangs.

"M-my God." Warren shoved the thing defensively with his good arm and forced it off balance, then backed quickly away. One step. Two.

"Warren."

The coarse voice grated in his ears, and he readied himself for Chuck's attack as he backed into the nearest yard. Chuck stalked him in the flickering yellow light, and Warren avoided his gleaming eyes, trying to remember that he and Emily were the hunters, not the hunted. He longed for the cross he had left at the hospital.

The car door opened, and the vampire swung around to Emily as she jumped out and ran back toward the fire.

"Emily!" Warren yelled, taking a step toward Chuck.

Her feet pumped hard into the street as he watched. Then a shadow darted and Warren turned quickly as the thing that had once been his friend lunged at him. It snarled as it knocked him to the dead grass.

"Warren . . ." sang the vile intonation. *"Join me. . . ."*

Chuck cackled inhumanly, bending down, chilling him with a raw breath.

"No!" He threw out his casted arm desperately, smashing the grinding jaw and sending Chuck sprawling. Pain shot through his shoulder, and he gasped and pushed himself back to his feet, his arm throbbing from the misuse. "In Christ's name." He gasped, then stopped the prayer, knowing that that weapon might drive the monster off, but that he didn't yet have the will or ability to kill it that way alone. If Chuck retreated, it would be nearly impossible to find him again until he returned to his grave at dawn. By that time Chuck would have found another victim for tonight. An unknown victim.

The vampire was up then, his horrible features of death and lust illuminated in flickering yellow brightness. Warren steadied himself, searching the yard for a piece of wood he could use as a stake.

"Warren," whispered Chuck seductively, "I'm your *friend*. I only want your help. You said you'd help me keep Carmen as mine, and I can't reach her inside that hospital. You must help me. Look into my eyes." Chuck stepped forward. *"Look into my eyes,"* it hissed.

The tone compelled him more through sick curiosity than its fledgling power. Warren bit his lip, remembering the false vision he's seen in Susan. But looked anyway.

Chuck. He saw the friend he'd known—a man he'd shared a part of himself with, a man he *trusted*. Warren's will heaved and disintegrated, ignoring the cries of his soul. He couldn't help himself, looking at the face of the man who'd always listened attentively to the sermons he preached. Chuck had always been ready to listen to him . . . and he offered that now, eternally. *Chuck was his friend.*

"Get away from him!"

The trance shattered in Emily's scream, and the taunting visions dissolved as Chuck became a pale, heartless creature dribbling saliva. He jerked toward the shrill command, and Warren flinched at the sudden loss of the man he'd known. Frigid sweat broke out on his forehead.

Emily stood in the wavering street shadows, advancing confidently, her hands holding two smoking pieces of lumber in the form of a cross. They glowed in the raw power of a furious conviction that he would hardly have believed existed in her, and that strength flowed over Warren, impelling its focus and sanity through him. With a start the vampire backed away, stumbling with croaking despair.

"Get back!" Emily yelled hotly, clutching the makeshift cross while she advanced into the yard.

Warren stumbled lethargically to help, more than a dozen feet back when she suddenly charged, slamming Chuck hard in a mad rush. The corpse wrestled with her to keep his feet, dragging his nails into her cheek as she fell instead, the wood flying from her flailing hands.

"You fucking bitch!" spat Chuck, leaping at her.

Warren knew he couldn't reach them in time. Chuck's arms were clutching at her clothes as his body covered her. Warren prayed hard, trying to believe—as Emily had said sarcastically— trying to believe him back into the ground.

"God, please—" he gasped, repeating words that disappeared as he whispered them, and then he knew he couldn't do it. He staggered, slogging ahead fearfully, trying to hurry as Emily groped the shadowed ground for the charred pieces of wood. She brought one against herself, panting, and rammed it furiously into the hideous demon's chest even as he drove against her with a bloodcurdling scream. The whine broke into the night, overcoming the crackle of the distant flames and the commotion of the firefighters. The stake tore through the vampire as Emily shoved it harder, and the creature fell on top of her.

"Damn you!" Emily screamed, rolling out from under it. Her face dripped with its slime. *"Damn you!"* She pounced on top of Chuck, shoving his face into the chilled ground—driving the wood into his body until it ripped through his back.

Warren stepped beside Chuck's twitching body as Emily rose. Greenish yellow embalming fluid covered Emily's smoke-blackened face. Overcoming nausea, he took her right hand, then knelt between her and Chuck, her touch giving strength to his slow words. " 'Our Father, which art in heaven,' " he wheezed with a dry throat, feeling his voice grow, " 'hallowed be Thy name . . .' " He looked up at Emily and licked his dry lips.

Chuck began to steam and wither. " 'Thy kingdom come, Thy will be done . . .' "

" 'On—on earth as it is . . . in heaven,' " whispered Emily. Chuck's skin shriveled and popped, boiling into a fog more frigid than the night as it spread across the ground.

"Forgive us our trespasses . . . in Jesus's name," Warren finished.

Emily clenched his fingers.

Chuck was dust, and Warren blinked at those blowing remains while he let Emily help him up. They held each other tightly.

"Are you okay?" she asked.

"Yes." He pulled a handkerchief out of his pants to wipe the stinking ooze from her cheeks. "What about you?"

She blew on her burned fingers. "It stings pretty damn bad."

"I'll take you to the emergency room."

"No—they'll just use medicated lotion and gauze. We can buy that ourselves." Then she coughed and slumped against him tiredly. "I just want to get out of the cold, Warren."

He frowned at her, dabbing at her forehead. "Can you drive with your hands like that?"

"Like what?" She tried a strained smile.

He smiled back. "Come on. We'll get some medicine and aspirin, then find a motel for the night. Tomorrow we'll have to go and consecrate those graves as Ben planned to."

Emily's voice was as coldly logical as a child's. "Warren, what if it leaves and we can't find it?"

He replaced his dirty handkerchief as they walked back to the car. She was right, and if the vampire was as coldly logical, it would seek the course she suggested. As in a game of hide-and-seek they were beaten unless they caught it. It only had to stay free while its victims died in their time, and infested the world, damning more than the single vampire ever could alone.

Warren shivered. "We have to go. The same thing that could happen here is already happening in Freeport. It's not like we have a choice, Emily."

They stared at each other; then Warren lowered his eyes. He saw the vampire's plan against them clearly.

"We can at least consecrate them in the daylight, can't we?" she asked hopefully, getting into the driver's seat.

"Yes. then we'll come back. The vampire *missionary,*" Warren said flatly, remembering its fiendish threat and praying the vampire would hold true to it, "has much work to do *here.*" She started the car as he got in, the shadow of the smoking house playing through the interior.

"I just want this to be over," she said in a small voice.

So did he.

2

When they were a hundred miles out of St. Louis, Emily shook her head. "Warren, I've got to stop. My hands . . ." She frowned in the dark car, feeling the tight, fiery skin under the gauze bandages. "Can we stop at that motel ahead?"

Warren looked out the windshield, then finally nodded. "Okay."

Thankfully, she pushed the pedal harder, biting her lips as she steered onto the exit ramp. "I'm sorry."

He chuckled. "Look at me . . . I can't even drive."

"Not funny." She turned off the ramp and passed the gas station there, then parked under the Ramada Inn sign beyond it. "We'll have to leave early tomorrow so we can finish by sunset," she said.

"I know." He yawned. "Come on. I'm beat too. I need this rest myself."

They stood beside each other and stared down the deserted highway. "God," Emily said, "it's hard to believe any of it out here. . . ."

"Yeah," he agreed. They went to the long building's office to check in.

The motel room was small, and dim in the nightstand's light. Warren turned up the heat as Emily sat on the bed farthest from the door, then took the ice pail out to fill in the big gray machine they'd passed. She unwrapped the gauze cotton he'd bandaged her hands in earlier, disliking the texture of the gooey first-aid cream. Her palms were still red and bubbled, though not as badly as she'd first feared. Warren had tried to insist she go to the emergency room.

The room was painted a drab yellow, and discolored framed prints of wild birds hung on the walls. It was all happening too quickly, Emily thought, and the only consolation was that this kept her from thinking about what had happened to Mom and Dad . . . even Aunt Joanie.

The door burst open. "If it was any colder out there," Warren gasped, hurrying inside and bringing a gust of the frigid air to prove his point, "we could just let you stick your hands outside and they'd turn to ice."

"Ha-ha," she muttered sarcastically, glad he was back to keep her mind off the past hours.

He brought the ice pail to her bed, then sat beside her and took one of her hands, brushing the discarded wrapping onto the floor.

"Ouch!"

"Sorry," he told her, letting go of the blistered fingers. He rubbed his hand on his slacks.

"It's okay," she said, trying to relax. "It just hurts . . . like my frigging hands are on fire."

"I told you we should have a doctor do this."

"No." She flexed her fingers and held the hand out again. "It's not that bad. We can't afford to take that much time."

"We can afford it for this."

She shook her head. "This is enough. Go ahead and rub it in." She held her jaw tight. "I guess little girls shouldn't play with fire, huh?"

He smoothed the cream lightly over her skin. "I'm very thankful."

She laughed to mask the pink blush flooding her face. "I didn't want you to be hurt, Warren." Her eyes became serious. "I told you; I don't want to be alone with those . . . *things.*"

"Well, *I* told you I'd need you."

Her jaw tightened with pain.

He laid her hand on the bed and took the other one. "Here. Rest your hand on my cast."

She did as he asked and felt him flinch. Hitting Chuck had probably hurt his arm badly. "I just hope your bone didn't break through the skin again," she said.

He squeezed the tube, wiped the ointment on his palm, and began spreading it over her raw fingers. "Huh?"

"You're not listening, Warren."

He glanced up at Emily sheepishly. "I'm sorry—what?"

"Nothing." She inhaled sharply. "Hey, what do preachers do, anyway?"

"What do you mean?"

"What do preachers really do in between Sundays?" She smiled. "When they're not chasing vampires, that is."

"That depends on the day of the week."

"Okay—but like tomorrow. We're going to be gone all day."

"We'll be gone two days, maybe three," he said. "There may be people killed by the vampires tonight. They won't be buried immediately."

"Hey, I told you that." She flinched again as he came to a sore, stinging spot. "But don't you at least preach on Sunday?"

"The associate pastor is taking care of everything until I'm well. With Susan's death and this arm I guess they figured even a minister should get time off." He grinned at her and squeezed her palm gently with a laugh.

The sudden, blinding white flash burned like lightning up her arm and she opened her mouth in a scream that shattered every thought. "God . . . damn . . . it!"

"I'm sorry. I'm sorry." Warren gasped, his eyes big as he let go of her and moved back. "Emily—I'm sorry!"

A minute passed before the the pain receded enough to let her think, and she gritted her teeth to hold back the curses hanging on her lips. "It . . . just stung a . . . little," she finally managed to say.

He shook his head. "More like a *lot*, Emily."

She managed a shrug. "Like I said . . . little girls shouldn't" —she winced—"play with fire."

"You're a wonderful person, Emily. You're a wonderful woman."

His words rushed out in the moment, making her smile, and she turned away so that all he would see was her long and dark black hair, frizzed by its visit to the fire. She gulped while he finished medicating her hand, then let it rest beside her.

"Thank you, Warren," she whispered, avoiding his eyes. "I— I haven't been called wonderful by anyone in such a long time, not unless it was some guy trying to sweet-talk me into bed." Tears glistened in both her eyes. "No one"—she passed her gaze around the small, plain room—"no one has ever called me a *woman.*"

"I'm sure your parents—" He stopped himself quickly. "I mean, I—"

"I don't know if my parents loved me or not," she said, almost to herself. The hatred of her life swept through her, infesting her thoughts with bitter memories. "I convinced myself they didn't, so I could hate them. They never talked to me like *that,* not after I was little. But they sure let me know it when I displeased them." She looked at her gooey hands and tried to hold in the sobs that pushed into her chest. "It was almost like they thought I'd be spoiled if they showed affection to me"— her lips quivered—"so they didn't."

"They must have shown you some love," Warren interjected. "They must have shown some—"

"They didn't. Not the kind you'd recognize and expect." She raised her slick hand to wipe her eyes, but stopped short. "But they *must've* loved me, or they wouldn't have paid for my college and—" She stopped and bowed her head, letting the tears slide relentlessly down her cheeks. Warren touched her shoulder lightly, then brought his arm around her waist.

"I loved them," she blurted out, releasing the sobs. *"I loved them."*

3

The wake-up call seemed to come far too early. Warren dropped
the bright yellow receiver in its cradle after thanking the motel
operator. The dark sky outside proved the call had come at the
right time. It was three A.M., and if they left now it would be
noon before they arrived at their destination, less than six hours
before sundown. It would take time to consecrate each grave,
and neither of them knew how many there would be.

Emily turned sleepily on the other bed. "Who was that?" she
asked with a husky yawn.

"Time to rise and shine," he said grumpily, propping himself
up. The action sent a sharp searing pain to replace the dull throb
he'd grown used to. He tried to twist and take the pressure off
his hurting arm.

Emily was out of her bed and at his side quickly. "Are you
okay?"

He shifted the arm again and the sharpness disappeared as
suddenly as it had come, leaving him with a dizzy nausea. "Uh
. . . yeah. . . ." He tried to control the tremble.

"It's your arm, isn't it?"

Slowly, he lay back on the bed until the queasiness subsided.

"I think you must have rebroken it last night, Warren. When
you hit that thing it must have unset the bone." She turned on
the light to examine his dirty cast. "Don't move, okay? I don't
think you're bleeding, but we've got to be careful. Does it feel
like you've torn through the skin?"

Did it? He'd hoped the intense pain would be gone this morning. Since it wasn't, he knew he might've done himself real
damage instead of just a slight jarring. Concentrating on the
alarmed senses of that limb, he sought the sensation of wet
blood where the constricting stitches were sewn. But he hurt
too badly there even to guess. If she couldn't see any, he'd just
have to hope. There wasn't time to have his arm X-rayed and
run the risk of being put back in the hospital.

"I don't think so," he replied at last. "I'll just have to be careful. When we get back I'll have it seen to. Get four aspirins for me, okay? We've got to get going."

She frowned, then walked to the bathroom, returning a moment later with the pain reliever and a sloshing glass. Her clothes looked even more rumpled and dirty than last night, and her hair now stuck out at odd angles. She opened the plastic bottle gingerly with her gauze-covered hands and fed the tablets into his mouth. "Here." She held the glass to his lips and tipped it, spilling a little down his chin.

"Thanks." He swallowed it all. "God, you're a sight. You need some clothes to change into, Emily." He belatedly remembered that she was hurt too. "How're your hands?"

"They sting, but not as bad as last night. You don't look so great yourself."

He lay back on the pillow, yawned, and stretched his left arm to her. "If you'll help me, I think I can get up now. Just don't touch my arm."

"Okay."

A strand of her hair fell across his lips when she bent over him. Carefully and slowly, he got out of the bed.

She held on to him until he was steady on his feet. "Okay?"

"Yes." He pulled her against him, pressing into her body, then bent his head and lightly touched his lips to hers.

For a long moment they stood still, almost a part of each other, and then he moved back and released her with embarrassment. Her face was red, too, and she looked away self-consciously.

Warren smiled and touched her cheek. "You're not doing such a hot job of making me eat regularly, Emily. Let's check out and get some coffee and breakfast. I'm starving."

"At least we don't have much to pack." She smiled back.

XVII

1

By twelve-ten they were within thirty-five miles of Freeport. Warren sighed wistfully. The drive had been almost pleasant; would have been if not for his arm and the shadow of their duty. Even so, it was a relieving change of pace, and he used the time to understand Emily better, and tell her about himself. He wanted her to know him, and wanted to know her. He wanted to help with the trauma still hovering over her life.

"Almost there," Emily said. "I think the tire's going to hold."

Warren nodded. At their last stop the attendant had reminded him the back left tire was bad, recalling that day last month when Susan had asked him to have it changed. He regretted not having listened to her now more than ever. The station was busy, though, and the job would take too long now. Warren made sure the spare was up and they went on. The sun was already high.

Emily smiled. "I should've knocked on wood when I said that."

"Here." He held out one of the stakes and they both laughed; then he relaxed and watched the remaining miles go by, his heart quickening when they came to the outskirts of a small town. A dozen cars were lined up behind a traffic light at the expressway entrance.

"This is it," Emily spoke up. "If we don't get off quick we'll miss the whole place. The only thing here is the college and a processing plant. If it weren't for that there'd hardly be a thousand people living here." She turned onto the ramp, passing the stacked-up traffic going the other way. Each car seemed packed with suitcases. "The only cemetery's a couple of miles from here," she told him, "on the other side of town."

"There's a lot of people leaving."

Emily shrugged. "It's Sunday. Small-town people still take Sunday drives."

"With suitcases?"

"I don't blame them."

"No," he replied. "It may even make our job easier."

They turned onto another street, and she drove on. "God," she whispered. Only one other car was in front of them, and nothing was coming in the opposite lane. "It's like a ghost town."

"Maybe I should say grace over the whole place," he joked lamely.

But Emily stared as the empty driveways gave way to empty parking lots. "Shit," she breathed. "Do you want to go to the graveyard first?"

"No. Your house first. I wonder if they're evacuating."

She shook her head. "The newspaper I read said they wouldn't do that unless the killings went on another week, Warren. I think the people are just scared. They're leaving. A lot of them were talking about it. I wanted to leave."

An old man was walking a tiny poodle down the sidewalk—one of the few signs of life.

"My house, you said?" she asked Warren.

He nodded, hushed by the devastation and upheaval. "We'll need to make preparations before we start to work. I'll need something that will hold a good amount of water, then I'll need to ask blessing over it."

"Like at your house?"

"Yeah."

She turned the wheel awkwardly with her wrapped hands. "We have two or three pitchers in the cabinets. Dad bought them to keep orange juice and stuff in, but they never used them after I moved out—he and Mom didn't like to mix it up. They bought the bottled stuff."

"They'll be fine."

She continued down the street and then her face darkened, as though something unpleasant had stepped into the road.

"What's wrong?" he asked.

"Oh . . . not anything, really. I was wondering." She looked in the rearview mirror at a brick-and-glass tower behind them. "I just wonder if Karen's all right."

He nodded, remembering the name from their earlier conversation.

"Her name wasn't in the obituaries, but . . . I'm sure people were killed last night."

"You can call her," he suggested.

"I will." She sighed, passing a police car. "I just wish I'd told her what was going on."

"Would she have believed you?"

"I doubt it. I could have tried, though. If anything happened to her it'll be my fault."

"I don't think that's true." He shifted with discomfort and stroked her arm. "She wouldn't have listened. We're doing the only thing we can do now. You've done the best you can, Emily. We're only human beings. We make mistakes. All we can do is ask forgiveness and go on." *Susan.* He took a breath. "All we can do is try, and keep trying . . . and leave the rest to God."

"That's easy for a preacher to say." Guilt lined her face.

Those words struck Warren hard. It had once been easy, but not now. Before, he'd preached that each person had to work out his or her own salvation through the gifts God gave them. He'd told it to Susan, to Chuck, even to Carmen. But he'd been wrong, and he had failed.

"It's easy to say," he told her timidly. "It's just hard to remember. But . . . it's the truth."

She watched the street, not speaking. Warren kept the silence. Before he knew it, Emily was pulling into the driveway of a pleasant house not more than ten years old. She parked, opened her door, and got out.

A defensive distance in her eyes kept him quiet as she came around to help him to his feet. Warren watched her closely, suspecting she was dealing with her guilty memories.

She opened the front door with uneasy reluctance. At the

entrance to the front room a pool of dust and a stained fence picket blocked the way. When Emily turned back, she swallowed hard, and Warren saw unfamiliar lines etched in her forehead. She bypassed that room, her eyes carefully avoiding the dust.

"That was my Aunt Joanie," she said thickly.

Warren nodded and closed the door behind them, then followed her through the bright hall to the kitchen. Still withdrawn, she opened a lower cabinet, took out two plastic half-gallon pitchers, and filled them with tap water. When she was through, she wiped the linoleum countertop meticulously. "I'll make us something to eat."

The low unemotional tone made him go to her. "Are you okay?"

"I think so. Where do you want me to put the water?"

"Doesn't make any difference. Anywhere will be all right."

She took the pitchers to the living room. Warren followed and took the New Testament he'd found in the motel out of his coat, locating the passage he wanted with one hand. "Thanks, Emily."

She nodded mechanically, then started back to the hall.

"Emily."

She looked back with dull eyes.

"You *are* a woman. A strong woman."

Her expression remained neutral.

"I admire you."

Her face twitched and she disappeared down the hall without a word.

2

As the sun descended, they passed Emily's car where she and Ben had left it and entered the graveyard. Warren had tried to urge her to take a few minutes to clean up and change clothes. When she'd refused, he'd offered to apply more ointment to her stinging hands.

"There's not time," she'd told him, then took the tube and did it herself quickly and painfully.

Ben had said she had guts. Warren only hoped he could match her strength. He steadied the sloshing pitchers between his legs as they bumped along the narrow, twisting drive and gasped as some of the cold water splashed onto his pants. He turned up the heater, dreading the outside temperature. The car finally coasted to a halt, and Emily studied the lengthening shadows.

"That's where I first met Ben," she said, pointing across the wooded yard.

His eyes followed, and he nodded.

"I hope we can hurry," Emily said, coming around to help him out.

"Uh-huh." He gave her the pitchers hurriedly, and moved too fast as he got out. He found himself holding the door with white knuckles.

"Are you all right?"

"Yeah," he sniffed. "Yes . . . I'm okay."

"You shouldn't move so fast."

"I'm okay." The grounds were empty but for two or three people at the other end. He was glad the large graveyard was flat and visible as he peered at the naked trees, large marker-stones, and ground plaques. The cemetery was old, too, and he suspected they would have no trouble distinguishing the recent graves from the others.

"Let's do it," said Emily, an eye on her watch.

Warren felt goose bumps. "Look for the new graves. We don't have time to go over the entire place."

She pointed out a clean white tombstone nearby, the earth before it black and loose. "It shouldn't be hard at all. The grass won't grow now to cover them. We're lucky it's winter."

He nodded, his body chill from his open coat. "That's the only good thing about it right now."

"At least it's not that cold today." She led him to the grave. "A good thing, too, or you'd be blessing this place with holy *ice.*"

They both smiled, then Warren forced himself back into a serious mood. "Sprinkle some of the water over the grave," he told Emily.

She did as he asked, cupping her palm to dip it, letting the water drip from her hand to the dirt.

"Hallow this earth, Lord. Purify it and let no evil pass through it. Bless this ground, and let it imprison the evil it covers so it cannot rise. 'Greater is He that is in me than he that is in the world.' I stand on that promise, and claim Your grace as power: 'My grace is sufficient for thee, for My power is made perfect in weakness.' I claim that grace, Father, and purify this grave in the name of Christ, Whose blood was shed for me. Amen." He was quiet in momentary contemplation, then closed his Bible. "Sprinkle some more on the grave, please, Emily."

She did as asked again, hushed by his prayer, then copied the headstone's name onto a scrap of paper and followed him to look for another grave.

3

Closing the New Testament for the last time, Warren made it to a nearby tree and let it support his weight. His arm ached terribly with the afternoon's exertion, and he felt ill. "Are you sure that was the last one?"

"I'm sure." Emily walked to his side and delicately rubbed her chapped, gauze-wrapped hands against her jeans. "I checked the whole graveyard, and we've been to every one that's been dug since the grass stopped growing. You blessed them *all* in the mausoleum." She showed him a piece of paper with names on it. "I wrote them all down so we'd be sure, and checked them off. You did it, Warren."

Relief soared through him, and he watched the sun low in the sky, with a sigh. *"We* did it. You, Ben, and me."

"And God," she said unexpectedly.

He nodded tiredly.

Bending, Emily picked up the two pitchers at his feet. She

peered into the one still half-full. "Do you think we should wait and see if this really works?"

Her doubt teased Warren, and he thought of the tap water he'd prayed over to hold vampires—demons inhabiting dead bodies—down under the earth where they could do no harm to anyone. *If only my old pals back at seminary could see me now,* he thought. At one time even talking of this kind of thing would have sent him into howling laughter.

He blushed with shame.

"It'll work," he said finally in a low voice, taking her hand. "It'll work. But we'll wait to be sure we didn't miss one."

"Then what?" She brought her hand out of his and watched the setting sun.

"Just a minute." They watched the fiery orb in the evening's silence. A slow conviction that they had forgotten something and that the graves would suddenly come alive grew in his gut.

"Are you sure?" asked Emily. "What if . . . ?"

The unfinished question made him acutely aware of his doubt. Ben had been fearless in his angry faith, and without such faith the consecration would *not* work. Warren's uncertainty bulged— *he didn't know if his desire to help people gave him the strength to destroy evil.* He soundlessly recounted scriptures and held tight to their power in his own experience, striving to rebuild courage and the strength of his trust. "Yes," he told her quietly, "I'm sure."

A minute later the sun dropped behind the horizon. Emily pressed close and Warren wanted to push away the distraction her soft body brought him. He shut his eyes to offset those feelings and the growing urge to doubt.

"Warren," Emily whispered, "it's working, isn't it? There's no mist—*nothing. Nothing's moving.*"

He clenched his left fist. *And what would happen if I stopped believing?*

"Warren?"

What would happen? Uncertainty surged into him and he faced the sickly desire to throw off his responsibilities and quit fighting. To unleash himself to the dark lusts deep inside, the dark lust offered him by the traveling salesman.

The earth beneath him trembled.

A sudden vision of the ghouls arising all at once filled his inner eye. To block out the image he grabbed his cast desperately and shoved it away from his body until his mind shrieked in thoughtless agony, driving those cries through his clenched teeth. He shuddered and crumbled to his knees as Emily tried to support him, groaning shaky verses of reinforcement aloud, over and over. But he no longer knew if he was praying to hold the vampires under the frozen dirt, or for the faith he needed to bring that about—

Or to stop the horrible pain he was bringing upon himself.

"Warren . . . I really think it worked." Emily sighed, bending down to him.

He gritted his teeth, his knees stiff on the ground, letting the verses form themselves automatically as he rode the waves of pain.

"Warren?" Her soft voice comforted him. "It worked, Warren."

The verses dropped off and he opened his eyes to the dusk surrounding them. "Yes," he murmured.

She reached into his pocket to take out the aspirin. "Here," she offered, opening the bottle to feed him two of the tablets.

He swallowed with a dry throat, remembering the pitchers. "Give me a drink, too, please?"

Emily's eyes were wide. "That's—that's the holy water, Warren. You blessed it."

He smiled crookedly. "Yes. It's okay, Emily. We bless our food before we eat it, why not water?"

She raised the pitcher to his lips and smoothed back his damp hair with her other hand. "Is that something you learn at seminary?"

After two long sips he turned away from her, feeling much better.

"Now what?" she asked.

Warren let himself relax. The dusk had turned to dark night and the cemetery was silent. He had believed, and the vampires had not risen.

"Now what?" Emily asked impatiently.

A burst of pleasure came from him in laughter. "God," he murmured, and rose his eyes to the starlit sky. "God."

The pressure of her insistent nudge brought him back to himself, and he gazed affectionately at Emily. With reluctance, he remembered that their task wasn't yet over. "Now what?" he asked for her.

She nodded.

"We'll have to stay over and do this again tomorrow when those people killed last night are buried . . . for however many days it takes." That knowledge made him think of Carmen, so far away now, and renewed those worries. He looked at the stars anxiously.

"I wish you could just bless the funeral parlor."

Warren wished that too. "The police are watching the bodies too closely. Besides, I don't know if it would work."

"Neither do I," she replied. "Ben said the infection didn't take full effect until after they're buried or have the funeral ceremony. But I can still wish. . . . Okay. What will we do until then?" She shifted the bulk of the pitchers in her arms with exasperation.

Carmen. "Have you got a suggestion?" he asked.

"How about taking you to a doctor?"

The pain still inside him urged him to that decision, but he shook his head. "They'd really want to put me in a hospital now, I think," he grunted, and started to pull himself up with his left hand in hers.

"Easy." Emily reached down and helped him to his feet as gently as she could. "I'll at least take your temperature and see if I can clean you up. We'll both get cleaned up."

"It'll be a long job," he muttered.

"Then maybe you can pay me back with dinner at someplace nice? Something to get our minds off all this?"

Something to get his mind off his doubts. He felt a lethargic grin and saw the surprise it gave her, and the pleasure. At least *that* made him feel good. "I think I could handle that," he drawled.

Despite Warren's pain they walked more lightly than they'd arrived as they went back to the car, and Emily's off-key whistle proved their success.

They had won this round. Yet still he could not eliminate the nagging fear for Carmen, and the greater task looming. It dampened his exuberance, but not the self-confidence he had begun to know, or the fondness he felt for Emily.

4

Warren slept hard that night when they got back from the restaurant, and awoke late. Although he moved as fast as he felt he could, it was already after two when they reached the cemetery again. They repeated their rituals at the sight of the day's first funeral and waited stiffly for the next one to end. The last ceremony didn't begin until four-thirty, and the night's chill was already settling when they went to the recently turned dirt there, waiting until the last mourners drove away.

The minor physical exertions exhausted him, though. He gruffly vetoed Emily's desire to eat out once more, and when they got back, he struggled up the stairs to her parents' musty bedroom, kicking off his shoes with exhaustion. He sat on their bed listlessly now. He was tired, and woozy as if he had the flu.

Warren caught sight of himself in the mirror on the closet door. His eyes were bloodshot, and he had several days' growth of beard. He was beginning to look as bad as Ben had.

A light tap came from the bedroom door.

"Yes?" he grunted.

"Dinner'll be ready in about ten minutes, Warren."

"Thanks." He frowned at the pleasant note in her voice.

"Do you . . ." She seemed to read his thoughts through the closed door and suddenly sounded concerned. "Do you need help getting down the stairs?"

"I'll make it," he called.

"Okay. I've got to go check the hamburgers, Warren. Holler if you need me."

"Right." He stared at himself again, then walked to the door and went out, starting through the winding, conservative house that already looked like a besieged fortress. He passed the pictures of Emily dotting the stairway's walls and Warren saw her smile of innocence dim as she grew older in each one, becoming a melancholy adult. When he reached the bottom floor, he looked at the front door and the stakes Emily had stacked near it with a pitcher of holy water. The curtains down here were all drawn.

"What's cooking?" he asked, following the aroma that made his stomach flip-flop between acute hunger and nausea.

"Just hamburgers," she replied cheerily as he rounded the corner. "There's not a lot to choose from." Her smile faded then. "That's one reason I wanted to go out again. No one's gone shopping since Mom . . . died."

"That'll be fine," he said quickly. She'd changed into another brightly colored dress like the one she'd put on last night when they went to dinner. He snorted grumpily at her cheerful attitude, which seemed woefully out of keeping with their duties.

She smiled sympathetically. "Do you need some more aspirin?" She brought him a hamburger.

"If—if you don't mind." He sat and looked at the food.

She put two tablets beside his plate. "You need to see a doctor."

"When this is over." He swallowed the aspirin and dragged the open newspaper to his own side of the table.

She went back to fix her own plate. "They're burying four more people tomorrow. I've been doing my homework while you rested." She sat across from Warren and tapped the newspaper. "The first ceremony is at one, and the next one's not until three. The last two are late, at forty-thirty and four forty-five. The sun doesn't set until five twenty-eight."

"That's close," he said.

"No one was killed last night. At least that's a good sign." She met his eyes hopefully, then began to eat her hamburger while he picked at his, removing the onions and pickles. They ate in silence.

After Warren pushed his half-eaten meal away in the fear of losing what he had, Emily walked him into the living room and poured them each a glass of wine, then sat beside him.

Warren spread the newspaper on his lap. "God—it must be

like the Nazi death camps. Nothing but death everywhere. I didn't think of all the people that had died but hadn't been buried yet."

She nodded. "I—I guess it's lucky we decided to come when we did. I read that the governor said that if there's another murder, he'll shut down the town immediately. No one will be allowed to leave."

Warren took a tiny sip of his wine. "I'm surprised they haven't already done that." He remembered the front-page story she was referring to: it was believed that foreign—read Soviet—agents had been responsible for the numerous unexplained murders, picking victims randomly to tie up military personnel and machinery. Investigations were proceeding under the guiding hand of both the FBI and CIA. The necessary steps had already been taken to initiate a complete quarantine.

"I'm just glad those government people didn't want to hold up these last burials for later in the week."

Warren contemplated moodily the authorities' explanations and reaction to the disaster. It was almost as if they knew the true causes, almost as if they were trying to cover them up.

"Do you want to watch TV?" Emily asked him.

He glanced at her, trying to rid himself of his growing paranoia. "I thought your friend Karen wanted to see you."

"She did. Her boyfriend was one of the people who died the night before we came here. Thank God he wasn't from out of town. We were lucky there, too, Warren. All but one of the students who were killed lived here and are being buried here, and the one from out of state is going to be cremated. Karen's boyfriend is going to be buried tomorrow. She wanted me to go to the funeral with her." Emily bit a fingernail. "I told her I couldn't because I was leaving town again tonight. It—it makes me feel guilty, since she was so much help to me when Mom died, but if I went with her, I couldn't help you, and we wouldn't get the graves consecrated." She stared blankly at the wall. "She'll be the first one he'll come after."

"That seems to be the way of it."

Emily twitched uncomfortably. "I'll have to make it up to her when this is over with, but—but I'm kind of glad I can stay with you tonight." She laid her hand on his cast carefully, her fingers grazing his. "Did you try to call and find out how Carmen was?"

He shook his head glumly and had another sip of wine, hoping its effect would nullify the ache in his arm and soul.

"You might feel better if you checked on her," Emily went on, then laughed with a hollow pleasantness. "The way you worry about her it's almost like you're in love with—"

"I'm not!" He turned away, pulling his cast back painfully. He thought of Susan, and of how he'd spent the last nights of her life with Carmen instead of her.

"Warren?"

"What do you want?"

Her face clouded and she closed her mouth. "This is not some kind of a damn *game,* Emily!"

"I . . ." She looked crushed.

She looked *humiliated.*

Warren gasped; the sight of her burned him with the instant awareness of his harsh misjudgment. He'd tried hard to bring her out of the deep-rooted guilt feelings she battled with on their drive here. He'd urged her to put the past behind her and to find an inner happiness that would spread out to others, suggesting that as a means by which she might work her way out of depression.

And now he was chastising her for her success! It froze his heart as he understood, and he knew he was acting the same way toward her as he had acted toward Susan when she lost her fingers.

"I'm sorry, Emily," he said as honestly as he could, shrinking from the emptiness draining his soul.

She stood up calmly, but his hard words clung to her. She looked at her feet. Her hands were gripped together at her waist.

Shame mingled with self-bitterness made him put down his glass and push himself to his feet with more difficulty than he'd had since leaving the hospital. "Emily, I'm sorry."

Her eyes stayed on the floor, and he knew then that his impression of her as a woman was far off base. She was trying, but deep inside she was still a girl—more so than many her age. She was a girl with an insatiable need to be liked and loved—to be accepted. He put his arm around her. He *was* sorry.

"I'll go pack so we can be ready to leave," she murmured, slipping away at his touch. She wouldn't look at him.

"Emily," he pleaded.

"Don't, Warren."

She disappeared into the hall and out of his sight. The hurt of her expression stayed with him, though, and stung him. Even if he had once been an ace theologian and was becoming an ace at fighting one form of evil, he was failing in his combat with another. He was failing as a human being.

XVIII

1

They hardly talked. After Emily finished packing, she sat down distantly to read a psychology book, and Warren stayed timidly on the other side of the room. They both went to bed early and said absolutely nothing the next morning during breakfast. Warren knew it wouldn't do any good to apologize again. She wasn't listening.

After two they drove to the cemetery for the last time and consecrated the newly covered ground where the day's first burial had taken place an hour earlier. They waited for the next one at three, which was blessedly short, consecrating it after the minister, who lingered and studied them for several minutes, had finally left.

"Only two more," Warren said as the time passed four o'clock.

Emily nodded.

The first service lasted only fifteen minutes, but the mourners were still tarrying at its side when the final funeral began across the yard. Warren waited with Emily before the graves of her parents and moved his eyes from one knot of people to the other, seeing the unknowing colleague who'd stared at them earlier, presiding once more at the last ceremony. He tugged Emily behind a big oak tree and they kept out of sight this time. It was four fifty-five.

At five-fifteen the last burial was finished, and the small group drifted away to their cars while the casket was lowered into the earth and covered. A pair of women still waited at the other grave, and Warren nudged Emily. She stared at the two stragglers.

It was thirteen minutes until sunset.

"What is it?" he asked.

"Karen's there," she whispered. "I think that other woman's her mother."

Karen knelt as her companion took her arm and tried to urge her back up. She was shaking her head, then pulled fiercely away with a scream that carried over the distance.

Emily bit a fingernail.

Warren put his hand on her shoulder. "Come on," he said. "We'll take care of the other and do that one last."

"I think they were going to get married," Emily said softly.

"Come on!" He released her and marched heavily across the ground alone, then heard her hurrying to catch up.

"I'm sorry," she explained, "I just wanted to try to help."

"You *are* helping her," came his tight words, "but we've got to hurry! We have to stop them *all* today, or there'll be more tomorrow!"

"Yes," she whispered.

The sun had met the ground when they finished and started back. Warren saw Emily's friend in a station wagon winding down the narrow road to the exit. He looked for the gravediggers who would lower the coffin and complete the burial, but the sacred rite was already done. "Hurry," he snapped, pushing his own stride. Emily kept up with him, sloshing the remaining water in the single pitcher they had brought.

"Warren! Watch—"

It was all Warren heard before his toes exploded in pain when they caught the granite slab. He pitched forward and crashed into the dry earth. His broken arm jammed up into his belly and red agony attacked in the crushing wrench. He gagged, sour spit forcing its way through his clenched teeth, the dead yellow grass fogging before his eyes and turning black. He blinked furiously, gasping, his good arm working futilely against the ground.

An anguished howl exploded from his lungs and soul.

"Warren!"

He opened his eyes to the fading light, feeling Emily's hands slide around him. There was still time.

He put down his good elbow and pushed with it, nearly blacking out once more. Cold fingers touched his heart, it pumped erratically and he gagged, unable to give force to the moaning screams that stung his lips.

"Warren," Emily cried, "the sun! We've got—"

With her help he struggled to his feet, and he clung to her, swaying from side to side. Emily grunted with his weight, and they lurched ahead to a gravestone for support. "Where's the holy water?" he rasped dryly, nearly gagging in his stomach's sour surge.

She braced him over the waist-high stone and hurried back, retrieving the pitcher. "Come on!" she called.

He tried to hold up his head, staring at the silver casket beyond the miles of gravestones on the downward slope. His heart thumped.

They wouldn't make it.

The single remaining vampire here would melt into the darkness, beginning the evil cycle all over again. Freeport would be closed down, and St. Louis would be dying before they returned. There would be no end to the evil.

"Warren, help me!"

Their eyes met, and he couldn't contain the savage defeat. "I can't do it."

She looked at the disappearing orange glow behind the trees, then across the yard. "We've got to, Warren—*we've got to keep Karen safe!*" She started toward him, then hesitated with a quick, frightened breath. "I'll be back," she gasped, running with the pitcher to the open grave.

Warren watched her pass through the growing shadows, groping for the strength to call her back. His shaky fingers dragged at the smooth stone when she stopped at the pile of dirt and hurried to sprinkle the water over the shiny metal coffin. Then he blinked. Even the sun's faint glimmers were gone! His heart thudded grotesquely and he tried to call to her again, but only a feeble yelp escaped his lips.

Mist seeped through the air above the coffin, bare inches from Emily, assuming a man's shape. Warren tensed, praying for her desperately through his pain, then saw the gaunt vampire materialize almost upon her.

"Oh, God!" he moaned. It was too late—too late! A horrid vision of Susan's laughing, icy face at this final victory brushed his thoughts, and he struggled to overcome the weakness in his legs. But one step brought him to his knees. He prayed desperately, then stopped short in gaping surprise.

Emily's lips moved faintly, and she threw the pure water at the bony hands stretching out for her. The lurching shape faltered, then met the clear liquid in a collision that flashed a blinding white. The vampire jerked, exploding into a new mist of steam with a tormented wail that tore through the twilight's peace. Warren tried hard to believe in the sanctified water's power over it. The billowing essence faded into the dusk.

Emily dropped the pitcher and walked slowly back up the slope.

"Are you okay?" she asked, reaching out to him.

Her arms supported him, and he relaxed into them. "Are you?"

"It's destroyed," she said thinly.

"Yes, I'm glad you were able to keep your head."

Her eyes searched him carefully, and he felt her tremble as she helped him to the car. He clenched his teeth as she squeezed him into the passenger seat. They'd done it! Emily had physically doused the evil with the water he'd blessed, and his desiccated faith had given it enough power. They'd done it. "It's over, here."

She smiled at him politely, and the car lurched ahead.

Though his arm burned, he felt better now. Much better. "Emily?" he pleaded, wanting to get things right between them, to get her right. He wanted her to go back with him—especially now. The knowledge of the fire he'd have to pass through alone frightened him, and he didn't want to face it knowing he'd failed her. If he left her with her unsolved problems, she might be up against an unknown greater than his. He knew she wouldn't be able to handle herself alone for long. Looking at the side of her face, he tried to see under the unemotional mask that dragged at the corners of her lips. "Emily?" he said again.

"What is it?"

"Will you come back with me, Emily?"

For a very long minute she was silent, facing the empty street and dark homes, then nodded. "I—I'll have to. I'm afraid to stay."

"It's safe now."

"I'm afraid to be alone, damn it!" She waved her hand at the unpopulated driveways leading to silent houses.

He touched her leg. "I'm glad you want to come, Emily. I'll need you."

She shook her head. "You don't mean that, Warren. If you hadn't fallen, I'd just have been the one to carry the water for you, that's all. You don't need me. You just need *someone*—someone to act as your arms and legs." She stepped on the gas, making the motor roar. "I just want to prove myself to you. I want to prove myself to me."

"You have, Em—"

"No!" she cried out, swerving the car in her anger. "Not until you need *me*!" All at once she lowered her voice: "What I want is to have someone need me—*me*. I want someone to need me for myself . . . and what I am."

Struggling, Warren tried to fathom her thoughts. It was as though she wanted him to believe that she'd destroyed the vampire through her own belief. Could that be? Could her faith have done it rather than his?

Long minutes passed and she turned the car, drove past too many darkened houses, and then turned again, this time into her driveway. She parked and sat silently.

"I—I accept you, Emily."

Her taut face softened and she shook her head. "You don't, Warren. You don't yet. But if I try hard enough, maybe you will." She helped him inside, walking him to the divan to rest.

"I'm going to bring our things out to the car," she told him.

Warren watched her go, laying his head back on the cushion. His head throbbed numbly and he didn't want to think—especially not about what they were going back to. It would be so good just to forget this and go on with life somewhere untouched by the vampire's vile shroud.

But where would that be? What place had been infected before this town? The victims would die and rise up as vampires in their own right unless the traveling vampire was destroyed first.

Exhaustion tried to limit his thoughts, but Warren could not let them go. He drifted in those questions that would not be avoided. He was afraid of their answers, for he knew that if he found them, he could not live with them.

How long had the salesman been peddling his wares?

How many others existed like him?

2

Freeport was far behind them, but their experiences there hung over every plan they made as Emily drove. They would find someplace to stay first so Warren could try to regain his faded strength and call the hospital to see how Carmen was. Somehow they had to learn the vampire's hiding place, and then maybe they could go to it during the daylight to enact the consecration they both knew now by heart.

"What are you going to do when this is over, Warren?"

He squinted at the headlights coming toward them across the central barrier of the highway. The words were Emily's first real attempt at conversation since his harsh words to her. Perhaps it was good that she felt responsible for the destruction of that last vampire. "I'll get this arm fixed first." He chuckled.

"How's it feeling?"

"Now it only hurts when I breathe."

She allowed a smile, then was serious. "With that fever you have, you've probably got an infection."

"I'm okay. What are you going to do?"

A faraway look came into her eyes. "I don't know. I don't know what I *can* do until this is finished. Things that used to be so important aren't." She flushed, settling deep in the creaking seat. "I can't see things the same way I did. I've learned a lot about myself . . . and about others."

"So have I."

She smiled at him again, but it was only a ghost of her previous smiles. A seriousness marred her youth. Her happiness, vibrant only last night, before he'd destroyed it, seemed gone forever.

"I'm sorry about last night," she was continuing. "I didn't mean to make you so upset."

"It's okay."

She shook her head. "No. I knew you were worrying about that woman, Carmen. I just . . ." She took her hands off the steering wheel and shook them.

Warren blushed. He felt her pain as well as his own and knew hers was more horribly far reaching. And he had helped inflict it on her, bringing to a head the sense of unworthiness she'd been battling so fiercely.

As he had done to Susan.

3

The tire was low when they stopped for gas. Warren limped to touch it when he returned from the rest room and groaned bitterly at this new delay. It resurrected his worry for Carmen, and that worry was proof that he was defeated in his faith, that she was no longer under its protection.

"Can you change it?" he asked the serviceman at another pump, furious with his useless arm. He couldn't begin to ignore the recurrent stabs it brought now.

The greasy attendant chewed a plug and spat at Warren's feet. "Shit, man," he cracked. "I'm running this damn hellhole myself tonight. I gotta full service and fix a cracked radiator in my garage. Helluva lot more money in that."

As Emily walked around the concrete-block station toward him, Warren fished out his wallet and counted the remaining bills. "I'll pay you—"

The man drew his heavy coat closer and grinned. "Tell you what. You just rest a spell inside and I'll get to you soon as I take care of the radiator."

"What's wrong?" Emily asked. She shivered, rubbing her hands together briskly.

"What's not?" He sighed. "This tire might go out on us down the road."

"Ain't that difficult to change a tire," chuckled the serviceman as he stopped pumping gas and walked back to his building with a credit card.

Emily stared after him coldly. "This man is *sick!*" she called back angrily, then looked at Warren with stiff pride showing in her raised eyebrows. "This is one thing I *can* do," she told him. She helped him move to the side of the car and opened the trunk to take out the jack, then the spare. Its tread was thin and it wasn't in much better shape.

"I wish I'd thought to have this done at the filling station *yesterday.*"

"I can do it," Emily repeated testily. She worked quickly, and they were on the road in half an hour. But in that half hour Warren's uncertainty overtook him until he could think of nothing else. He thought of Carmen wistfully, remembering the quiet beauty that had nearly seduced him. It hurt him that the words he'd spoken to her in the hospital and his prayers for her sake were useless. He'd failed her and could add her name to the lengthening list that already included Susan . . . and Emily.

He'd failed himself.

4

Warren was barely able to stand when they stopped at the crumbling motel in St. Louis where Ben had stayed. It was seven A.M. Forcing himself to walk inside with her, Warren leaned silently on the scarred front desk while Emily got them a room, and then handed over his credit card to the gum-chewing desk girl's raised eyebrows. He felt too ill to think, signed the receipt with an illegible scrawl, and pocketed the room key. Emily led him back to the car. Warren could barely put one foot after the other, and sank back into the car with relief. He wanted to just sit there as he had since they'd left the service station, and try to regain the strength that was slipping away faster and faster. When the car began to move again, he closed his eyes to the rising sun and laid his head back on the headrest with relief, wanting to sleep.

But the car stopped almost immediately, sliding between a scratched, unpainted pickup and a dented station wagon on the single-story motel's northern side. Warren blinked in the light of pink dawn, feeling searing needles as Emily pulled him out of the cab. Forcing back the hot nightmares that had drained his attempts at sleep while they were driving, he tried to keep in step with her.

"I'll get you inside, Warren," she said uncertainly, "then I'll get our things in. You need to lie down and rest."

"Okay," he mumbled, slumping into her as she forced him ahead. The endless hours in the car had left him more weak and exhausted than when they'd started out. His forehead burned with increasing fever.

"Just a second." She unlocked the numbered door and pushed him in. He tried to help but could only moan as she dragged him to the tiny discolored bed. He felt the squishy pillow under his pounding head with a relieved sigh, but red pressure crushed his thoughts.

"You need a doctor, Warren," she said.

He shook his head, feeling it with awful exaggeration. "I've got to call"—he tried to pull up, reaching for the phone on the end table with a shaking hand—"I've got to find out how Carmen is."

"I'll do it," she insisted, pressing him back down and setting the phone on the lumpy bed. "Do you know the number?"

Gasping in difficult concentration, he pressed the lighted buttons clumsily. She put the receiver to his ear. "Thanks," he said, then waved her back. "I'm okay."

"I'll bring the stuff in," Emily murmured, unable to hide her distress. She gave him a long look and went back to the door.

The earpiece was cool against his face and Warren sighed in the faint pleasure, then listened to the familiar ring.

"Riverview Hospital," a professional unisexual voice answered after the third ring.

"Yes. I wanted to check on one of your patients—a Carmen Richison. I can't remember . . . the room number."

"Just a moment, sir," replied the voice, and he held his breath. Ice spilled into his guts and shivered up his backbone. He forced his breath.

"I'm sorry, sir. Carmen Richison passed away two nights ago."

"What?" The agony of the truth mixed with his fears and his pain. Vertigo rushed over him, and he clawed the phone with a slippery hand, cold sweat covering him. "Wh-when?" he gasped.

"Two nights ago, sir. I don't have the exact information. You'd have to—"

"What—what about the funeral arrangements?" he burst out anxiously, his throat raw.

"I don't know anything about them, sir. You'd have to find that out from one of the relatives."

He dropped the receiver. The chill inside him grew and grew, its tendrils enveloping his ragged soul. *Carmen was dead.*

"Warren?" Emily said. "Are you all right?"

He found her through the dimness of his vision and shook with shame. Carmen was dead. Dead two days! His faith had never protected her. He felt the hot tears and cried out. *He had no faith!* And yet he planned to go out and take on the fiendish demon that was devouring the souls of so many. *And Emily would be brought down with him.*

"Is she—"

He howled the pent-up anguish and sank into the mattress, unable to speak . . . unable to breathe . . . and slipped into hellish darkness.

XIX

1

The damp cloth on his forehead brought Warren to a sensitive awareness, and he slid his eyelids open to the dim light. Memories darted back and forth, fading slowly into the outlines of the strange, unknown room. He felt his loss and moaned. "Carmen's dead," he heard his own unsteady voice say. Ben's desperate motive had drawn Carmen more deeply into this, but it was *his* own failure that brought her destruction. The totality of his life's work burned with futility: he had withdrawn from Susan to advise Carmen, and now, Carmen was dead.

"Are you all right?"

He slid his face along the sheet until he saw Emily seated beside him, a dripping white washcloth in her hand. She laid it over him again, and he flinched at its cold.

"Warren?"

The far wall was spiderwebbed with cracks. "Carmen's dead," he said again.

"I know. You've been saying that. You've been saying it over and over." She furrowed her brows. "How're you feeling?"

"I . . . hurt," he told her quietly.

"You need a doctor."

Hopelessness weighed inside him . . . and he was tired. So tired.

"I'm going to get help."

He tried to think of something he could do, but it was all over.

His limbs ached so stiffly, he couldn't even move. With the growing understanding of his limitations, the long drive had torn away every feeling of victory. *They could not win.* He was sick —very sick, and very tired of fighting. Carmen was dead because of him. She would become a life-sucking ghoul now, because he hadn't protected her. Because he had failed.

Failed.

Emily picked up the phone and dialed. "I have to get you to a hospital, Warren."

The words sank in slowly. *Hospital.* Hope tried to rise against the painful throbs. The doctors would repair him and nurture him until he was strong again, able to deal with what had happened. It would give him time to rebuild the faith he'd let slip away. When he got out they could— He closed his eyes and saw a world stricken as he convalesced, the streets of St. Louis as empty and deserted as in the small town they'd left.

"Yes," Emily was saying. "Can you give me the emergency number for an ambulance?"

"No!" he shouted.

She stared at him.

"No" he repeated hoarsely, driving his hand to break the phone's connection.

"Warren." She tried to make him lie still, the panic alive in her eyes. "Warren—"

"No doctor." He gasped. "I'll rest tonight. Tomorrow I'll be better." He let go of the tense adrenaline and felt the sticky dampness of the bed under his shoulders. "Aspirin," he breathed.

"But what if you're *not* better?" She got up with a wretched grimace.

He grabbed her hand. "Please, get the aspirin."

She went to the bathroom, and he tried to keep her in focus. She came back a few moments later with a glass and took the plastic bottle from his coat.

She propped him up, letting him take each pill from her open hand. He knew he *had* to get better. There was no time left.

"But if—"

"We'll see." She eased him back and he closed his eyes in misery. His thoughts roamed and buckled; he fell into a stupor.

His mind was flying apart and back together in the red tingling of pressure. Warren slept, drifting in and out of consciousness until he didn't know which was which. He cringed in that subconscious solitude as the hell of his nightmares loomed ever nearer, hotter. He saw the evil salesman laughing at him, filling his soul and the world with vampires that preached dark, evil sermons of decadence and lust.

Your own God has let you fail, preacher. The thought-words dripped in his mind. *Your feeble victories buy only the short moments you have lost already. Your God has victimized you once more in the span of your short life! I have centuries to overcome your tiresome meddling. Your life is so short and grows shorter each second. You have failed Him too! He created you to fail; he gave you these lusts you fight and He laughs as you battle them. You are merely His entertainment.*

"No . . ."Warren whimpered, feeling the truths he was burdened with overwhelm him.

He *had* failed. His attempts to help others were never enough, only intellectual dialogues ignorant of human emotions. He cared, but kept himself from showing that concern in his own personal life. He could tell others how to act . . .

But he couldn't show them. He couldn't even let himself sympathize—and he knew he was guilty of every sin he'd condemned in others!

"No!" he cried out, wanting to deny the accusations. He jerked up dizzily, dazed by the shadows of his restless sleep. He squinted in the fading light from the windows and knew he'd slept the day away. It was becoming dark.

Dark. It crawled over him with grim fascination, making him purposeless: Carmen was gone and beyond protection. The endless struggle loomed, barely diminished—but he was much weaker. The world around him was growing darker by the minute, imitating the heaviness in his soul.

The vampire was right. He was living on borrowed time, and it was not enough.

It was too late, despite his every effort. His works had been nullified by his physical limitations and spiritual infidelity, leaving him in the solitude of his own bleak abyss. Struggling to sit up, he tried to focus on the fuzzy room. "Emily?" he whispered, wanting someone—*anyone.* Then he saw the scrap of paper on his chest. When he touched it, it fell away and he watched it float away with sudden fear—knowing she had left him too.

Emily was not there.

Straining his eyes in the dim shadows of the ancient, musty room, he was more alone than he had ever been.

He was alone with his horrid betrayals. He'd enshrined himself falsely, bringing down those around him, elevating his mission of love and sacrifice above love itself. He could not even overcome the evil within *himself.* Then, as the tears were dripping down his burning cheeks, he heard the light tapping.

He stared, feeling the eerie cold of that sound. The tapping grew louder inside his thrashing brain. "Come in," he heard his own voice say, unbidden.

"It's locked, Warren," came the muffled, husky voice.

He pushed himself to edge of the bed in the sudden hope that it *was* Emily, and that she had only left to get something to eat, but the tone stirred him uneasily as he slid off the mattress, and he knew better. His legs shook with each faltering step, and only an inner fervency impelled him to the door. When he got there, though, his hand hesitated in heavy reluctance.

But he wanted to open it. Loneliness burned with his fear. He willed his hand upward, to the knob; closed his fingers around it.

"Warren, I want *you.*"

At that last moment he felt lust's saturation and sinister promise in the whispered words and almost stopped. But in his loss of meaning he wanted the lure of that dark tone, and knew that want and his failure proved him deserving of this fate.

The door opened and he staggered back with it, face-to-face with his dreams, with a beauty more potent than he'd ever known, with a raw sexuality that overcame every warning of his soul.

Carmen floated fluidly through the door and bolted it, her long gown clinging tightly to rounded hips. She giggled, majestically removing her wrap to firm, full breasts, erect nipples poised under the tight silk. He reached toward her, admiring her perfect color and alluring build, compelled by her flawless, dainty face. Her features relaxed in tender anxiousness, and she paused with a smile of expectation. Warren gasped, knowing that she was here to surrender herself to him completely and enact the fantasy hidden in his heart for so long.

Without a word she pressed her lovely cool skin to his, draining his pain magically. The lust he had refused guiltily became unbearable and he pushed forward to meet her lips with a frantic kiss. Then, as one, they slid together to the bed and he let her press him onto it, their tongues still together. His fingers were trembling on her shoulders when she pulled away leisurely and began to loosen his clothing. He struggled back into the embrace that would unite them and tear him out of the awful solitude. He yearned for that moment, reveling in her touch—forgetting everything but her—groping as she lifted her gown and lay above him, grinding her naked, downy flesh over his, guiding him, opening to his straining lust. Pushing desperately, he felt her moist power surround him, and then the incredible release he'd gone so long without.

He sighed.

Carmen stroked her fingernails delicately across his scrotum. "You've imprisoned yourself, Warren. You locked yourself away and then threw away the key. You denied me, but you were only denying yourself." Her voice was soft. "But I've always wanted you, Warren. You've always wanted me, though you didn't dare admit to it . . . even to yourself. You made yourself into the God you worship, and tried to make us all into the creatures you wanted us to be." Her tongue slithered over his cheek, then she drifted down his body, her long hair caressing his hips. "You killed Susan . . . then you killed Chuck . . . and even Ben Dixon." Her tongue intrigued and urged his revival, though he was barely over the last ecstasy that battled to overcome the crushing humiliation of her words. Her temptation made him arch his back and push to give her what she craved—what *he* craved. Her hot breath aroused him to new strength and he shuddered with urgent desire.

Her lips closed smoothly around him and he knew the wondrous ecstasy of her tongue's earnest manipulation. He breathed hard, pulling her face closer and pushing inside her throat as far as he could—*and felt his groin explode into sudden, excruciating fire that shredded his veins and tore through his soul.* He howled with shock at the piercing pain as it drove out the

shadowy and superficial pleasure, and knew the ghastly realization of his self being ripped from his body, sucked out of him
with his very blood, the hot red of it smearing Carmen's dead
lips. In that terrible instant she became a horrid, pale corpse,
her pallid flesh taut over rigid bones that creaked their grating
dryness. Filmy yellow eyes bulged in shadowed sockets, and
her flabby, shriveling breasts sagged grotesquely in death.

She laughed with vulgar disdain. "But you're not God, Warren. You're just a lonely, whimpering fool!"

Warren howled again, screaming into the licking and gurgling
as Carmen fed on his blood, *his life*. Wanton evil flowed in and
he felt as though all his insides were being shredded, replaced
with scalding acid.

And then, without warning, it stopped. She raised her head,
his blood drooling thickly from her dark, wet teeth. Her vicious
eyes expressed a fury greater and more horrible than even her
lust. "You . . . are not ready . . . yet." Carmen gurgled, dribbling the warm blood and then catching it with her tongue before it ran down her chin. *"You are not mine yet!"*

He sighed, relief and regret tangling inside him. He wanted
the evil joy he'd begun, yet the disintegrating harness of past
hopes she'd tried to dismantle inside him kept him from calling
her back. *He could not beg her to finish with him.* Drifting fog
filled his head and paralyzed him between the two struggling
goals of his life. He could only gasp his hunger.

"Perhaps tomorrow," she angrily taunted, moving off the
mattress and standing beside the bed as a lover, regaining completely the beauty she had entered with. "Yes"—she smiled,
exposing her terrible stained teeth—"perhaps tomorrow you
will be worthy, and we can unite as we both always wanted—as
we couldn't in life."

She turned away and he tried to reach out after her but was
instantly crushed by the agony flowing back into his arm and the
new sharp throb from his bleeding abdomen. His nerves disintegrated under the force of his pain, and the evil inside him
merged with the shadows of life and death fighting for him.
Among the violent twistings, a small spark struggled to remain,

but he could not move against it or for it in his exhaustion, could only fall away from that battle into the misty darkness of sleep and enter willingly, praying he wouldn't awaken.

2

Standing behind a huge woman bundled in an overcoat that made her yet larger, Emily waited anxiously. It had been far too long since she'd eaten. The hamburgers and fries she was waiting to order smelled so good, they almost made her sick. She looked back over her shoulder into the night.

Warren was alone.

Alone.

And though she was only separated from him by the two-lane street and could see the motel's neon sign through the restaurant windows, she felt alone too. Even more than when watching his sleeping, sweating body in their room while he tossed and turned and moaned words that were indiscernible fragments of the fever that had been throttling him more and more viciously these past hours. Time and again she had tried to pick up the phone to call an ambulance, but each time the sound of her voice seeking help had stirred him back to sanity. He insisted that they must go on and he must stay free.

The glass door beyond the empty tables opened then and a man with two noisy children pushed in, shivering and rubbing his hands as he stopped behind Emily. He smiled dismally at her and sniffed, then wiped his red nose, watching his boy and girl scamper to a video game at the far side of the big room.

"Colder than hell out there," he muttered.

A louder sniff came from Emily's other side and she glanced at the big woman, who narrowed her eyes at him, extending her criticism to Emily too. The woman took her food and carried it off to a far corner, sitting by herself to eat with her back to the room.

Alone.

"What can I get you?" asked the teenager, wiping the grease on his hand over the emblazoned Wendy's emblem on his striped shirt.

"A hamburger," she whispered, rebelling at the emptiness Warren's anger had drilled into her. He had attacked her verbally and painfully, just like Mom and Dad, and she had held tight to the familiarity of that hostility, holding it against him.

It had made her past swing close, and she wanted to hate him. The thought made her remember when Ben had killed Dad. Hate.

At her table in the corner the woman crumpled her wrappers purposefully into a tight ball.

"Wait!" Emily called out, leaning over the wide linoleum counter.

The teenager glanced up, brushing a long blond lock back under his cap.

"Two—two hamburgers; make one a double," she told him, her hunger increasing as she said it.

"Two?" He grinned. "For a little girl like you?"

Emily smiled. "I've got a very hungry friend."

3

"Oh my God!"

Warren awoke with a labored gasp as the sensation of his arm overturned his other senses, then disappeared into the grisly tumult of his soul.

Emily dropped the paper sack she was carrying and ran to him. *"Warren! Why— What . . . can I do?"* She stared at him with horror.

He looked down weakly at the torn flesh of his lower stomach and cringed at the evil festering there, then was overtaken by the foulest pleasure—the destruction of his old life and the

promise of the new one he'd seen in Carmen, the promise of a
power that could bring him away from desolation and into the
total fulfillment of lusts he'd never even imagined: the consumption of another's life and blood.

His eyes were hungry for Emily; he longed for her taste and
youth. *Her innocence.* He wanted her, and reached out to her
shirt impulsively, pulling it away from her pink, naked flesh.

"No!" She slapped uncertainly at his hand and tried to pull
away.

Laughter welled in him, and he wrapped his fingers in the
material insistently, then tugged.

"No!" she screamed, and this time tore from his grasp with
anger. "Warren, no." She staggered back, tears shining in her
eyes, and at last, her love and fear for him drilled through his
despairing need, proving itself as she held out her trembling
hands to touch him. Her touch ran deep, breaking through the
evil surrounding what he once had been, reaching the love and
goodness still breathing inside him.

"Warren," she said, "please. . . ."

He fastened to the shrinking spirit he still possessed. "Emily," he managed weakly.

She touched him with frightened caution. "What happened?"

"Carmen." He gasped.

"Oh, how could you!" she blurted, pressing herself tight
against him until her familiar scent stung the evil thoughts trying
to reclaim him. "Oh, God."

The anger in her words drooped with the fear etched in her
forehead. Her concern added to his flickering strength, helping
to break the evil spell. With a slow understanding he stared at
the blood trickling onto the sheet. He had failed again and again,
but she was his final chance to be the man he pretended he was.
Despite everything she had come back. He was not alone. But
without him she *would* be alone against all this. *Alone.* He shuddered, understanding that hell too completely. "Emily . . .
you've got help me . . . got to stop the blood. We've got to
stop them . . . we *must* stop them *tonight*!"

She pulled back from him. "How can you do it?"

He raised his torso awkwardly, rolling to the edge of the mattress that tried to suck him back into its wheedling defeat. He

grabbed the sheet, dragging himself up to thrust his legs over the side, and panted, drooling thick spit down onto his wound.

"Bandage me," he ordered.

Gritting her teeth, Emily found a towel and mopped up the blood. She threw it aside with distaste and went back to the bathroom, returning to him with a clean towel and her purse. She took a small bottle of peroxide from the handbag and sprinkled it over his tingling wound, curling her lips.

But he could barely feel the clear liquid. "The—the holy water . . . we brought back," he rasped, shaking. The ghastly throbs bit deep . . . and deeper . . . into his soul.

Her face flickered with hope, and she went to a sack in the middle of the floor, taking out the almost empty pitcher. "There's a little," she breathed.

"Pour it on the wound"—he gasped—"and a little into my mouth." She did as he asked quickly while he shivered in an uncontrollable vertigo of agony. He forced his mouth open and felt the trickle of scalding purity spill past his tongue, gagging him. Slime boiled up from his butchered skin. The flesh stretched magically to repair itself in the healing sanctification. He coughed, blacking out as his spirit was torn between the forces inside him.

It seemed that hours passed in that subconscious struggle, but when he opened his eyes, he found himself still sitting on the bed, feeling as clean as when he was the boy his mother bathed in the tub. The world he saw around him in the suddenly bright motel room was sharp edged and new; Emily a bright, central light.

The magic brought him back—brought back the semblance of what he'd been—though it was barely enough. The evil will fought to contradict him and he tasted its bitter malevolence still, through the sweet freedom. Some part of him cried out, shrinking with his disappearing wound.

Emily covered his nakedness with a towel and brought water and the bottle of aspirin. He held out his hand, felt the tablets as they dropped. Four of them. He brought them to his lips and chewed them sourly, swallowing with the cool water she gave him. He knew it wouldn't be enough.

"Help me . . . stand. . . ." He dropped the glass to take

her hands. He had to move now, to find Carmen and destroy what she'd become to save himself—for Emily. Only his redemption would enable him to face their final nemesis—the demon that had begun it all.

The traveling salesman.

4

"You don't dare face her, Warren."

Opening his eyes, he looked at Emily across the car seat. She seemed far away to his distorted vision and he blinked to bring her into focus. "I have to," he murmured, feeling almost beyond fear now, but remembering. He studied her drawn face and knew that much of the worry expressed was for his sake—for him.

"I can do it," Emily volunteered slowly. "If you don't kill her, Warren"—she crushed the steering wheel in her fingers—"if you fail, you'll be one of them!"

Her soft words were like hammers to his aching head. "If I don't try, I'll be one them," he growled. "I'll be worse off than Ben was . . . and she will come for me no matter where we go. She—they—will come for you too. They can find us through me."

Emily looked back to the road. They had already discussed the terrible heightened sense Carmen's attack, only partially dissolved by Emily's action, had brought him. But Warren kept his other inner feelings a secret. His soul was bound to Carmen's by their unholy union, the damned blood marriage he had willingly taken part in. He could not help but sense his evil partner's presence.

"Are we getting closer?"

Warren closed his eyes again, letting the vile consummation bring his soul to Carmen. It made him wince, remembering her astride him on the motel bed as he wanted her and gave himself to her in useless despair. He reached out to Carmen on that supernatural plane they were joined in, then choked as she passed through him—and withdrew. The terror of that brief meeting opened his eyes wide, and he winced at his own panting breath. "She's near. . . ."

Emily slowed down and put her hand on his.

He shook his head, unsteady with weakness. "We must hurry."

"Which way, then?"

Her trusting voice burned his ears with shame. She relied on him even now. He shut his eyes and forced himself to search the blot of entrenched sickness. "Turn right at this street," he managed to gasp, guiding her with an outstretched hand.

Emily steered under his direction as the surges in his soul grew more virulent, threatening the relative cleansing he'd received. His thoughts were intercepted more and more by the strange and elusive urges of the hot lust and decadent hope Carmen awakened throughout his traitorous mind. They dragged at him through the evil coupling of their souls, reaching into his thoughts with her own single-minded hunger.

But that induction into darkness had begun to show him the plans against them. The fearsome link showed him how he, Emily, and Ben had been watched minutely as they were probed for weakness on that dark level inside them all—the darkness each man hid from himself that tied him to evil. It was a tie that left them open for observation and attack. It had calculated Warren's reaction to Carmen and sent her—it—to destroy him.

The bent paths of his mind knew this yet couldn't resist. Only the slight purity remaining was unknown to their enemy, and that slim advantage was scarcely a match for all that was arrayed against them. Although hope was all he had, there was precious little of it. His wounds—both from Carmen's bite and those he had inflicted in his own spirit these past years—stood tall against him.

"How close now?" whispered Emily's voice.

Warren withdrew into himself again to detect Carmen's proximity. The raw vileness of how she craved to gorge herself on his life's hidden desires nearly overwhelmed him.

"How close, Warren?"

He pushed up barriers between himself and the evil with a horrid awareness, and looked up through the windshield at the dark street and the white church spire looming ahead. *His church.* His dazed dreams. Darkness had infiltrated even this once holy building, overwhelming its symbolism. The diluted truth he'd helped make it had been overpowered by a pure evil that only an opposing purity of real love could stand against. His heart fell as he recognized the church as his own self.

"Warren, that's a church! Those fucking bastards!" Emily stopped the car with a screech, and her eyes sank into his.

"There was nothing . . . to keep them out," Warren told her thickly. "A symbol not backed by truth and love is only an idol." He wished back the time he'd spent explaining away and adjusting the Will and Word of God to man rather than adjusting men —and *himself*— to God. "We must . . . drive them out."

Emily eased ahead, turning the car into the parking lot. She laid her hand on the sack of sharp pickets between them, and Warren's skin tightened. But there was no other exit for either of them now. The stain was upon him, even if physically removed. It had been inside him for years, and Emily's soul was equally marked. They had to go on. To escape now would weaken them them for the fight that would be waiting, and only prolong their fear until they were at last caught.

"Let's go."

She leaned across the seat to him. Her lips brushed him, then were firm against his mouth. She kissed him with a sweet love he wasn't prepared for, and its power nailed down the sinful appetites seeking sensual expression, even as its strength sparked a focus of his true purpose.

At last they parted, and he gave a small smile.

"I think I'm ready," she whispered.

"Yes." The thankful surprise he felt contradicted the confused, dirty self-righteousness bursting inside.

"Come on, Warren." She got out and went around to his door, opened it, and lifted him to his feet.

The old architecture of the church sent its own chill into the cold air. The building was dark, and the air outside seemed to pass through their very beings. They stepped forward together. He grunted at his weak legs, but her arm kept him steady. When they were at the door he lifted his hand to the broken lock, and the door opened easily. Emily looked at him and pushed it wide, and they both stepped inside.

Warren wished for Ben. He was afraid. Despite the bare triumphs he was *afraid.* So much of his ability when he'd met the evil before had stemmed from the older man's faith. Even when Ben was broken and wavering, torn by the memories of his past, his courage had brought Warren to peak in that final showdown. He'd lived off the dead man's intensity and knowledge while consecrating the graves. Now he no longer could.

He took in the familiar decorations of the entry hall and the whitewashed walls. The front lobby dripped with the cold cruelty permeating the very air, and Warren hobbled to the literature table, squinting off to the right and left down long, darkened halls. Ahead waited the closed double doors to the sanctuary, their glass windows formed in the shape of crosses. The knowledge that the evil had passed through them without flinching stabbed his soul.

"I can feel them in here," Emily said.

He nodded, ignoring as best he could the mass of pain overtaking the right half of his body. Sweat drenched him and he clenched his teeth behind torn lips.

"Are you okay?"

"I'll make it." He moved on through the dim lobby, toward the source of evil drawing him.

Emily followed, her breaths fractured, and they passed the ornate stairway, arriving at the inner sanctuary door. The stench of raw sewage became steadily stronger, driving into his nostrils.

Carmen's potent will was closing over him, strong and commanding.

Emily touched his hand, then dragged one of the heavy doors open. He staggered into the room's umbra. Vile cold penetrated his clothing, freezing his heart, and he coughed as the stink of decaying flesh filled his lungs. Gagging, he switched on the lights, blinking in their sudden flash from the ceiling.

The pews stretched through the pillared, expansive room to the altar and pulpit, creating strange shadows. The baptistry behind the pulpit was surrounded by a thick, red puddle, and more blood spilled into it from the tall, ornate cross moved to stand against it. Warren opened his mouth with nausea and saw its burden of a naked man, his stomach sliced wide to drain his life into the bapitistry's obscene pool. He recognized the sallow, agonized, and dead countenance of his blond-headed associate pastor in a ghastly new despair that drugged his soul. Then his eyes were on Carmen.

She giggled and raised her hand in victory as she waited expectantly behind the shining wooden altar, her eyes gleaming her invitation. "Warren," she hissed, "have you come to me so soon?"

His devilish compulsions dragged him down the center aisle as he fought desperately to surmount them. He clenched his shivering fingers around the back of a pew and squeezed fiercely. "I—I have come *for* you!" he shouted hoarsely.

Shrill, gleeful laughter shook the great room, echoing as the thing that had been Carmen glided up the aisle toward him, its arms open. "Yes, for *me*," came the dry words. "To be mine. You *will* be mine." She waved her long fingers back at the desecration. "You must. *Your* lies of love have already made your own ministering brother a sacrifice to Truth! And now your only companionship lies in me."

The horror of the sight made Warren sag. His useless sermons had stripped away God's protection. He was *already* damned. Her voice tugged at his memories of futility and began its seductive work.

"I will give you comfort, Warren, comfort in the long dark night—"

"Warren!" Emily shrieked, driving her cry into his fogging thoughts. *"Don't!"*

The traveling salesman was right. The lie he had preached and lived was all that was left of him. He had sold out.

"Please, Warren!"

He heard Emily behind him, running, and suddenly his inner visions broke into the memory of her sweet, trusting kiss. "It's too late," he wheezed as Carmen came nearer. "Too . . . late."

"Fuck you," Emily screeched at the vampire, her black hair flying as she bolted past him. *"We have come to destroy you!"*

Carmen laughed again as Emily closed, raising the stake and hammer high. Carmen's eyes flashed as she darted forward and struck Emily full in the face. The blow resounded against the paneled walls as Emily stumbled, then fell on her face with a grunt, spasming. Carmen cackled. After a short second, she turned back to Warren, then drifted in the saturating stink to stop two feet from him.

"My God," Warren moaned, wanting to do something against the weakness of his past. It surged into him mercilessly from Carmen's deep-set eyes, but it was everything he could manage to keep his feet and stare at the beautiful woman he'd been unable to refuse. She slipped the shoulder straps of her gown down, exposing her naked breasts and standing nipples. Then she licked a finger and stroked them with that glistening wetness, moistening her lips with her tongue. "Not two hours ago I lay with you, preacher, and consummated the passion for my body you had hidden since our first meeting. I fucked you as you had dreamed it, and sucked you as you had never *imagined.*" Her eyes became small, filled with the fire of truth. "Why didn't you destroy me then, rather than enjoy what you would not take pleasure in while I lived? You are too impure to join your fellow in a sacrifice of life-giving blood. Now your life is *mine!*"

Warren shuddered. Emily lay still on the hard floor. "N-no," he croaked.

"Must you first taste evil before you condemn it?"

"You—you *forced* me!"

"I forced nothing, you self-righteous bastard. You wanted me. You wanted me and you fucked me as hard as I fucked you. You *wanted* me. You always *wanted.*" Carmen's mouth twisted into a smile made bitter by the terrible teeth it revealed. "You want me now." She slipped to him quickly, her arms outstretched. "Now you are ready, Warren," spoke her coldly wicked voice. "Now you *are* mine."

The breath was icy on his neck but Warren could do nothing but lean to her, no longer aware of her as a dead creature, but as Carmen, the beautiful woman he wanted, the woman who promised him everything he desired, and his hand stroked her smooth buttocks when she pressed him to her, raising the gown so he felt her cool, naked flesh. She dragged his fingers back across her hip, and pushed them into the dampness between her legs, her touch drawing away his pain and increasing his longing. Her lips brushed his neck lightly and he felt the soft needles of her teeth, but forgot them as the juices of her sex dripped over his fingers.

"No!"

Carmen released him, wheeling around. The spell was instantly broken and with a cry he dropped to his knees and squinted through pounding torment to see Emily stagger to her feet and hurtle forward, ramming the stake between the vampire's perfect breasts, knocking Carmen to the floor. Carmen's shrill cry exploded in his ears when Emily brought the hammer down onto the stake, and it sank deep, ringing against her breastbone, sending Carmen into shrieking convulsions as Emily slammed the hammer down again. The wood crunched, ripping through the heart and sending a reddish-brown jet of blood into the air. Warren fought nausea, knowing the blood was his own. Vomit filled his mouth and he gagged wretchedly.

Emily's hammer thudded loudly into the wood, again and again, and finally the horrid screams and their echoes faded. The church was silent, the scent of invaded death wafting foul through the air.

"I did it, Warren." Emily knelt beside him, breathing in short gasps. Her trembling hand caressed his neck where it seemed he could still feel the deadly teeth resting. "It's dead."

It was. The illusion of life and beauty was disappearing from Carmen, trickling from her veins and the mangled hole between her sagging breasts. The lips he had adored cracked and split, flowing with steaming pus, and her once tempting flesh shriveled before his eyes, rending itself to expose crumbling bones. The remains bubbled with gore-filled pimples that popped and spewed until her body was covered with their stink. He turned away, sick, barely able to appreciate that the shackles harnessing him had been extinguished with its doom. A peace tried to find rest in his soul.

"But what have you gained?"

Warren looked up sharply at the crackle of the words and drew back from the black figure that had suddenly appeared at the altar. A shiver drilled him. It was the vampire, its red eyes laden with fury.

"What do you hope to gain by stopping me?" The thing paused. "I am already inside you, preacher. *I am inside all men.* I come to bring you what you dare not wish for. I am here to sell you only those things you crave. I look into your heart and offer you the unspeakable fantasies you dream, filling you with their truth. The false morals of men hide their dark needs but do not extinguish them. *I bring you your own truth.*"

Emily wiped her face of the blood she was covered with and tried to get to her feet.

"Your false words and actions have brought you only misery, *preacher.* I offer you the satisfaction of your lusts." The vampire laughed and lunged quickly to Emily, clenching his gnarled fingers around her shoulder and throwing her down again. "And you, little girl . . . what have you to gain?" The tall figure stepped close to her and extended his other sallow, sinewy hand. "You've killed your mother and father and now regret it. You speak of love, but their blood stains your hands. Your hate killed them long before their flesh grew cold. Will you prove your love and join them now? Will you not join them to give the comfort of their beloved daughter?" Brittle laughter erupted from the dead throat. "Don't you wish to ask their forgiveness and be with them once more?"

Forgiveness.

The forgiveness of grace. Ignoring the demonic voice, Warren's heart awakened to the answer with that thought. He grunted with the feeling of peace that desired to console him even now, and faced his own self-condemnation, which had come to life in Carmen's accusations. He crawled to touch Emily. She had destroyed Carmen. For *him.* Tears shook him at the recollection of his failure of all the others and of his misconceptions. He had preached love, read of love, and contemplated love. He had claimed love, but he never allowed that love to claim him. His compassion had been one of duty and intellect, but not of true feeling.

"Come to me, Emily," the vampire said softly. "Come to *me.*"

Gripping Emily's foot, Warren howled with the pent-up and buried passions he'd hidden so long. "Emily—forgive me!"

But Emily was transfixed by the vampire's eyes, and without releasing her the vampire chuckled greasily. "You are beyond the forgiveness of others." It bent over her.

His head pounding, Warren realized that love *had* torched him tonight through Emily's innocent kiss. He already had her forgiveness. If he was beyond the sympathy of others it was only because he was beyond that point for himself.

"Emily!" Warren yelled, pushing away his self-serving notions as life rushed into him with new understanding. *"You forgave me! We are both forgiven of it all. We have to accept the forgiveness of Grace!"*

Triumphantly, the vampire clutched Emily's trembling body, ignoring Warren completely. It ripped at her clothing and forced her flat on the cold floor, easily overcoming her struggles. The hard thin fingers squeezed into her arms and she screamed, her eyes wide in unbroken fear. The vampire stared back silently, its face ageless with malevolence and cruelty. It lowered its head to the bare flesh of her breasts. Its black tongue slithered to taunt her nipples, dripping foul yellow saliva.

Warren pushed himself up to help her, though the yard's length between them seemed like miles. Ignoring the fire in his arm, reaching for her sake beyond the fear of his own safety, he touched the evil creature's shoulder without the dread that had shackled him, the new love flowing in his gentle touch. It ran from deep inside him through his fingers, blasting into the hate and evil.

The vampire jerked back, baring its long, evil teeth. Surprise and anguish furrowed its face.

"I"—Warren nearly shrank away so near to the wicked visage —"I am *forgiven! In that salvation I sanctify this house of God in Christ's name.*" He followed the spark inside that led him softly but powerfully, filling him with potency. "I sanctify the floor you stand on, demon! You have no place here. *You cannot exist in the Love of God that is His house.*"

The undead thing's face contorted further, wrinkling as the eyes darted back and forth in confusion and agony. It snarled and leapt at Warren, grabbing his cast—and jerked back its hands with a scream.

"I am sanctified," Warren said, feeling the unfolding myster-

ies grow inside him and moving to embrace them. "And in that Love I sanctify you, *vampire*. I offer you the Love you refused, the Love that surrounds you!"

"Y-you cannot destroy me—with *love!*" it shrieked, inching away from him to the door. Its hands scratched the empty air savagely. *"You cannot!"*

Warren came closer. "In spite of your sins I welcome you with Love."

As he backed into the lobby, the vampire's countenance flared in a confusion of hate and panic. He touched a stack of colored pamplets on the literature table, scattering them into the air where they burst into flame. The vampire grabbed them as they burned, hurling them at Warren.

Warren stepped aside, far removed now. "You can't stay here unless you accept Love." He sprang forward with the new energy, fluidly taking a small cross from the table and blocking the way. He held the cross up. *"And you cannot leave."*

"No." Electricity charged the air and the stairway erupted into blue flame as the thing tore at its own dead flesh. "No!" it howled wildly, seemingly unaware of the putrescence it brought oozing from its torn body. "I can offer you freedom from the false morality you are *bound* with! *I can sell you your own soul!"* it pleaded, its fingernails plowing more savagely into its own self, scraping out fragments from its face in raw panic.

"I offer you *Love,"* Warren replied. He walked to the vampire unflinchingly, his own past buried in grace. His hand held the symbolic cross high, and it glowed brightly in his belief. "I can face you now without *this—without fear!"*

The vampire searched for an escape, cringing as Warren came closer. It cried out, struggling with ebbing strength as Warren pressed the cross down to its open, drooling mouth. Great pummeling winds blasted from it to make the air crackle hot with the searing waves of fire. Warren pressed the cross deeper as the undead thing sank unwillingly to its knees. He pushed the cross farther, past the evil teeth, holding it in the stinking throat as fire engulfed the walls and ceiling, the vampire bubbling with putrid blood and its mouth beginning to crumple, the process creeping across its flesh until it was consuming the entire body.

It tore at itself weakly now, regurgitating odorous bile and blood onto Warren, its voice a shrill note of unendurable agony.

With the end of the terrible scream the furious wind began to die and the supernatural fire around them smoldered. Bits and pieces of the creature's decomposing flesh, gorged with the blood of its victims, loosened and dropped wetly to the ground, boiling with awful sulfuric stench. Its hair fell out and still it tore into itself, until at last its fingernails themselves raked off with liquid laceration, dripping rivulets of thick dark blood.

"D-damn . . . you. . . ." gurgled the vile voice. "D-damn . . . you to . . . hell!" It stared defiantly, and its bubbling eyes began to steam, mixing with the smoke still filling the church.

Warren felt a sympathy for the rotting thing before him he wouldn't have believed himself capable of. "It is not too late," he heard himself say. "Repent of your evil and know Love."

A hideous bellow welled up from the creature's deteriorating lungs and its skin shrank and tore in stringy pieces, exposing a ruptured, decayed heart and stinking intestines that foamed around the disintegrating and blackened bones. The wind was gone now, as was the fire. Lingering traces of the putrid smoke and steam disappeared as though they never had been.

Emily staggered to Warren's side, her face pale. "That . . . fucking shit from hell," she whispered, but her arms moved around him tenderly and they both waited in silence until the stained carpet before them was covered with benign dust.

XX

They were back again.

Putting down the new book she was indexing, Elizabeth Potter followed the progress of the man and young woman walking past the library desk to the stairs. They had come here that day weeks ago, leaving those books on the table and creating a ruckus. They'd been here every day this week, and last.

She watched them like a hawk now. She watched them as they reached the partial second floor and walked along the overlooking rail. They stopped at the newspaper room, as before, and went in.

Strangely, the man reminded her of that other one who'd come here last month—the derelict. His activities were similar, and his face bore a similar haunting.

Similar, but not quite the same. The derelict had been borne down with a nervous despair, while this man walked with the sense of a victory—and more strangely, of compassion.

Her curiosity unsatiated, she wished she could know his ends, and the ends of the girl with him . . . or what he was doing with a woman so much younger than himself.

Then she wondered if maybe they knew the derelict, remembering the day he'd left and never come back. She laughed at the idea, but remembered the impression she'd had, that he'd been looking for a job. Her assumption was that he'd found one and never returned. It might be that this other man and girl were up to the same thing.

Letting her hostility slip slowly, she found herself echoing the compassion she'd noticed in him, and rather hoped they would find one.